Deli's Take Out

Bad Boys of Beta Squad series, Book 4

Siobhan Muir

ISBN: 1-947221-09-4
ISBN-13: 978-1-947221-09-3

DEDICATION

Dedicated to Mary Decker, logical confidante and Raven's Brew Deadman's Reach connoisseur. Thank you for your encouragement, your humor, and your unfailing faith in this story. I raise my mug of black gold to you, and hope you love Deli.

ACKNOWLEDGMENTS

Writing a book is never really a one-person job, and writing a series is especially difficult alone. Keeping track of details is so much easier when you have help. Not only does it take a great deal of hard work, editing, and research on the part of the author to get things correct, but without my compatriots, there'd be a lot more mistakes.

Great thanks to Silver James for checking over my military and police procedures so I get them right. Huge thanks to Mary Decker for reminding me that Military War Dogs have specific commands and they're *not* in English. Thanks to Marcelo Angiano who I met in 2015 and he gave me the face of CPO Eugene "Deli" Rubenovich. You were totally perfect for this character! And great thanks to Kris Norris for designing the cover with such a tough image to balance. You rock.

As always, great thanks to my readers for cheering me on – I recall the "Deli! Deli! Deli!" chant on several of my live posts. Y'all make my writing worth the detailed effort.

GLOSSARY OF DOG COMMANDS
(Pronunciation)

Come – HERE

Find or Track – ZOOCH

Go Ahead/Escort – GAY WEETER

Heel – FOOSE

Relax – VOL-NO

Release (the bite) – POOST

Sit – ZITS

Stand – SCH-STAY-EN

Stay – BLEEBEN

CHAPTER ONE

"MEDIC!" Deli roared into his radio as he dragged Master Chief Petty Officer "Bones" Skelling out of the line of fire.

The man had taken several rounds to his legs before the branches from a tree behind him fell on his head. Bones lay out cold and bleeding while Deli hauled his huge ass to cover. As the smallest man on SEAL Team 9, Bravo Squad, CPO Eugene "Deli" Rubenovich had taken his share of shit from the bigger guys. Good thing he could drag his larger comrades through hell and high water.

They'd almost reached the tertiary LZ when a tango with a purloined M-16 opened fire on their retreat. Furious impacts peppered the ground behind them as Deli ran for the helo, and he swore a blue streak. *Mom would be appalled.* Thank glory his mother never came anywhere close to a warzone.

The two gunners in the helo opened fire on their backtrail and Deli pushed harder to get to the bird's deck. A black shadow came out of nowhere and latched onto Bones' other arm as he started to slide off Deli's shoulder. Deli damn near tucked and rolled, dumping Bones to the ground, before he recognized Petty Officer 2nd Class Eric

"Padfoot" Farkas. The man earned his nickname by being so damn silent he gave Ghost a run for her money. That, and he liked to read Harry Potter.

They nodded to each other and dragged Bones the last steps to the helo as the rest of the team came streaming in.

"All boots on board, captain! Let's haul ass." Retro's voice came across the coms.

Deli and Padfoot helped move Bones to a clear spot on the deck where Chief Warrant Officer Todd "Magic" Hunter could work on him. The helo lifted off while CPO Leo "Strafe" Metzger laid down cover fire. Deli wished he could watch the little bastard who'd shot at his retreat get mowed to the ground, but he helped get Bones strapped in.

"Everyone get in, sit down, strap in, and hold on. Things are about to get squirrely."

The pilot's voice came over the coms and Deli shared a look with Padfoot. "Aw fuck."

"You got that right." Strafe threw himself into a harness beside Deli. "I saw what's comin'. High canyon walls and anti-aircraft weapons. It's our only way out of this fuckin' mess, but it's gonna be hell."

"The only easy day was yesterday." Padfoot clipped in and tightened his lips.

"Fuck yeah it was." No one laughed as the helo lurched upwards then tilted left.

Deli gritted his teeth. Damn, he hated when they had to do aerobatic maneuvers. The idea that they could tip over and lose the cushion of air holding the bird up gave him the heebie jeebies. He kept his jaw locked and his gaze on Magic working on Bones.

Come on, man. Don't bug out on us so soon. Bones was new to the squad, but Deli liked him a lot. He had an easy way with anyone in the SEALs. Including the arrogant cocksuckers and humorless tightwads. He seemed comfortable in his own skin and the quality was rare to find, even in the SpecOps community.

Deli hadn't prayed in years, leaving his parents' religion at the door of the enlistment office, but he sent up a few words in hopes someone was listening. *Please watch over Bones. The man's too good to be lost yet. Please.*

The helo twisted and turned in the air, dodging missiles and flak as they made their escape. He bet the pilot white-knuckled it through most of it, but eventually they leveled out and headed for their cover ship. Their escort helo covered their tail rotor as they shot out to sea. *Thank glory.* While most things didn't scare him, getting tossed around in a flying brick put his usual calm to the test. Now all he had to worry about was Bones making it.

Deli shot a look at Magic and his teammate nodded, but he wore the mask his wife Chris called the "Intense Tight Look." It meant he had someone wounded and he didn't know how it would turn out. Hell, they never knew, but usually "Magic" would pull a miracle out of nothing, so Deli chose to hope.

"Five mikes out." The pilot's voice sounded calm and Deli checked his gear so he could get out as soon as they set down.

"Thank the Goddess." Padfoot dropped his head back and closed his eyes.

Deli found his prayer odd, always invoking the Goddess instead of god, but Farkas was solid as a fighter and a teammate. *Must be a Wiccan or Pagan.* It didn't matter as long as he had their backs.

They touched down on deck and quickly disembarked. Magic turned Bones over to the medics on the ship and joined Bravo squad for debrief. Despite their wounded and narrow escape, the op had been an overall success. The debriefing went as expected. They analyzed what went right and what needed improvement. *Yeah, it would've been better if Bones wasn't hit.* Deli scowled as he headed for the showers and his bunk. He'd stop by the infirmary to see how Bones was holding up as soon as he could.

Deli made his way through the labyrinthine corridors to the cabin they'd been given as temporary housing on the ship. He didn't have to duck, a benefit to being the shortest guy on the team, but he damn near cracked his shins on the knee-knockers at each port. He threw his gear on his bunk and checked it over one more time. While they weren't likely to go out again in the next twenty-four hours, he wanted his equipment ready to go. He sharpened the blade of his K-bar when he found nicks in the edge, and took apart his M-16 to make sure no dirt marred the inner workings of the weapon. He cleaned and packed away all his gear carefully before setting it in his locker and leaning his forehead against it.

Come on, Bones. You gotta pull through.

Deli didn't often entertain fatalistic thoughts, but Bones' stillness when they headed home ate at him. No one should be that still unless they were dead. And he'd seen the man breathing.

"Fuck!" He slammed his fist into the locker door.

"Something eating at you, Deli?" Farkas appeared beside him, his arms crossed over his chest. "Or did the locker insult your manhood?"

Deli met the other man's eyes and scowled. "Nothin'. I'm fine."

"Oh sure. I've seen that kind of fine. Fucked up, Insecure, Neurotic, and Emotional." Farkas nodded. "Or maybe you're just F'NE, 'cause I don't think you're insecure about anything."

Deli wanted to pummel the smirk off Padfoot's face, but he couldn't argue with his assessment. He was emotional, but he usually kept it bottled up and diffused it with furious exercise or hardcore sex. Neither of which looked to be on his radar any time soon. He growled and shook his head.

"Listen, I know you don't need me butting into anything you got going on, but maybe now would be a good time to ask for leave."

"What the fuck are you talkin' about? Why the hell would you say that, Farkas?"

"Because you've gone through a shit-ton of teammates recently what with Brickman and Killian getting medically discharged from fighting status, and Anderson retiring. It's hard to switch gears so often." Farkas shrugged. "You've never let up and given yourself a break."

"I'm a goddamned SEAL. That's what we do."

"Yeah, I know, I went through BUD/S too, remember? Got the Budweiser." Farkas tilted his head, his expression serious. "But we all need some real down time. Don't try to tell yourself different. And you can always carry around your electronic leash if you're needed. Go ask for some leave before you're useless to the rest of us."

Deli growled. "You know I still outrank you."

Farkas nodded. "Yup, but I'm pretty sure you're smart enough to know when you need to clear your head. If you tell me to fuck off, I will, but give yourself permission to step away if the leave's available. Sir."

Deli wanted to snarl and howl about fucking off, but the anger only stemmed from knowing the man was right. "Sonuvaprick!" He closed his eyes and took a few deep breaths before squaring his shoulders and meeting Farkas' gaze.

"Why the fuck do you care, Farkas?" Deli didn't understand the man's insistence. They were SEALs. They never gave up, they never took it easy, and they never quit.

Padfoot sighed and shot a look toward to door as if someone could walk in at any moment. "I joined Bravo Squad because I lost all but two members of my previous squad dealing with the Daesh. It was a shit time and I broke more walls and plates than I can count. I damn near broke my fiancée and that's when the scary hit home."

Unease settled into Deli's gut. "Holy shit. Was she all right?"

Padfoot nodded. "But it was a close thing and I was put on mandatory leave before I killed any innocents." He looked away again and muttered something like. "I damn near did." But when he turned back some of the blackness in his expression had lifted.

"What I'm explaining badly is we can only be superhuman for a short time, but then we need breaks. We need to be vulnerable and angry and scared. I know, you're probably thinking I'm a pansy-ass for admitting that, but fuck, we're SEALs and that means we're the best at everything. So why the hell should we be substandard humans? I learned the hard way that ignoring the emotions fucks you up worse than acknowledging them."

Padfoot shut up and ran his hands over his head with a guilty look. "Sorry, I'm sure you didn't need the lecture. I just didn't want you to take the same path I did."

Deli opened his mouth to blow Farkas off, but the words stuck in his throat. He didn't like to be vulnerable or scared or angry, but it seemed to be with him more often than not these days. *All right. I'll talk to Whittleton.*

He clapped the man on the shoulder and nodded. "Thanks, man. As much as it pains me to say, you might be right."

Farkas didn't grin at his words. "Yeah, I hear you. Talk to Whittleton and go on vacation or hiking or some sort of outdoor shit when we get to port. We'll be here when you get back."

Deli bit his bottom lip. He normally didn't get into all the personal crap they carried around with them, but Farkas seemed like he had his shit together a lot better than he did. "Can I ask you a question? Whatever happened to your fiancée?"

Padfoot's jaw tightened and he took a deep breath in through his nose. "She left."

"Aw, hell, man. I'm sorry."

He shrugged and shook his head. "Don't be. She

wasn't the right woman for me, both for me as the man and me as the SEAL. She couldn't handle the not-knowing of a SpecOps spouse."

Deli nodded. "Yeah, I'm thinkin' those kind of women are few and far between."

"Roger that. You gonna talk to Whittleton?"

"Yup. My next stop. Thanks, Padfoot." They shook, grasping thumbs, and Deli squeezed in appreciation.

He squeezed back. "You're welcome. Get your head screwed on straight and I'll catch you on the rebound."

"Copy that."

Deli turned his ass around and headed back to the situation room where Whittleton had set up his temporary office. Hopefully the man hadn't hit the rack yet. Most of the officers kept weird hours just like their crew, but sometimes they actually got to go home once an Op ended.

Fortunately, Whittleton leaned against the table, chewing on a soda straw as he reviewed his notes. Deli knew he'd been trying to quit smoking after he watched his brother die of emphysema.

Deli stuck his head in the portal and rapped on the door with his knuckles. "May I come in, sir?"

"Sure, Chief. What can I do you for?" Whittleton's gaze met his as he closed the folder he'd been reading.

"I, uh, I wanted to talk to you about taking some leave when we get back to Coronado." He stood at parade rest to hide his unease, suddenly feeling like a wimp.

Just remember what Padfoot said.

"All right, let's talk about it. Something happen to your family?" Whittleton's gaze sharpened.

"No, sir. But today was a close call and Bones got injured pretty bad." He resisted the urge to scuff his toes on the floor. "And to be honest, it's been buildin' up. First Brickman, then Killian and Bronco, now Bones...I don't like askin', but I think I need some time to get my head on straight once we get back."

Whittleton didn't say anything for a long time, but his gaze never moved from Deli's. It was unnerving how still the lieutenant-commander could get. The man hadn't been in the field in over a decade, but he still had many of the SEAL traits from his active career. He'd gained the nickname 'Whistler' because he was fast and quiet, and many of his teammates had been hard-pressed to keep up with him in his youth.

"Everything okay, Chief?" Whittleton's voice filled with caution.

"Yeah, yeah...no, not entirely." Deli frowned, trying to make his thoughts coherent. "I'm too much in my head and it's pissing me off. My teammates are on the injured list or gone and I'm having a tough time focusing." He swallowed hard and met his commander's gaze. "I need some time before I fuck up so badly someone gets hurt or killed."

"You think you're that close?"

"Yes, sir. Nothing has happened yet, but I'm feelin' twitchy and I can't find my usual calm. If we're not on for the next bit, I'm requesting leave to find my center, sir."

"All right, Chief. I'll have the paperwork ready to go in the next twenty-four. Last I heard, we were on the down rotation, just training, but nothing serious once we finish this sail." Whittleton nodded, his expression grave. "But keep your phone on you. Shit heats up pretty fast around here, as you well know."

"Yes, sir. Thank you, sir." Relief cascaded through Deli and the tension in his shoulders released.

"Dismissed."

"Thank you, sir."

Deli retreated from the office and headed back to his cabin to change into his workout clothes. He'd use the ship's gym to work off some of his frustration. He didn't need to have a meltdown in front of the squad. And Farkas was right. If he didn't get out now, it could go a lot worse for him and his team.

CHAPTER TWO

"Get the hell off my land."

Caroline cocked her father's Henry .22 rifle and aimed at the tie hanging in the middle of the frontman's chest.

"Now, Señora Atherton, I'm sure we can—"

She took aim and fired into the stump no more than four feet from him, making him swear and jump back toward his black SUV. The dogs in the yard behind her facility set off a cacophony of barking in distress. She cocked it again.

"I'm done talking. This land has been in my family for over a century and it's paid off. There ain't no back taxes or liens or hidden provisos on how it's used. All my permits are in order and I got copies. So no, I'm not selling and no, you can't overpay me for it. Now get off my land." She aimed the rifle at his chest again. "And if I see you here again, I'll make sure to tag your vehicle with a little redneck decoration."

"This isn't over, Señora Atherton." The man snarled as he opened the passenger door. "I will be back and next time we won't be so nice. Maybe we will call the ASPCA and tell them you run a filthy facility. Or we will come and take your dogs ourselves. It's smarter to just sell your land."

Namby-pamby suit can't even drive himself.

She shot at his feet, making him yelp and jump.

"Oh, it's a done deal, honey. The ASPCA is on my speed-dial and knows me better than you. And if you come anywhere near my dogs, I won't just shoot at your feet. So, you just run along to your boss and tell him to find land elsewhere. I'm not selling." She glared daggers back at the suit.

"You don't know who you're dealing with, Señora Atherton. You'd be wise to reconsider. No one says no to our money. Not even the cops, *comprende?*"

She lifted the rifle to point it at his head. "I know the cops, too. I'd be within my rights to shoot you dead right here. Want to test me?"

"You will regret this." He snarled as he slammed the door and the SUV peeled out of her gravel drive.

Good riddance and get the fuck out. She held the rifle at the ready until they disappeared around the bend in her driveway then lowered it with a sigh. She suspected they'd be back eventually.

"Are they gone?" Daphne stepped out from behind the screen door and peered over Caroline's shoulder.

"Yeah, they're gone." Caroline leaned the rifle against the wall and shook her head. "I'm sorry they came back, but I'm glad I was here this time instead of having to be called. How are you doing?"

"Better now that they're gone." Daphne trembled more than usual and Caroline wondered if she'd had one of her PTSD attacks.

"Did they trigger something in you?" She pushed a bit of Daphne's hair behind her ear.

Daphne grimaced and nodded, turning her gaze toward the trees creaking in the breeze coming off the mountains.

"He had an accent like those people who drugged and kidnapped me."

That news had Caroline's eyes narrowing. "Are you

sure?"

"Yeah. I might not remember much, but I remember the voices and he spoke just like them."

Two years earlier, Caroline's niece had gone to a job fair on her community college campus and signed up for an interview with a company called Data Pool. When she got the job, she'd been so excited. The only hang-up was she had to move to L.A. Caroline had worried about her in such a big city, but had been pleased for her niece.

But when Daphne stopped returning calls, emails, and stopped posting on social media, Caroline had gotten worried. She'd reported her missing to the police, but they did nothing. It had been frightening and frustrating. No one would do anything and calls to the company produced no results.

Caroline had given up on Daphne's return when she received a call from the Coronado police department who'd picked up her case. It turned out Data Pool was a front for a human trafficking ring using the job fairs at local colleges to obtain "product" and Daphne had been rescued with a few other women her age. Caroline didn't care too much about the how or the why, just that Daphne was safe and the faux company was shut down.

But her niece had come home with nightmares and PTSD just like the dogs Caroline rehabilitated at her Last Chance Dog Sanctuary. She was their last chance, whether to get new homes, become service dogs, or just to survive their own traumatic experiences. Not all the dogs were from the military. Some she received as pups to train into service animals. She'd been successful, too, especially when Daphne came to stay and help, and actually bonded to one of the recovering dogs.

Beryl, a boxer, leaned against Daphne's leg and stared up at her with utter devotion and focus, the dog using her physical weight to bring Daphne's panic back down. She closed her eyes and reached down to touch the dog's head, taking deep, shuddering breaths.

Caroline swore under her breath. The sense she got with those assholes in the black SUVs was that time was running out for them and they needed Caroline out of the way. Unfortunately, she had no intention of leaving. If she'd learned anything in her forty-five plus years of life, when some men didn't get what they wanted, they grew desperate and violent.

What the hell am I going to do now?

"Let me make some of the chamomile tea for you." Caroline pushed through the screen door and put up the rifle in the rack. "Then I'm gonna check on the dogs. They got pretty riled up with those jackasses here."

Daphne nodded. "Dogs always know when something's wrong." She patted Beryl's head again.

"Yes, they do, which is why I like them better than people in most cases." Caroline headed for the kitchen to set the kettle to boil. "You just settle in and I'll bring the tea to you after I check them."

"Okay."

Caroline grimaced when Daphne's voice sounded so small and scared. The young woman had been through too much and should've been safe in the northern California woods. But now Daphne had to face more stress and threat. Caroline sighed and turned on the stove before heading outside.

The ranch had been set up with a large house, a matching barn, and corrals. Caroline had modified the barn to house equipment and supplies. The horse stalls could be used for both storage and extra living spaces for anyone who needed to stay overnight when training with the dogs. She'd taken out two corrals to build a kennel barn and a covered arena for obedience and agility training. They were connected to the house by a covered porch. She'd used it for Daphne's dog Beryl, but also for some of the other dogs to regain strength and stamina from injuries. The rest of the corrals she'd converted to dog runs with chain-linked fences to allow the dogs to see the trees and open spaces clearly.

She let herself into the kennel building and breathed deeply to calm her energy. She'd often been called a lola-granola hippy for her description of energy, but the dogs were more sensitive to unspoken cues than most humans, and they knew when she was upset.

"All right, everyone. We're okay. The intruders are gone and we're okay." She spoke in a calm measured voice and the barking slowed. "That's it. We're okay. You all did a good job in protecting us."

The barking diminished and tails began to wag. She checked on each occupant in the kennels before she headed out to the dog runs. Two dogs had been in the runs when the SUVs arrived, but only a shivering bluetick coonhound with his tail clamped to his hindquarters greeted her.

Oh dear, where's Sergeant Trace?

She moved to the empty dog run found the gate unlatched. *Dammit, not again!* She shot a look toward the forest. *I'll have to move fast if I want to catch her.* She spun and headed back to the house to grab a leash, hoping the dog didn't hurt anyone on her walkabout.

Daphne poured tea as Caroline came in the door. "Did you want some tea?"

"No, not at the moment. I have to go find a dog." Caroline shook her head as she pulled a ball cap on and snagged the leash.

"Oh no. Which one?"

"Sergeant Trace."

"Oh glory. Do you want some help?" Daphne set her mug aside and swallowed hard.

"No, honey. I need you to stay here, lock the doors, and keep an eye on the dogs. I won't be long." *At least I hope I won't.* She waved her phone at Daphne. "I'll take my cell with me. Call or text if you need anything."

She headed out the door with the leash and scanned the ground around the dog run to see if Trace had left tracks.

****

Deli turned off the main road onto a dirt forest road heading up into the hills. His turquoise Jeep Wrangler Rubicon Unlimited rumbled up the washboard road, churning up the miles as much as he churned up his thoughts. His anger over his teammates' injuries hadn't abated, but being away from the base and out in the open helped.

The weather had cooperated with his leave and the sunshine stained the trees in golden light. They'd had rain the night before and the forest still held the scent of water in the air. He bounced along with the windows down, enjoying the smell as he pulled into the trailhead.

Because it was a weekday, the area sat deserted and he could park as close to the trail as he wanted. He switched off the ignition and climbed out, ready to be moving on his own power rather than stuck in a vehicle. He yanked his backpack out of the Jeep and settled it on his shoulders before locking the doors.

Inhaling deeply, he closed his eyes to find his center as the anger surged again. *Fuck, it's exhausting.* He'd been exhausted for weeks, his sense of loss corroding the pride and joy he took in being a special operator. Now he could barely face the next op.

Focus on the good things. He released his breath slowly and opened his eyes, taking in the trail. According to the map it wound its way through the forest and hills in a big, five mile loop, with a lake at the apex. He'd chosen it for its location away from most people and for its shortness. He had enough gear to camp if the weather got bad, but he didn't expect it to take him more than a couple of hours.

But I'm gonna go slow. He checked his pack to make sure he had all the water and food he needed before he set off. He'd picked up some junk food at the convenience store where he last got fuel and smiled at himself. *We didn't buy them when we were kids.* His parents were sticklers for kosher foods, and Cool Ranch Doritos weren't on the list. Despite his parents living on the East Coast, he felt a twinge of guilt for buying the cheap treat. *But I'm gonna enjoy the hell outta them.*

Deli set off at a good clip despite his intention to go slow. The pace allowed him to focus on his body and let his bothersome thoughts go. It also allowed him to let some of his deep truths resurface. Like acknowledging he'd lost the drive to participate in scheduled violence. And he wanted to have something more permanent to come home to when the ops were over. He had his Beta Squad brothers and sister, but they had families of their own now. It took him a few breaths to realize he was the last member to know the story of why they had the nickname of Beta Squad.

Padfoot, Gabe "Keys" Szellem, Bones, and Strafe had filled in the spots Ghost, Bronco, and Bam-Bam left behind. Yeah, Magic, Retro, and Rimshot were still there, but it wasn't the same. They rarely called themselves "Beta Squad" anymore, and an odd sadness spiked. It was something special they'd shared, but now it was fading.

He rolled his shoulders, trying to loosen the tension in them as he hiked. If he was completely honest, it wasn't the ending to "Beta Squad" that saddened him, it stemmed from an inane jealousy he had about his friends. They all had someone special in their lives now, and he wanted someone special waiting on him to come home after missions.

And I want a dog again, dammit.

His enlistment was up in just over seven months and the easy thing to do was simply re-up. But he'd grown tired of the constant missions and injuries. *And death of teammates*. The problem was, he didn't know what to do with himself afterwards, and he had no one permanent to share it with. Sure, there'd been women to take the edge off, but no one who really made him want to share what he could. With his memories and knowledge of being a SpecOps member, he didn't know how to be anything else, but the life was starting to pall.

His heart rate elevated as the anger and frustration merged with his uncertainty, so he forced himself to pull his speed and to slow down his breathing. *Remember what Farkas said.* The man had reminded him that they had emotions and those emotions had to be acknowledged. And frankly, Deli was pissed that his friends were getting hurt or getting hitched, and he was scared he'd live to the end of his enlistment with nothing to show for it but more scheduled violence.

What the fuck am I going to do?

He tried to enjoy the scenery, but he couldn't keep from pushing his body against the flood of frustration and his strides ate up the ground. He kept his attention on his surroundings, noting the changes in wind and temperature as his own heated up. The birds kept him company and he heard the shrill whistle of a red-tailed hawk somewhere above the canopy, but when everything fell silent, he paused.

Predator. And it isn't me.

He held his breath as he scanned the forest around him. The wind had settled and the birds had grown quiet. After a few seconds he heard a low growling that made the hairs stand up on the back of his neck. *What the fuck is that?*

Settling into his own predator mode, Deli moved as quietly as he could toward the sound emanating from around the next pile of boulders. The trees thinned a little and the trail cut across a meadow filled with spring wildflowers. Bushes lined the edges of the meadow with ripe berries hanging like Christmas ornaments.

The growl sounded again and Deli froze, turning only his head to check his peripherals. A sharp bark and a matching growl filled in the air. A large black bear stood on all fours facing a much smaller blue heeler dog with a truncated tail. The dog faced the bear with its hackles up and its teeth bared, its snarl as menacing as the bear's growl.

Oh shit, now what? The bear rocked its weight between its two front feet and roared. The dog responded by crouching and leaping to the side, taking the bear's attention with it. Deli suspected both animals knew he was there but had more immediate concerns. He watched the ursid try to outflank the canid, but the dog appeared to be leading the bear toward the far end of the meadow.

Away from me...

The dog's tactics pulled up a memory from his time in the Navy before he joined the SEALs. He'd been a dog handler, working with the animals who'd go into the field as SAR and bomb sniffers. He'd helped train several dogs from shepherds and malinois to a few Labradors and a couple of short-haired collies. But one dog stood out in his memory of his time at Joint Base San Antonio-Lackland. Her name had been Sergeant Trace and despite her muttly appearance as a blue heeler with a black spot covering her left eye and ear, she'd been smart, determined, and loyal, and she'd often drawn attackers away from her handler when threatened.

Deli focused on the dog and the markings on her coat while she teased the bear away from his position. *Holy shit, that's Trace.* The way the dog moved showed her age and her experience, but the same moves Deli had seen in the pup who came to the JBSAL played out in front of him. The question became, how did he save the dog without endangering the bear? California took dim views on people who killed protected species and the black bear was on the state's flag. *Shit, I might as well kill a bald eagle.*

17

He still hadn't come to a decision when movement at the other end of the meadow caught his attention. A woman stepped out into the clearing and froze, her hands wrapped around a rifle. "Trace!"

"Stay back. You'll catch the bear's attention." Deli shouted, hoping he hadn't done the same.

"Are you all right? Did she hurt you?" The woman kept her gaze on the developing conflict, skirting the animals toward Deli.

"No, but that bear's pretty damn frustrated with the dog, and liable to take it out on anyone it notices."

She nodded. "I'll try to call Trace to me before I get off a shot."

Deli scowled. "Are you going to shoot the bear?"

"No, of course not. I just want to scare it away." She matched his scowl. "Be ready."

"Let me call the dog. I have the ability to get out of the way if the bear follows." Deli shrugged out of his pack and dropped it. "On three?"

"Wait, how do I know you can do what you say? I don't know you and I've got the rifle." She narrowed her eyes at him. "And I know Trace."

"You're not the only one." She shot him a surprised look but he'd already moved into a position to call Trace to his side. "Be ready. When I give the command, she should come to my side. When she does, shoot into the air. I'm hoping it'll distract the bear and spook it. You might have to shoot twice, just aim somewhere other than the bear or me. Copy?"

She shook her head. "What if it charges you?"

"We'll cross that bridge when we come to it. Ready?"

"I don't think—"

"One…" Deli moved toward the trees to give him a better chance to use them as interference. "Two…" The woman swallowed hard and raised the rifle, her gaze on the dog harassing the bear. "Three! Trace! Hup, *here*!"

The dog's head came up and her gaze switched to Deli's as the bear roared.

"*Here*, Trace. Hup, hup!"

Time seemed to slow down as the dog made her decision, but the bear had started to move. Deli held still only because his training required it, but his gut crawled up to his throat as Trace shifted to charge to his side. Unfortunately, the bear had already closed the distance and swiped at her with one massive paw.

Trace leapt over the paw, twisted mid-air, and came down on the other side, bolting for Deli. The bear pivoted after her, its hindquarters bunching as it prepared to lunge for Trace's non-existent tail. Deli kept his gaze locked on Trace and hoped the woman would fire the rifle before the bear hit its stride.

Come on, come on, do it!

A rifle shot shattered the air, sending birds into flight and making the bear falter. Trace kept running until she skidded to a stop at Deli's side, her gaze still locked on him. The bear grunted a complaint, its head swinging from side to side. The woman cocked the rifle and sent another shot into the air accompanied by a loud scream rivaling a Banshee.

The otherworldly shriek seemed to do the trick. The bear pivoted again and headed for the woods away from the trail. Deli grasped Trace's collar to keep the dog at his side as he watched the bear disappear into the trees. Crashing sounds came from the forest, but Deli didn't wait.

"Trace, *foose. Sch-stay-en.*" The old commands felt natural as Deli retrieved his pack. Trace fell in beside him, the dog's stance vigilant. Damn, he missed working with MWDs. "Good girl."

He swung the pack onto his shoulders just as the woman approached. "Trace, *here.*"

The dog looked at Deli then back at the woman before she whined, but held her ground.

"Trace, *here*." The woman pointed at the ground beside her.

"She's not gonna do that until I release her from her task." Deli met her gaze and watched anger and frustration flash across her face before she settled for cold seething.

"Who the hell are you?" She probably wanted to say more, but she closed her lips over her teeth in a tight line. "Give me back my dog."

"Your dog?" Deli raised his eyebrows.

"That's right, mine. And you didn't answer my question. Who are you?"

Deli shook his head. "How is she your dog? This is Sergeant Trace, a U.S. Military War Dog. She doesn't belong with a civilian."

"I know exactly who she is and she's been medically retired from the military. She's my dog now and I've sworn to take care of her. Now, let go of her, because she's comin' with me." The woman stood her ground. She didn't point the rifle at Deli, but he suspected she wasn't far from doing so if he pushed.

Deli glanced at the dog, still staring up at him with trusting golden eyes. "Okay, Trace. *Vol-no*."

The dog lost some of her vigilance and her tongue lolled out of her mouth in a relaxed doggy grin. Deli's tension went with Trace's.

"How did you get an MWD after she'd retired?"

"How about you let me have my dog back and identify yourself before I tell you anything?" The woman raised her chin and stared him down, her eyes the same golden color as Trace's. She had golden-blonde hair pulled into a ponytail, with the tail stuffed through a baseball cap. She stood just about his height with full breasts and long legs. *Holy shit, she's beautiful.*

He cleared his throat and brought his wayward attention back to the present. "I'm Chief Petty Officer Rubenovich, U.S. Navy."

"What are you doing so far inland, Chief?"

"I'm taking some R and R."

She nodded. "Sorry to interrupt, but thanks for the help with the bear. *Here*, Trace. Let's go home. Hup."

"Let me come with you to make sure the bear doesn't return." He knew it was a lame excuse, but he didn't want to be parted from the woman and Trace so soon. *What the hell's wrong with me?*

She snorted. "I'm the one with the rifle, remember? Besides, the bear isn't likely to come back after that display."

"That may be, but there are more predators than bears out here."

She shot him a piercing look. "Oh, I know there are."

The way she held her body and the hard expression she wore told him more than he wanted to know. He'd seen both in the mirror before he'd left the base. The wary, defensive look that suggested she didn't trust easily or often.

The urge to win that trust, to help her, rose in his chest and he shook his head to negate it. He'd known her for a total of ten minutes. She didn't need to trust him or have his help. She snorted and rolled her eyes before retreating down the trail, Trace following along like the good dog she'd been trained to be.

"Wait." He launched into motion, catching up with her in a few steps. "Please let me come with you. I don't mean any harm and I'd like to see where Trace is now. I worked with her a few years ago while she still served. It'd be good to see how she's getting on."

"I don't know you, Chief Rubenovich." She paused and turned to face him, her rifle held across her chest. She scanned his body as if categorizing the threat he represented. "Anyone can claim to be active military. I don't trust random guys who show up in the woods and try to take my dog."

"Trace isn't your dog. She's a member of the U.S. Military."

"Oh, for the love of everything holy." She turned on him, keeping the rifle between them as she stared him down. "Trace is retired and has PTSD. I don't see the U.S. Military steppin' up to take care of her when she has an episode that makes her tremble and cower. I did that, and I did it through proper channels." She held up her hand when he opened his mouth. "Thanks for the help, but in a few more feet we'll be on my land and we'll be safe."

Deli wanted to argue that "safe" was a relative term in the wilderness and he needed to see how she cared for Trace. But she didn't know him at all and though he always trusted a dog's judgement when it came to people, she might not. She definitely wouldn't know he wasn't just another scumbag trying to get something from her.

"But the dog—"

"Was adopted through proper channels by the Last Chance Dog Sanctuary." She narrowed her eyes at him. "If you're really in the military, give your intel group a call and see what happened to Sergeant Trace. I have the paperwork all in order. You can check for yourself."

He held up his hands and stopped. "Roger that. Just wanted to help. You have a good afternoon."

"Thank you." She turned away and stretched her legs to get distance from him without looking back. Trace went with her, still alert as if watching out for the woman at her side.

Take good care of her, Trace.

Deli looked around to decide where he'd go next, but the peace from his hike had eroded away and he really wanted to get off the mountain to his Jeep. Maybe he'd get a hotel and a shower and splurge on a big meal with a good draft beer at a local alehouse. *And check into the Last Chance Dog Sanctuary* And the prickly woman who claimed to run it. He should just ignore them both and get on with his life.

But he couldn't quite get either woman or dog off his mind as he stomped back down the trail.

CHAPTER THREE

Caroline brought Trace home, her mind full of the big bear and the man she'd met. Trace carried herself like a true warrior and now, though alert, seemed more settled. She didn't bolt away from Caroline, but trotted a few feet in front of her doing what Caroline had learned meant "casting."

I might have to do some of my own recon on Chief Rubenovich. The man hadn't been tall or broad, but he had presence and power, and just looking at him had made her catch her breath. She'd wanted to trust him, but when he'd balked at releasing Trace, her hackles had gone up. No one took her dog from her, no matter how handsome or well-meaning. She'd liked the way he protected Trace while dealing with the bear and the cadence of his northeastern accent. And he'd filled out those hiking clothes just fine.

But then he had to go and ruin it by doubting me and my claim to Trace.

Memories of her father doubting her ability to run her own business without the help of a man had reared their ugly heads. Right along with all the boyfriends she'd had who couldn't deal with a woman who was too driven. *Yeah, it's only good to be driven if you're a man.* They'd expected her to be biddable, pliable, and accommodating.

I've never been accommodating.

But the way Chief Rubenovich had interacted with Trace showed kindness and focus and had made her want to trust him despite her natural reserve around strange men. If he truly knew Trace, he'd be more than welcome to come to the sanctuary to visit her.

And I wouldn't mind seeing him again, either. His brown eyes full of sharp intelligence had set him apart from most of the men who lived in and around Cascade Breaks. Combined with the dark scruff on his cheeks and she'd damn near swooned when she first saw him.

She snorted as she let Trace back into her dog-run. "Let me get you some water, Trace. And maybe a milk bone for taking on that bear to protect the Chief."

The dog sat down and looked at her with intelligent golden eyes.

"Good girl. Yes, you impressed me."

The dog huffed and blinked, and Caroline swore she was asking Caroline's thoughts on Chief Rubenovich. *Great, now I'm anthropomorphizing a dog.*

Caroline shook her head. "I don't do random men. Heck, I don't do even the men I know at the moment."

She moved away to fill the dog's water bowl with the hose. She sometimes wished she had a man around, someone with a beard, chest hair, and muscular physique. But she hadn't found one she liked well enough to be with longer than a few months. They always got frustrated with her determination to save the dogs, calling her too focused. She snorted. *I am that.* To be honest, she hadn't found a man she liked enough to split her time between him and the dogs. He always fell short.

CPO Rubenovich is already short. You could fall for him.

She groaned and turned off the hose before carrying the water bowl back to Trace. The dog didn't look down at the bowl, but stared at Caroline with patience and eerie understanding.

"What?" Caroline set the bowl inside the dog run. The dog blinked as if waiting for her to understand. "You're telling me I should give Rubenovich another look?"

It's what you want, isn't it?

Caroline shook her head and pointed at the water bowl. "Drink."

Trace gave her another slow blink before she dropped her head and lapped at the bowl. *I'm going nuts and talking to a dog.* Except she'd been taking to dogs since she was a little girl and they always seemed understand each other. It was why she'd started the Last Chance Dog Sanctuary. She could tell what they needed because she could hear them, in a way. She hadn't told anyone about her ability–glory knew she didn't need folks thinking she was crazy–but she had capitalized on it to help those who needed it.

And sometimes I like dogs better than people. The dogs usually wanted to be helped. People, not so much.

"Good girl, Trace. I'm glad you're here. You did a good job protecting us from that bear. Thank you for your work. But next time I'm gonna latch and padlock the gate."

The blue heeler looked up, gave her a slow blink that equated a dog's wink, barked, and bounded off to do dog things. Caroline watched her go with bemusement, shaking her head. *I'm definitely reading things into this.* She coiled the hose and went to check on Daphne inside.

****

After the day she'd had, Caroline simply wanted to soak in the tub, but her shipment of dog food wouldn't arrive until the next day and the squirrels had gotten into their supply of fortified kibble for one of her bitches. The Rottweiler female was pregnant and puppies would be arriving soon, but she needed to eat to bring those puppies safely. Fortunately, the feed store in town carried it and they stayed open later than the rest of the town.

Might help that they'd combined the feed store with a bar.

Why anyone thought alcohol paired well with a shop selling farming equipment was a good idea, she didn't know, but it made it easier to get feed for emergencies like this one.

"Daphne, I have to run into town for dog food for Tallulah." Caroline threw on a light zip-up sweatshirt and grabbed her keys. "I'll take the Cherokee. Be back in about an hour, 'kay?"

"Yeah, okay. I'll have dinner ready by then."

Dinner? Caroline rubbed her face with one hand as her stomach growled. Damn, the day had gotten away from her and she'd forgotten to eat. Again. "Great. I'll see you then."

She snagged her purse and headed out to the SUV, wondering if she should grab something quick to tide her over since she hadn't eaten since...*Was it breakfast?* She couldn't remember and she didn't have the luxury to let herself get sick. The dogs and Daphne needed her to be strong. *Especially if those assholes come back.* She had no illusions about their tenacity.

The twenty minute drive soothed some of her concerns and she made it into Cascade Breaks without trouble. The little town had been home to her grandparents and she'd happily moved back when her parents retired to San Diego. The town boasted a post office, a gas station on either end, a Travel Lodge motel, the Cascade Breaks Feed Store & Bar, a sheriff's station, an old Safeway grocery, and a Loves truck stop. Most of the town catered to tourists hiking the trails or the truckers on their way through to somewhere else, but the farming community just down the road kept the feed store going.

And the bar. It was the local meet-and-greet place which allowed the locals to do their shopping and their drinking.

Caroline parked her Cherokee and eyed the big trucks in the lot. Saturdays at the feed store/bar were always busy and crowds made her nervous. But Bert and Mable who owned the store usually kept the business separate. Taking a deep breath, Caroline grabbed her purse and headed inside.

The bell tinkled over the door and Bert looked up from organizing some dog food cans on one of the endcaps. "Hey Caroline. How are you?"

She smiled, relieved she wouldn't have to wait for service. "Good. Well, kinda." She grimaced. "I'm out of food for Tallulah. Damn squirrels got into it."

"Damn, woman, you need to get a cat." Bert grinned as he stood.

"Oh yeah, that's a good idea at a dog sanctuary."

He limped down one aisle to the dog food section, his prosthetic foot giving him an uneven gait as he laughed. "Gotta keep them dogs in shape, right?" He winked. "Lullah's due to whelp any day now, isn't she?"

"I think so. I'm expecting a dog food shipment on Monday, but she's gotta eat this weekend."

"She sure does. Hmm, we don't have any out here. I'll have to check the back." Bert shook his head. "I know we got some recently and no one else has a dog whelping at the moment. Be back in a minute."

"Okay." Caroline walked around the store to see if there was anything else she needed to pick up. Maybe a toy for Trace, though the dog wasn't much for playing. Treats always went over well, but the dog had learned she had to earn them and Caroline didn't want to break her training. She meandered back to the counter and admired the fun hand-painted welcome signs hanging on the wall. She particularly like the one with the German Shepherd standing at attention.

"Hey, honey, ain't you a pretty thing." A rough voice

damaged by cigarettes and drinking reached her ears just before the scents of cheap cologne and alcohol hit her nose. "What's a lovely thing like you doin' in a place like this?"

Seriously, do they really think those lines work? Caroline shifted away from the hulking presence sidling up beside her and craned her neck to see where Bert was. *Hurry up, Bert.*

"You don't say much, do you, sweetheart?" The man beside her wore a grimy baseball cap and a plaid short-sleeved shirt barely covering a gut big enough to hide his belt buckle. From his scent, he hadn't bathed in a while, and the alcohol had helped him overcome any reservations about approaching women. "Whadya say you come over for a beer with me and my buddies?"

"Thank you for the offer, but I'm just here to get dog food before going home." She didn't meet their eyes, just turned her head a little to acknowledge the invitation.

"Oh, come on, now, sweetheart. It's Saturday night. Take a load off. The dog can wait." He reached for her and she dodged away, but one of his friends shifted to her other side. "Come on, it'll be fun."

"No, thank you." She kept her expression neutral and her arms at her sides, but they'd hemmed her in. "I really just would like to get my dog food and go. Thanks."

"Well, we'll let you do that once you've had a drink with us. Come on, don't be rude." He reached for her again and she had nowhere to get away.

Deep breaths, Caroline. The only way to get out of this was to be calm.

"I'm pretty sure the lady said no to you twice." A new voice joined the conversation as CPO Rubenovich stepped up behind the guy. "While other situations might be confusing, I think she was clear on declining your invitation."

The pungent man turned and looked over his shoulder before smirking. "Well lookee here. A midget has come to her aid. What are you gonna do about it, little man?"

The other men laughed and she expected Rubenovich to show fury or irritation over the remarks about his height. But he gave them a half-smile and raised his chin.

"First, I'm going to ask you to leave her alone, then I'm gonna ask you to leave the store." He shrugged. "After that, you can do what you want."

The laughter turned derisive. "Go away. There wasn't nothing wrong with asking the lady to join us for a beer."

"Nope, nothing wrong with that except for not taking no for an answer." Rubenovich shrugged his shoulders. Under the black t-shirt, they looked strong. "She said no. Not hard to figure out what to do next."

"Yeah, leave us the fuck alone."

Rubenovich shook his head. "I can't do that. She told you to leave her alone, but you won't. You told me to leave you alone. Guess what I'm gonna do?" His mouth quirked up in a grin.

Caroline would've laughed if the situation wasn't so serious.

"All right, little man. We're gonna teach you to mind your own business."

"No." Rubenovich shook his head. "You're not going to have a fight in this store just to shore up your bruised egos. You want to do this, let's go outside."

Caroline didn't think the men would go for it and wished Bert would return to back Rubenovich up. She didn't even have her bag of dog food to use as a deterrent.

The guy who'd approached her barked an ugly laugh. "Okay, little man, we'll kick your ass outside."

Rubenovich snorted, but nodded. "After you."

"I don't think that's a good idea." Caroline reached out, resting her hand lightly on the rigid muscles of his forearm. "Please, it isn't worth you getting hurt for me."

The crow's feet around his eyes crinkled as he grinned. "It's my job. Usually it's for the whole country, but today I get to do it for a specific citizen." He nodded to the men filing out of the store. "Even if they're currently serving in the military, which I don't believe they are, this is a teaching moment."

She raised her eyebrow. "Teaching moment? And what are you going to teach them?"

"Two lessons." He headed for the door and she followed out of sheer curiosity. "One, don't underestimate a small person. Just because they're small doesn't mean they're helpless or easily beaten."

"And the second lesson?"

"When a woman tells you no, lick your wounds and take her at her word to leave her alone." He nodded to her and pushed out the door to join the other men.

At that moment, Bert came back to the counter carrying the dog food bag. "What's goin' on, Caroline?"

She bit her lip and retreated to the counter. "Five guys propositioned me and CPO Rubenovich stepped in to deter them. They're all outside getting ready to fight."

Bert blinked. "Should I call the ambulance for him?"

She shook her head. "Not for him. For them. I suspect they're going to need it."

CHAPTER FOUR

Deli found the men waiting for him in a semi-circle, their expressions avid for gratuitous violence. They saw him as weaker and smaller prey. He almost grinned at their lack of foresight, but reined it in before it got him in trouble.

"Thank you for being so understanding about causing damage in the store." He nodded to them as he stopped a few feet from them.

"Yeah, yeah, whatever. You ready for an ass-kicking?" The lead thug sneered as he narrowed his eyes.

Deli held up one hand. "First, I want to give you a chance to leave with your pride and bodies intact. You still have time to walk away and write this off as 'not worth the trouble.' It's something you should consider."

"All right, it's been considered. Now get ready for an ass-whoopin', little man."

The others gathered around him with smirks, so certain of their success. He took a deep breath and nodded. "Okay then, don't say I didn't warn you."

The scene reminded Deli of one from a movie about a guy who'd become a Samurai while in 19th Century Japan. The words *too much thought* came back to him and he settled his mind. He doubted the screenwriter had gotten the fight scene right, but the advice held wisdom and it stuck with him. *Don't think, just react. The body knows what it's doing.*

The first guy came at his back and Deli spun to the left, back-handing the guy in the kidney with a closed fist. The man went down with a gasp as the second man tried to grab Deli's shoulders. He dropped and rammed his fist up into the man's groin, making him bend in half, and Deli finished him off with a blow to the back of the head.

The main belligerent thug roared and threw a punch at Deli's head. Deli leaned back and grabbed the thug's arm, jerking him off balance and sending him sprawling into his friend who hadn't expected the move. They collapsed in a heap of snarling, swearing limbs, and Deli focused on the last guy who'd stood back, watching. His eyes grew round as Deli met his gaze and tipped his head. *You comin', jackass?*

Kidney-guy staggered to his feet and came at Deli from behind again, this time using his foot to slam into Deli's back. But Deli twisted sideways and grabbed the guy's foot, dragging him forward a few hopping steps before swinging him into his last friend standing. Deli listened for the others as he put the doors to the feed store to his back.

Belligerent-guy finally scrambled to his feet and came at Deli again, snarling and screaming about assholes and punks. Deli saw the punch coming and blocked before landing his own punch into the guy's midriff. As he went down, Deli clapped his hands against the guy's ears, and he collapsed hard. Deli threw his foot down on the back of Belligerent-guy's neck and held it there as he listened for the others.

"Now that we've made it clear this wasn't a good idea, you wanna let it go and move on?" He met everyone's gaze who remained conscious. "You can have your friend as long as you leave quietly. No one needs to get more hurt."

Apparently, they weren't listening because the friend who'd collided with Belligerent-guy came at Deli with a walloping right hook that landed on the left side of his head before he could duck. It sent him sprawling into the dirt with his ears ringing like a bell. *See? Too much thought.* Yeah, yeah. Deli ignored his screaming lungs and rolled, coming up with an angry snarl. While the jackasses were gloating, he used their distraction to fight dirty and shot back into the fray with a hard jab to the 'nads that took the guy down.

Deli stood back and waited to see if anyone else wanted to come for him. His head rang like a gong and his vision shifted in and out of focus, but he waited, the adrenaline pumping through his veins like liquid fire. A new sound came to his ears, but he wasn't sure if it belonged to the ringing he already heard or something else. *So much for R&R.*

Flashing lights hit his peripheral vision as the ambulance and cops finally showed up, but he kept his gaze on the other men just in case they wanted to try one more time. When the emergency vehicles stopped, Deli relaxed marginally, still far enough away to take on anyone threatening. The only thing he didn't expect was the light touch on his shoulder and he spun, fist cocked.

A feminine gasp made him pull his punch, but the dizziness that came with his spin took him down to his knees. He tried to keep his gaze on something still, but ended up with an eyeful of breasts and his brain went into pleasure mode.

"Are you all right, Rubenovich?"

Pretty. He wanted to shake his head to set his mind straight, but all he could focus on was the lovely woman in front of him. *Don't let my guard down. Enemies remain.*

"Fine. You?" How was he down to one-word sentences?

"I'm all right, but you don't look so hot."

He snorted. "Sorry. Will try to be sexier."

She rolled her eyes and shook her head. "Not what I meant. Will you let the EMTs take a look at you?"

"I'll be f-f-f-fine." Why did his head feel like it was spinning?

"And my name's Mary Poppins. You're gonna let the EMTs take a look at you and then you're staying the night at my place. No argument. Copy?"

"Copy that, ma'am." He didn't mind staying with her. Maybe she'd nurse him back to health. And then some.

He allowed her to drag him over to the EMT to check him out. He answered the standard questions and let Caroline do all the talking when the deputies showed up. He just agreed to her version of the events. The EMT said he had a concussion and shouldn't move around much for the next twenty-four hours, to which Caroline stated he wouldn't. Deli inwardly laughed at her vehemence but kept his mouth shut. If he wanted or needed to move because he was recalled, he'd move. But for now, he'd let her baby him. It was nice to have a woman go all mother-hen over him.

"All right, Chief. I think we got enough. Sorry you had to set those boys straight. You sure you're gonna be okay?" The deputy eyed him with a frown.

"Yup. Just need some water, some food, and some rest. I'll be fine tomorrow." He didn't nod, but he gave the deputy an encouraging smile despite the continued ringing in his head.

The guy nodded. "You wanna press charges, you can come on down to the sheriff's office tomorrow."

"Will do. Thanks, Deputy."

He tipped his hat before he headed off to help his fellow deputies load the men into their vehicles. Deli didn't have the energy to smirk. Those guys would need medical attention before they were booked. *More so than I will.* Still he wasn't looking forward to reporting back to Whittleton. The CO wouldn't be pleased with him getting injured on R&R. He grimaced and Caroline frowned in concern.

"Come on. Leave your vehicle here and we'll come back to get it tomorrow. You're in no condition to drive." She grasped his arm and pulled him to his feet.

"I don't need help to walk."

She nodded. "Oh, I know you don't. I just need escorting to my truck so I don't get accosted by anyone else."

He narrowed his eyes at her, but that only made his vision more blurry. He instead focused on putting one foot in front of the other without falling over. *Damn, I just want to sleep.* But he forced himself to keep awake as she helped him into the passenger side of her Cherokee. *Hell Week was harder.* He thought back to what kept him going then while she loaded the dog food into the back of her vehicle and climbed into the driver's seat.

"Ready to go?"

"Yes, ma'am."

She snorted with a smirk. "I like the sound of that."

He laughed even though it made his head ring.

****

Caroline tightened her lips in concern as CPO Rubenovich's head nodded, his eyes closed. *Dammit, is he asleep?* She had to keep him conscious at least until she got home. She almost reached over to tap him when his head came up and his eyes opened. They didn't appear to focus on much, but at least they stayed open.

She'd make sure he survived the night and tomorrow he could go on his merry way, leaving her and Daphne in peace.

Oh, hell, Daphne.

She pulled over to the side of the road and parked,

scrounging for her phone. She hadn't thought about her niece when she offered to take care of Rubenovich. The younger woman didn't deal well with men after her time in South America, and here Caroline was bringing one home. She shook her head. *Smart move, Caro.*

She dialed the house line and waited for the answering machine to pick up. "Hey, Daphne. I wanted to let you know we'll be having a guest tonight. Long story and I'll tell you when I get home. Should be there in about fifteen minutes."

She stowed the phone and got back on the road. Hopefully, it wouldn't be a big deal and she could get him into her room without too much fuss. Daphne wouldn't even have to interact with him.

Caroline sighed. She'd have to watch him all night long, waking him every few hours to make sure he recovered. *Damn, it's gonna be a long night.* Why the hell did she do this to herself, taking in every hard case and sob story thrown at her? For some reason, she couldn't dismiss Rubenovich. He reminded her a little of her dogs, never giving up even when they'd taken a beating, but still needing care and rehabilitation.

Not that he wasn't in fine condition, physically. His body looked toned and fit, despite the bruising caused by the fight. But something about him suggested his mind needed a respite from something dogging him. *Yeah, nice pun there.* She couldn't shake the feeling he needed as much recuperation as the MWDs. *I'll do what I can, Chief.* She just hoped it would be enough before he had to return to active duty.

She kept her attention on him for the whole way home, but the usual drive sped by. By the time she reached her place, she was more stressed about what Daphne would say than by taking care of a man she barely knew. *Even if he is a hot one.*

As soon as she parked, Daphne appeared on the porch

with Beryl, her lips tight. "What the hell happened, Caroline?"

Caroline blinked. "Bar fight, kinda. Unless you're talking about something else. Did someone come back while I was gone?"

"No, but Sheriff Tanner called and said you were having trouble with someone at the feed store. Are you okay?" Daphne usually didn't go all mama-bear unless pushed to the limit and she didn't like folks hurting her loved ones.

"Yeah, I'm okay. Did you get the message on the machine?"

Daphne shook her head.

"Oh, well, we're going to have a guest tonight. Can you come get the dog food while I help Chief Rubenovich out of the truck?"

"Sure." Daphne paused at the bottom of the steps. "Wait. Who?"

"Chief Rubenovich, U.S. Navy. He decided to take on all five of the assholes who wouldn't take no for an answer." She shook her head as she opened the passenger door. "Can you walk under your own power, Chief?"

Rubenovich opened his molten fudge-brown eyes and she tried not to get sucked into them. *He's a guy who's probably like all the others. Don't get hooked.*

"Yeah, I'm good. Where are we?" He turned his gaze to take in her home.

"My place. The Last Chance Dog Sanctuary I told you about. Looks like tonight I won't be taking care of just dogs." She was too tall to shove her shoulder under his armpit, but she locked an arm around his ribs, trying to ignore the hard body she grasped. "Come on, let's get you inside and into bed." *Glory, he smells good.*

"Moving kinda fast, aren't you?" He smirked as he leaned his weight on her.

She rolled her eyes, but kept him moving toward the

house. "Funny. You'll be sleeping in the extra bedroom."

He laughed anyway before he winced and some of her frustration faded. He'd gone into battle for her and sustained enough of an injury to deserve some compassion. She helped him up the steps to the porch while Daphne watched with wariness until she got a good look at Rubenovich's face. She gasped and jerked upright, her hand coming to her mouth in surprise. When Caroline raised her eyebrows, the younger woman shook her head, but continued to watch them as Caroline helped him inside.

"The bedroom's down the hall, second door on the right."

"Second star on the right, and straight on till morning." His mumbled words made her smile. Who knew the badass Navy man read classical literature?

"Yeah, well, you're not getting the 'straight on till morning' routine tonight. I'll have to wake you up every couple of hours to make sure your concussion isn't too bad." She didn't look forward to that, although getting to see him that often might not be awful. She snorted. *Rein in the hormones, missy. He's too young for you.* "What directions did the EMT give you for taking care of yourself?"

"Aw, you know, the usual. Don't sleep too long and call them if anything seems off." He shrugged like he'd gotten the spiel a few times and had it down.

She sighed and helped him down the hall to the extra room. She hadn't made the bed with clean sheets recently, but no one had slept in it since their last guest a few months ago. At least they'd cleared most of the storage totes of miscellaneous crap out to the barn. *Thank glory for small favors.* He staggered straight for the bed and settled into it like a man twice his age. *How would I know that? I don't even know how old he is.*

"Oh, damn, this is a comfortable bed. Is it yours?"

Caroline shook her head as she helped him take off his

shoes. "No. I'll be in mine."

"Why? Isn't this one comfortable?" Rubenovich leered, though it was spoiled by the grimace of pain as he settled back.

"This bed is fine, but you need to rest alone tonight."

He frowned. "I don't make you nervous, do I?"

"That depends from what you think my nervousness stems." She helped him under the light covers.

His leer disappeared. "I'd never hurt you, Caroline. I swear. I'm not that kind of guy."

She didn't laugh, nodding in understanding. "I didn't think you were. I'm more worried you won't make it through the night. That guy clocked you pretty hard and brain injuries are serious. Even the football players are coming to understand collision isn't a good thing for your head."

"I'm gonna be fine. I've had worse."

She sighed. "It's not about that. It's about right now. Your past only brings a cumulative effect to the present. You might have done this before, but that could mean this is worse than then."

"You worry too much."

"And you don't worry enough." She clenched her hands into fists and swallowed hard. "Look, I don't know your past and I don't care, but right now you're my responsibility and I'd appreciate it if you wouldn't die on my watch, okay?"

He smirked, but something in her expression must have registered because it died away. "I promise not to die on your watch and I'm grateful for your help." He reached for one of her hands. "I'm sorry to scare you. Thanks for lookin' out for me and Trace."

She snorted to hide the thrill of his touch. "I'll always watch out for Trace. She deserves the most love of all."

"So do you." He yawned the words so she could've misheard when he didn't continue.

"Get some rest. I'll be back in a couple hours to make sure you're okay." She paused to look back at him lying in the guest bed and he nodded.

"Okay."

She flipped off the light and left the room, wondering why she hoped she hadn't misheard him.

CHAPTER FIVE

Screams and gunshots filled Deli's dreams and he came awake with a start when someone touched his shoulder. He gripped the arm of his assailant and yanked them over his body, pinning them beneath him.

A terrified squawk brought him back to the present and he realized the body underneath him was soft, warm, and decidedly feminine. Several moments of heavy breathing cleared the cobwebs from his mind and he got his vision to work.

"Caroline?"

"Yes, Chief. Can you please get off me?"

He didn't want to move. She smelled good and cushioned his hard body better than the bed where he slept. But her heart pounded under his chest and he recognized barely-held panic in her expression.

"Sorry. Combat sleep. What are you doing here?" He rolled back over, releasing her.

"I'm waking you to check on you. Concussion, remember?" She scrambled off the bed and stood out of reach. "I see you're okay. Do you need anything? Water, tea?"

Deli almost shook his head, but the persistent

throbbing had set in after moving quickly. "What kinds of tea do you have?"

The question surprised him. He didn't drink tea, being a beer or coffee kind of guy. But something about the mild taste of hot, steeped leaves appealed to him at the moment.

Caroline bit her lip. "Dragon phoenix, a mixture of black and green tea in little balls. Or some chamomile. Or huckleberry."

"Little dragon and phoenix balls?" He smirked. "Yeah, okay, I could take a chance on that."

She rolled her eyes. "The tea is called dragon phoenix and it's rolled into little…You know what? I'll just bring you what I have." She spun and strode out the door before he could say anything else.

He chuckled but stopped it short when his head reminded him of his injuries. Damn, he had to move faster next time. If he didn't, either he or the members of his team could be killed. All humor fled as he remembered the dream. He could still see Bones drop to the ground and smell the blood from his wounds.

Deli squeezed his eyes shut, but it only made the memories clearer. Tears leaked out the sides of his eyes in a sudden burst of emotion. He missed his family, the other SEALs who made up his squad and their spouses. Rimshot and Bam-Bam had found their happily-ever-afters in women who understood them. Bronco was a dad with Lindsey. Hell, even Retro and Magic had snagged the same woman in Chris "Ghost" Brickman. They all had someone waiting for them to come home.

Where was the one waiting for him? *Fuck, my heart's getting dark.*

He rarely gave into the feelings of loneliness among his peers. Loving a SEAL wasn't easy in peace time, much less when they had to go out and disappear for months at a time. And when they came back, they couldn't talk about where they'd been or what they'd seen. *If we come back.* It took a very strong person to put up with that.

Despite loving what he did and his need to 'save the world' from the bad guys, he also wanted something specific to fight for. Or rather, someone. Family, his parents and his siblings, his squadmates and their spouses, they were important, no question. But for the first time in his life, he wanted someone who waited just for him.

Damn, this concussion has fucked me up.

Padfoot's words came back to him, bubbling up from his roiling emotions. *I learned the hard way that ignoring the emotions fucks you up worse than acknowledging them.* Deli didn't want to acknowledge them because doing so would only illustrate just how alone he really was.

But the tears and fears, once given the exit strategy, surged forward and spilled down his cheeks. Sobs filled his chest and damn near stopped his breath. Pain and loneliness sucked him down into the abyss of darkness and it only lifted when someone sat on the bed beside him.

He hiccoughed a sudden breath and opened his eyes to find a beautiful woman with a mug of tea in her hands. "Tea makes everything better. Drink."

He couldn't make his voice work to say thanks. He nodded and took the mug instead.

"I'll leave you to rest. Let me know if you need anything else."

She rose, but he grasped her trailing hand and held it. "Please stay a while."

He might not know her well, but he needed someone to keep him company. Even if she never said a word.

"You want me to stay?"

"Please." He didn't want to tell her about the nightmares or admit that they ate at him each time he tried to sleep. "Thank you for the tea."

"You're welcome. Drink it down. It will help calm some of the emotion, I promise."

He frowned. "What did you put in it?"

"Nothing. It's chamomile from my garden. It has natural calming properties." She squeezed his arm, a comforting gesture that drained the tension from him. "You can let your worries go for the time being. This is a safe place. No one here will hurt you."

Her words and body language relaxed him, but he worried it was more than simple relaxation and comfort. What if she'd drugged him with the tea?

"Easy. Relax. You're safe here." She watched him and he dutifully drank some of the tea.

It softened some of the worry almost immediately, but he set the mug aside and lay back in the bed to keep an eye on her. He didn't really want to break down in front of her again, but something about this place loosened his hold on the shit he kept buried.

"Come on. Relax. I'll stay until you fall asleep again." She settled beside him and held his hand, rubbing the back with her fingers.

Holy shit, that feels awesome.

He'd never enjoyed being touched unless it had to do with sex. Then he was tactile as hell. But something about the way she ran her hands over his skin settled him as if he'd taken a sedative.

She didn't say anything more, just sat beside him and kept up her repetitive motions. He closed his eyes and let himself drift, exhaustion threatening to overtake him. He couldn't let down his guard. He didn't know this woman at all despite his interest in her. Of course, Sergeant Trace liked her, and he gave high marks to anyone who was trusted by a Military War Dog.

Caroline didn't hum, but her breathing soothed Deli along with her hand on his. He fought long and hard to stay awake and present, but the chamomile tea and her relaxation techniques lulled him back to sleep.

****

Caroline knew the moment Chief Rubenovich dropped off to sleep, but she couldn't stop running her hands over his head. When she'd returned to the room, he'd been fighting tears and emotions, probably too long contained. Her heart had gone out to him, not in sympathy, but in empathy. She'd experienced much the same reaction when Daphne had been brought home.

Tea makes everything better.

She hadn't been wrong. She'd intended to bring him the dragon phoenix, but opted for her homegrown chamomile instead. He'd had a harrowing night and while she didn't know what he usually did in day-to-day life, everyone needed some downtime. Seeing his emotion streaming down his face had made her glad she'd chosen the chamomile.

She studied him in the light from the hallway. Dark lashes fanned his cheeks under thick black brows. He hadn't shaved and the short scruff around his elegant lips made him look rakish and sexy. Despite his shorter stature, he had a strong, well-built body and she shivered with the unbidden idea of having it under her hands.

Oh, for goodness sake, he's just a man.

Yeah, and she didn't need one. She had her robo-dick and fresh batteries in the other room. But when he'd let down his guard before she delivered the tea, his vulnerability had softened her heart. She didn't need a man, but she'd forgotten what it was like to simply want one around.

Why is your attraction so hard for you to believe? He's hot, sexy, and heroic. What more could she want?

The answer came back as likely as finding a unicorn. *I want someone who values me for me.* It had been a long time since anyone beyond Daphne had valued her, and no one romantically inclined. She shook her head. *Put wishes in one hand and spit in the other, and see which one fills up first.*

She retreated to her bedroom and set her alarm for a couple hours ahead so she could wake him again. Settling into the bed, she switched off the light, but sleep wouldn't come to her. She kept thinking of the man in the other room, a man who'd gotten a concussion trying to protect her from five redneck thugs. She grimaced and shut her eyes, determined to get a little rest.

But the next thing Caroline knew, the alarm was going off and she had to get up. She rubbed her face and sat up, unnerved by how dark and silent the room had become. Hadn't she left the light on in the hallway? She frowned and shot a look toward the window.

A shadow moved out of the corner of her eye and the muzzle of a pistol pressed against the side her head.

"Oh glory."

"Tell the little man he's not welcome. He can't interfere."

Anger surged despite the fear and she raised her chin. "He won't back down. He'll defend us no matter what. He said he's going to—"

"Let me explain something to you, bitch. We'll get this land no matter what you do, and we'll take down your little Navy man in a heartbeat. You can either vacate on your own, or we'll make you." The gun's muzzle pressed harder. "Say *buenas noches, perra.*"

A loud report ripped Caroline out of sleep and her alarm blared in the still room. *Holy shit, it was a dream.* She slapped the clock to stop it and scrubbed her face, relieved to see the light still on in the hallway.

She rose but her legs shook and she took a few moments to steady herself while her heartbeat slowly returned to normal. *Deep breaths, Caro.* She closed her eyes and took a few steadying breaths before raising her head and crossing to the extra bedroom. She checked on Daphne first to make sure her nightmare was just that.

Beryl looked up from the bed when Caroline opened the door and she breathed a sigh of relief. *Time to wake the chief.*

She found him lying in the bed with his eyes open. "Are you okay?"

His voice startled her and she straightened her shoulders. "Yes. Why?"

"I heard you call out. Are you sure you're okay?" His dark eyes scanned her body and she tried to hide the shiver.

"Yes, I'm fine. How are you? Would you like some more tea?"

"No, thanks. I'm not really tired." He scooted his body up higher against the headboard. "I feel pretty much awake and now I'm hungry."

"That's a good sign."

"Right?" He laughed and patted the bed. "Come sit with me a moment."

Caroline hesitated. "Let me get you some food before I go back to bed."

Rubenovich shook his head. "Sit down for a bit. I have a question."

She bit her lip as her gut clenched. "What's your question?" She settled on the edge of the bed near his feet.

"Who's threatening you enough to give you nightmares?"

She gaped at him. Had she said anything about the men trying to take her land? "What are you talking about?"

He shrugged. "You talk in your sleep. What's going on, Caroline?"

She gave him her best dismissive smile. "Nothing you need to worry about. You'll be up and around soon, and free to get back to your vacation. We're fine tonight."

"Were those guys at the feed store part of this problem?"

His question made her pause. Were those men part of the Casa de Catequil Cartel threatening to take her home?

She shook her head. "No. Those were just local yokels showing off their male entitlement."

"Male entitlement?" He raised an eyebrow.

"Yeah, you know. Every woman they see is meant for their entertainment and enjoyment? It doesn't matter if she says no. It happens more often than most people like to admit." She shrugged. "In any case, they don't have anything to do with my nightmares."

"Then what does?"

She gave him a vague smile. "Don't worry about it. You need to rest so you can enjoy the rest of your vacation."

He scowled. "I won't be able to if I think you're in trouble. Why don't you tell me what's going on? Maybe I can help."

"Why would you want to? You stuck your neck out for me once and you don't know anything about me other than I take care of discarded dogs with PTSD." She shook her head with a frown. "Why do you even care?"

He raised his chin and his gaze grew cold enough to make her shiver. "I'm in the U.S. Navy. My job is literally to make the country safe for its citizens. That's the whole reason I joined. But it sounds like you don't think you're safe. I'm here, I have the time, and the skills, to make you safer." He took a deep breath and his gaze warmed a little. "And I like you. You're helping Sergeant Trace and other dogs. That in itself is pretty damn cool."

Caroline studied his face, but all she could read was honest determination. She sighed and looked away, trying to decide if he was worth the chance. *He's a stranger.* He wouldn't be here long enough to make a difference. But he did have military training and maybe he could dissuade the thugs from the cartel enough for them to look elsewhere.

"It's not that I don't feel safe, per se." She ran her fingers over the hem of her shirt, trying to find a way to explain that wouldn't make him laugh at her. "A few

49

months ago some men with heavy Hispanic accents came here to offer to buy my place. Hispanic accents aren't that strange in this part of California so I didn't think anything of it. They wore fancy suits and shoes, drove sleek, expensive cars, and spoke well enough that I thought they were just real estate folks trying to buy up cheap land for the yuppies in the cities."

"They weren't real estate people I take it."

"No." She shrugged. "They offered way too much money for the land's worth, but it's been in my family for over a century and I wasn't interested in selling. This is my home and I'm doing what I love. They told me to think about it when I turned them down. But they came back again and again, and got angrier and angrier when I wouldn't take their offers, no matter how large they were."

"Why your place in particular?"

She shrugged. "I don't really know. I guess because we're kinda secluded up against the national forest with no neighbors. The last offer was something around fifteen million."

"Holy shit."

"Yeah. They weren't expecting us to turn it down."

"But you did, again."

"Yeah. They were so angry they stomped off, snarling in Spanish that the cartel wouldn't like it and something would have to be done." She rubbed her hands on her thighs, palms suddenly sweaty. "The next day I caught a news report about a new Columbian cartel, Casa de Catequil, House of the Incan Thunder God, was making inroads into California, buying up land for transport of drugs and sex slaves. I made the connection then."

Rubenovich's gaze hardened. "Are you saying the guys who want your land are cartel thugs?"

She nodded. "Yeah, I'm pretty sure. The last time they came was yesterday afternoon and I told them they already had my answer and to leave me the hell alone."

He shot her a half-smile. "You threatened them?"

"Only if they came back. I'm not going to hunt them down."

He shook his head. "No, but I suspect they'll hunt you down. That's really dangerous."

She narrowed her eyes. "And what was I supposed to do? Nod and smile and take their money while leaving my land to them? I can't. It's my home and business. This is supposed to be the United State of America, not the random state of cartelland."

"They're not going to give up."

She nodded, anger rising at his patronizing tone. "Y'think? How stupid to you think I am, Chief?" She glanced at his mug. "Do you need any more tea? I need to get some sleep."

"No, I'm good. Thanks."

She rose and nodded, not willing to absorb his pity for her. She protected her home and her land from rustlers, just like her father, grandfather, and great-grandfather. She wouldn't be run off just because some rich assholes wanted it. *The cartel is scary, but this is my home.* And woe betide anyone threatening a woman's home.

CHAPTER SIX

Caroline rose without a word and headed for the door of the bedroom. *Damn, the woman is prickly.* She understood the dangers of dealing with a foreign cartel, but she still shot at them. Now they'd be gunning for her on ego alone. And she didn't have the backup of an entire team of elite warriors or the equipment they used to fight the bad guys. *She's gonna get herself killed.*

"Caroline, wait."

"Look, Chief. I took you in because you needed someone to look after you while you recover. Tomorrow you'll be free to go wherever you like. You asked what was going on and I told you. I don't need your pity or disappointment. I get enough of that from my family. Just get some rest and I'll see you in the morning."

"I don't pity you, but I do think this is a bigger deal than you realize. You could get yourself killed."

"What do you care? You're on vacation and I'm someone you just met. Why should it matter to you?"

"It matters! It matters because I'm in the Navy and—"

"I know, you defend the country and its citizens." She sighed. "Look, it's not your fight. You don't have to do anything but relax. I'll take care of myself like I always have."

He gritted his teeth against the growl that wanted to erupt. "That's the point. I'm not sure you can take care of yourself."

Deli realized his mistake the moment the words were out of his mouth.

"Thanks for letting me know that, Chief. You have a good night." She turned to the door to leave.

Shit. "Caroline, wait, that's not what I meant." He shoved his temper down and took a deep breath to gather his thoughts. "I'm sorry. That came out wrong." He grimaced as her eyebrows went up. "I meant, in this situation, you might be outmatched." He held up his hand before the anger he read in her face poured out. "How 'bout in the morning, I help you come up with some ideas of how to handle the cartel's thugs when they come back? I have some experience with them and I don't mind helping out."

She sighed and shook her head. "Thanks for the offer. Right now, just get some sleep. We'll deal with whatever comes in the morning." She left the room, switching off the light as she went.

Deli rubbed his face with his hands and settled back into the bed. But his mind wouldn't shut down. Something about the name of the cartel wouldn't leave him alone, and the idea of her taking on a cartel scared the daylights out of him. She said she'd heard a report of a Columbian cartel moving into California, but that could be just about anyone.

And not necessarily the Team's previous vacation destination.

Bravo squad had visited Columbia and taken down the head of a cartel, but they'd had a different name and unraveled after the SEALs visited. *Yeah, but cartels are like hydras – cut the head off, and after some reorganization, at least one new one grows back.* He hadn't heard any scuttlebutt about the cartel they'd toppled.

Deli frowned. Tomorrow he'd call his buddy Rimshot

and see what the man knew about it. And he'd do all he could to help Caroline and her Last Chance Dog Sanctuary. He closed his eyes and courted sleep. Tomorrow would be soon enough to tackle Caroline's problems. But her disappointed expression chased him down into his dreams.

Morning had him up at the butt-crack of dawn and he swung his legs out of the bed. Too bad he hadn't convinced Caroline to join him there. *Yeah, after pissing her off, I'm sure she would've been okay with that.* He stretched slowly, taking inventory of the aches and pains, particularly his head. All in all, he didn't feel too bad, and he searched out his shoes to go for a run. No one else seemed to be awake, and he slipped through the house toward the front door.

Caroline's sleeping face on her bed arrested him before he made it to the living room. She lay fully dressed on her side, her hand cradling her face. She wore her exhaustion even in sleep and he found himself wishing he could take some of her worries away. He snorted softly. *If she'd let me.* Despite her fatigue, her innate beauty struck him still, and he realized he could sit there and watch her sleep, studying the planes of her face.

Great, now I'm a stalker.

Grimacing, he carried his shoes to the door and let himself out of the house, locking it behind him. She could let him back in when he returned. Or he could enjoy the sunrise if she wasn't awake yet.

He settled on the porch and shoved his feet into his shoes, wishing he could take Sgt. Trace with him on his run. He missed working with dogs, but his SEAL squad hadn't had a canine unit. He still had a few months until his enlistment was up, but maybe he'd get back into working with the MWDs or their retired brethren. He certainly wanted to reconnect with Trace.

Deli rose and stretched his body to loosen up the muscles. He groaned with how tight he'd become just from lying in Caroline's guest bed. *Damn, I'm getting old and soft*. Shaking his head, he took off at an easy jog, marking and noting landmarks to bring him back to the house easily. He'd always been good at navigation, his specialty in the Navy, and he never got lost, even in places where the directions seemed jumbled.

Despite being out of it the night before, he recognized the curve in the road around a large pink granite outcrop and the huge Ponderosa pine sentinels standing as a natural gate about two hundred yards from the house. The house itself was secluded and private, and he could see why the cartel would want it.

Makes for a helluva way station. No one would bother them or see anyone coming or going. Goods could be taken in and out of this place without detection. With the National Forest backing the property, they would have miles of open country where no one could find them easily. No wonder they were hounding Caroline to sell. More than likely they weren't going to take no for an answer. Fear for her well-being surged and gave him a boost to his run.

He had to figure out how to help her without pissing her off or tipping off the local authorities. SEALs didn't operate on domestic soil, but she'd be a sitting duck if he turned a blind-eye to her situation. And he was supposed to be on vacation. He snorted with amusement. SEALs never really went on vacations.

As his strides carried him down the road, he considered his options. Something bad was brewing up here in the Sierra Nevada, and he had the capabilities to mitigate it. Unfortunately, he didn't have official authorization or the gear to do some real damage. But his buddy Rimshot might know someone who did.

Having come to a marginal decision, Deli let his mind drift as he ran along. He settled into the rhythm of his feet hitting the packed dirt of the road. It felt good to push himself, especially after lying in bed for almost nine hours. His breath flowed in an easy pattern as he looped around

Caroline's homestead. He wanted to get a sense of how big her spread was and any locations a group could sneak up on her.

He found a couple of breaks in her defensive lines, but they could be easily shored up when the time came. In the meantime, he needed backup and some advice. Deli stopped at the Ponderosa Sentinels, as he thought of them, and pulled his phone out from his back pocket, letting his breath settle. He scrolled through to Kevin Stanton's number and hit call, hoping the squad wasn't already in the field.

"Stanton."

"Hey, Rimshot, what's up?"

"Aren't you supposed to be relaxing?"

Deli snorted. "Yeah, what the hell do you think I'm doin'?"

"I dunno, Deli. You're callin' me." Rimshot sounded amused. "Usually that means you're in some sort of trouble."

"Shut up." He grinned and shook his head, but refused to admit the sniper was right. "I'm not in trouble, but someone else is."

"Aw hell. You didn't rescue another lost puppy, did you? You remember what happened the last time, don't you?"

"No, I didn't rescue a puppy." *In a manner of speaking.* "And it wasn't my fault the dog escaped from an illegal dogfighting ring. I just followed the blood trail."

"Uh-huh. What have you gotten into this time, Deli?"

"Not me, but something hinky is going on up here in the Sierra Nevada. I ran across a woman who's being threatened by some cartel thugs." He scanned the woods around him to make sure no such thugs were in sight. "Normally, I'd be headed the other direction and let it go."

"Yeah, you should. But?"

"But she runs a dog rehabilitation center for MWDs,

and she's been bothered by these assholes who sound like they're comin' from our friends in Columbia. You remember those people?"

Silence met his ears on the other end of the line. He knew Rimshot hadn't forgotten. He'd had to shoot his own woman through the gut to help rescue her. She wasn't the only one they'd rescued, but she'd been the most memorable.

"Fuck. Are you tellin' me they're movin' shit up here now?" Stanton's voice held fury.

"I think so. It's a different name, and it could be a different group, but it's worth checkin' out. You still in contact with Master Chief Cyrus Finch, you know the one who had more intel on our Columbian buddies?"

"I'm not, but I think Bam-Bam Killian might know where to find him. I think the guy retired from the Navy."

"Aw hell." Deli scowled at his toes in the dirt. "The guy's probably out of the game and wants to be left alone."

"Maybe, but you know how old missions kinda stick with you. Give Bam-Bam a call and see what he says. If he can't do anything, you might have to get the Feds involved."

Shit. The FBI for all their skills, didn't have the firepower or the latitude to take down the cartel's thugs. But they could operate on domestic soil, along with the Department of Homeland Security. He didn't like either agency, but it was their job to protect the citizens. Maybe he should just call them.

"Yeah, I can tell by your silence you're all over that idea." Stanton chuckled. "Just call Killian. He might have better news for you."

"Yeah, okay, thanks, Rimshot. Say hi to the squad for me, and tell Farkas thanks."

"Thanks for what?"

"He'll know. Later." Deli ended the call and scrolled through his contacts to find Greg "Bam-Bam" Killian's number. The guy had retired from active combat duty after a bad arm injury. *Yeah, a bullet will do that.* Bam-Bam had become an instructor for the BUD/S program in Coronado.

Hopefully he's not out torturing recruits.

"Yeah, Killian."

"Hey, Killian, it's Rubenovich." Deli settled his back against one of the sentinels and kept his eye on the road. "I needed to talk to you about our little South American vacation. You got a moment or three?"

A short silence sounded before Killian responded. "Yeah, I got a few. What's going on?"

"I wanted to know if you were still in contact with Master Chief Finch, the guy who came to talk to us about our friends down south."

"Right, I remember him. I think he retired from the Navy."

Deli's gut sank. "Shit. Do you know who's filled in for him?"

"No, I haven't heard. But I did hear some scuttlebutt on him starting his own surveillance, security and rescue company, Ultimate Recon or some shit. You might try Googling it along with his name, Cyrus Finch."

"So you can take the man out of the SEALs, but not the SEAL out of the man."

Killian snorted. "Hooyah, Chief."

"Hooyah. Thanks, Killian. I'll definitely try to get in touch with him." He pushed off from the tree at his back. "How is the whole Instructor thing going?"

Killian chuckled. "Oh, it's going good, though not so much for the recruits. Between Ghost and me, they're wishing they'd tried out for the Marines instead of the SEALs."

Deli laughed at the thought of his two previous teammates harrying the BUD/S recruits. "You know, the only easy day was yesterday, but I'm kinda glad I don't have you guys for Hell Week."

Killian rumbled a laugh. "I keep telling them, "come on, smile, this is the easy part," but they just don't see it that way."

Deli snorted as he shook his head. "Little do they know." BUD/S was tough, but it paled in comparison to some of the shit they'd had to do on mission. *Like the last one with Bones.* He shoved the miserable memories away. "Thanks again for the info on Finch, Killian. I'll definitely look him up."

"Yeah, you do that. And let me know what you find out, especially if you need someone to watch your back."

"Roger that."

Deli ended the call and shoved his phone in his pocket. He'd check the net at Caroline's place to find Finch, but he paused and scanned the forest around him. He suspected the cartel thugs would be back and might come in a less civilized manner. *That's assuming I'm right about them being with the cartel.* The actions Caroline mentioned definitely seemed those of an organized group rather than an individual, but he didn't have enough evidence to say either way.

Check and recheck.

Yeah, that was the name of the game. He stretched his body as he let his senses take in the quiet morning forest. Birds chirped and moved around the canopy without their usual caution. *No predators lurking except me.* He finished his stretch and jogged up the road toward the house, still taking in his environment.

When he reached the house, he found a young woman seated on the front porch, a dog beside her. She looked familiar, but he had trouble placing her. The dog looked like a boxer mix, but instead of watching him, the animal laid its head on the young woman's thigh as she stroked the its head. She narrowed her eyes at him as he approached, but she didn't move from her seat when he stopped at the foot of the stairs.

"Hello."

"Hi." She nodded to him. "You must be Chief Rubenovich."

He bobbed his head. "Yes, ma'am. I'm visiting Caroline."

She snorted and shot him a half smile. "You mean recovering from taking on five guys at the feed store last night?"

Deli grinned. "That, too."

"Given your height, you're either overly ambitious or crazy."

The old irritation at his stature rose, but he beat it behind his eyes. *Can't change the truth, jackass.* "Maybe a bit of both. I'm just gonna go shower." He headed toward the door.

"Wait. I'm sorry. That came out really rude. My name's Daphne. Daphne Phelps." She gave him a grimace. "Do you recognize me?"

Deli blinked. She looked familiar, but his old training kicked in and he smiled. "No, ma'am. I don't think so. Are you related to Caroline?"

"Yes, she's my aunt, my only living family left." Daphne tightened her hand on the dog's collar, rubbing the colorful nylon with her thumb. "Are you sure we haven't met? I took an unexpected trip to South America a while back. It would've been about two years ago now. Does that sound familiar?"

Deli paused, taking in the features of her face. Two years ago, he'd been with the squad on their mission to Columbia, where Killian sustained his arm injury and they'd brought back some additional souvenirs. After studying her face a little longer, Deli recognized Daphne as one of the women they'd rescued.

But he couldn't discuss the op with her, not for love or money. He couldn't admit he'd even been there. It was one of the things that sucked about being part of the SpecOps community. Plausible deniability was the name of the game, even to those he cared about. He hated lying to innocents, but to admit his involvement could get him and his whole Team killed.

He gave her a polite, innocent smile. "I'm sorry, Ms. Phelps."

She frowned. "Are you sure? You seem really familiar to me."

He shrugged as his gut twisted. "Maybe I just have one of those faces. It's very nice to meet you now, though. I'm gonna take a shower." He bobbed his head and ducked into the house, wishing he could acknowledge her gut recognition.

"Wow, you're up and out early. How are you feeling?" Caroline's voice met him as he stepped into her living room.

Standing in the morning sunshine, she'd lost some of her fatigue and anger, and his body tightened at her beauty. Damn, she was gorgeous. *Like a rose. Prickly, but beautiful.*

"Yeah, old habits die hard. Felt like I needed a run this morning." He gestured toward the hallway. "You mind if I take a shower? I'm pretty sweaty."

Her gaze slid down his body and he felt it like a caress. His dick twitched and her lips quirked as if she aborted a smile, but she nodded.

"There are clean towels in the closet beside the bath in the hall, and shampoo and soap should already be in there. Afterwards, I'll take you into town so you can get your vehicle and continue your vacation."

He opened his mouth to tell her he'd be returning with his Jeep, but she'd turned back to the stove and the sounds of eggs sizzling in a skillet hit his ears. What was that old rule again? Better to ask forgiveness than permission. He wasn't going anywhere until the sitrep improved or he was called back to base.

61

****

Caroline turned her back to Chief Rubenovich and heard him head down the hall to the bathroom. She allowed the relief to course through her and settle her heart with his return. She'd awakened to find him gone and she hadn't known what to feel. Relief that he wasn't meddling in her affairs? Worry for his injuries? Disappointment that he hadn't said goodbye? She'd shaken her head to find the truth and hadn't liked what surfaced. What if he couldn't stand her so much he just up and left?

The last seemed stupid in light of his return. Hell, all those worries seemed ludicrous now, but the latter one stuck with her. She'd never been much of a pushover or the 'easy girl,' but she could be prickly when presented with someone who wouldn't listen. She didn't date often and most of the men she'd met before Daphne came to live with her couldn't understand her need to care for the dogs. She was driven and determined, and it had killed many of her human friendships. Add in her care for Daphne, and her dating life had ceased to exist.

She understood she wasn't easy to get along with, and she didn't put up with arrogance, disdain, disrespect, or selfishness. She knew what she wanted in her life and she wouldn't give up her efforts to get it. But sometimes she recognized her loneliness and wished she could bend a little to have a partner.

Rubenovich didn't strike her as a man who ran away from much. In fact, he tended to run toward danger. But that didn't mean she wouldn't scare the shit out of him, too. She drew up short as the eggs cooked in the skillet.

Why do I care if I scare him or not? It wasn't as if they'd connected on an emotional or sexual level. Sure, he carried a virile sexuality with him, but he hadn't shown any sort of interest in her beyond her care for Trace. She sighed as the screen door slammed with Daphne's entrance.

"I talked to our guest this morning, and I swear I've met him before." Daphne settled into a chair at the breakfast bar while Caroline dished up the eggs onto two plates. "I asked him if he'd been in South America two years ago, but he said he didn't recognize me." She shook her head as she salted her eggs. "But he seems so familiar. I'm sure he's one of the guys who rescued me from that place."

Caroline raised her eyebrows as she sat in the chair beside Daphne. "You think he was on the rescue team?"

Daphne nodded. "Yeah, I'd swear on a stack of bibles he was there."

Caroline sipped her coffee as she mulled over the bit of information. That would mean Chief Rubenovich was someone pretty darn sneaky, like Delta Force or Army Rangers. *Except he's in the Navy, dimwit.* He could be a SEAL.

"Hmm. From what I've read about the people who do covert rescue missions, they can't talk about where they've been or what they've done to ordinary people. Not even those they love and trust." She took a few bites of her breakfast while she listened to the shower in the hallway bath start. "You've heard the old line 'Loose lips sink ships'?" Daphne nodded. "It came from World War One, and people blabbing about ships carrying munitions. Of course, no one thought the Germans would sink passenger ships just because they were carrying weapons, but they did, and the propaganda was born."

Caroline nodded to the hallway bathroom. "If he's a covert Naval officer, I'll bet he can't admit he was there because that would mark him and his team as unsafe. It could get everyone he knows, including you and me, killed. Loose lips sink ships, and kill friends." She shrugged, despite the excitement of potentially having a real SEAL in her house. "If you recognize him, and know it in your gut, that's just fine. Just don't push the issue with him or anyone else. Because that could endanger the people who rescued you."

Daphne opened her mouth to protest, but shut it when Caroline raised her eyebrow. "But I know it's him. I know he was there."

"Then know it, deep in your gut. But don't ask him about it because I suspect he can't tell you. Even if he wanted to." Caroline turned her attention to her breakfast. "Don't live in the past on this one, Daphne. It's not worth it." She finished her coffee. "Besides, he'll be leaving here after breakfast anyway."

"What? Why?"

"Because he's on R and R, and he needs to get back to his vacation."

"Then why did you bring him all the way up there to our place?" Daphne frowned.

"Because he got beaten up on my account and didn't have a place to recover where someone would keep an eye on him if his concussion got bad." She ate the last of her meal. "I need to take him back to town for his car. After I drop him off, I'll be back up here to work with the dogs."

Daphne nodded, her shoulders slumping in defeat. "All right. Do you want me to let the dogs into the bark pen so they can run their energy off before you get back?"

"Yeah, that'd be good. Everyone but Trace. I'm going to take her with me when I run to town."

Daphne raised her eyebrows. "Do you think that's wise? Is Trace ready?"

Caroline nodded. "She's ready for a road trip with people she knows. I won't let her out of the truck unless I feel threatened. But I want you to keep the doors locked and let the landline go to voicemail. If I call you, it'll be on your cell. Okay?"

Daphne nodded. "Yeah. Why are you so worried about the phone and door?"

Caroline shrugged. "I had a dream last night where those guys from the realty place returned and threatened to kill us if we didn't leave." That wasn't quite true, but close enough. "It scared the daylights out of me."

Daphne shook her head, but her shoulders tightened. "It was just a dream."

Caroline nodded. "Could be, but it felt like a warning, so I want you to just keep the doors locked and don't answer the phone until I get back, okay?"

"All right." She turned her head as Chief Rubenovich returned to the main room, freshly washed and dressed in yesterday's clothes. Daphne turned her head away, a blush tarnishing her cheeks.

Curious.

"Can I make you some breakfast, Chief?" Caroline slid off her stool and carried her dishes into the kitchen. "I can make you some eggs and toast."

"Sure. Sounds great as long as I can get some coffee, too." He nodded and took the stool on the other side of the one she'd left.

Caroline snorted. "In this house, ain't no way the world gets started without coffee." She filled a mug and set it on the island in front of him. "After you eat, I'll take you into town."

He nodded. "Sounds like a plan."

She turned back to the stove to cook, unsettled with the disappointment at his easy acceptance. *Now don't be stupid. Last night you thought him an arrogant prick.* True, but after she'd calmed down, she recognized a man who had a good heart and didn't put up with injustice. She snorted. *Really, you're letting your inner romantic take the reins? Remember what happened the last time you did that?*

She remembered. She'd damn near lost her inheritance and her livelihood. Trusting men based on appearance and perceived heroism hadn't worked well for her. But something about Chief Rubenovich made her think he might be the real deal.

Doesn't matter. He's too young.

She shook her head as she finished up his eggs, belatedly hoping he liked scrambled. *Because that's pretty much the state of my mind at the moment.* She set the toast on the plate and settled it on front of the chief petty officer, meeting his smile. It warmed his eyes and made him even more handsome. She loved the scruff on his cheeks and chin, and her inner romantic served up a fantasy of what that scruff would feel like on the skin of her thighs.

"Okay, I gotta go check on the dogs and make sure they have food and water before we leave." She mentally smacked herself and turned her back on the handsome man eating in her kitchen.

It'll be better when he's gone. Yeah, didn't that just feel like a lie?

CHAPTER SEVEN

Deli kept his eyes on the surrounding woods as Caroline drove him back down the mountain into town, his mind cataloging all the landmarks along the way. He'd looked up Ultimate Recon on Google while he was at her house, but he hadn't had time to give them a call. His gut warned him they were nearly out of time and backup would be needed sooner rather than later. *I'll get my Jeep and call Ultimate Recon on the way to her place.*

Caroline hadn't spoken much after he'd gathered his few things and followed her and Trace out to her late model Chevy pickup truck. Her expression remained impassive and withdrawn as they drove, and he wondered if he'd done something to piss her off again. *Couldn't have. All I did was eat this morning.* His snark made him chuckle and she turned her head toward him.

"What's so funny?"

He shrugged. "Nothin'. Thanks for taking care of me and giving me breakfast this morning. Much appreciated."

"My pleasure." Her tone suggested that was her canned response. "Did you leave your car at the feed store or somewhere else?"

"Jeep, and yeah, I parked at what I thought was the

bar. I had no idea they were one and the same." He gave her a grin, but she didn't return it. "Hey, are you okay? Did I do somethin' this morning?" He gave her a half-smile. "I mean, I know I pissed you off last night, but I thought I'd been okay this morning."

She huffed a sardonic laugh. "Noticed that, did you?"

He laughed and her smile filled out a little more. "Yeah, I know I'm touchy on certain subjects. It comes from having to take care of things on my own with no one else to help. And most of the time, the guys in my life just wanted to tell me how it needed to be done rather than listen to me. I've fought hard for my independence."

"Yeah, I can see that." He nodded. "I just wondered why you'd gotten so quiet."

She sighed and her shoulders slumped as they came to the first stop sign before town. "I'm just worried about Daphne. She's suffered a lot of PTSD since her trip to South America, and I don't like leaving her alone long, especially if I take Trace with me." She shrugged. "I mean, she does have her dog Beryl, and the others, but they aren't much protection if those thugs come back."

"Yeah, about that. How about I come back up to your place once I get my own vehicle?" He patted Trace while he took in Caroline's profile. "I still have time on my leave and it's always good to have backup should anything happen."

She retreated a little, her expression tightening. "That's very kind of you, but we'll be fine. I don't want to take more of your vacation time from you."

"Hey, I don't mind. Besides, it'll give me more time with Trace. Right, girl?" He patted the dog between them and she tilted her head for more scratches.

Caroline's lips tightened and her eyes lost their warmth. "Tell you what. Why don't you take today to relax? You shouldn't waste your vacation on our problems. This evening, I'll meet you here at the bar around seven and we can talk about what you think needs to be done. Okay?"

"You sure? I don't mind comin' back with you right now."

She shook her head as she pulled her truck up in the parking lot to the Cascade Breaks Feed Store & Bar. "No, it's fine. I'm going to check in with Bert to let him know you're okay after last night. I'll see you back here around seven tonight."

"Yeah, okay. Seven tonight at the bar. Sounds like a plan." He unbuckled his seat belt and opened the door. "Hey, Caroline?"

"Yeah?"

"Thanks."

She raised her eyebrows. "For what?"

"For takin' care of me when I needed it. And for letting me help. I know you're used to doing it on your own, but I'm glad you're accepting help."

"No, I said I'd hear what you thought needed to be done." She gave him a real smile, though, and he counted that as a victory. "Enjoy your vacation day up here in Cascade Breaks, and I'll see you tonight."

"Yeah, okay." He nodded and slid out of the truck, his shoulders loosening for the first time since last night. "Have a safe drive home." He closed the door and waved.

She waved back before she pulled over to the feed store side and headed inside without another look toward him. He didn't want to disrupt the fragile truce they'd come to, but his gut said he couldn't wait even one day with the cartel. *Oh, yeah, it's gonna be more of the ask forgiveness side, I think.* He snorted and headed for his Jeep, happy to see his gear remained on the floorboards behind the front seats. He opened the driver's door and settled into the seat as he pulled out his phone.

He needed to stay with Caroline and the Last Chance Dog Sanctuary. The cartel had probably reached the limit of their patience, and no one ever told them no. He kept his gaze on Caroline's truck as he dialed the number for Ultimate Recon.

"Good morning, Ultimate Recon. How may I direct your call?"

"Yeah, hi, my name's Chief Petty Officer Rubenovich, and I'm tryin' to get ahold of Mr. Cyrus Finch." Deli watched Caroline come out of the feed store with a small bag of dog treats.

"I'm sorry, Chief. He's not available at the moment. Would you like his voicemail?"

"Yes, please. Thank you, ma'am."

"You're welcome." The line clicked over to a voicemail announcement and a cowboy drawl came on the line. "Hey, you've reached the voicemail for Cyrus Finch. No point in pussy-footing around. Just tell me what you need and I'll get back to you."

Deli couldn't help laughing as Caroline got into her truck and backed out of her parking space.

"Yeah, hi, Mr. Finch. My name's Chief Petty Officer Rubenovich and I met you a while back at Coronado. I was wondering if I could talk to you about the possibility of sharing some intel on a South American op back in the day. I got a friend who might be interacting with some tourists from there. Give me a call when you got some time. Thanks."

He left his number as Caroline drove out of the parking lot and headed back up the mountain toward her home. Soon after, a couple of guys came out of the feed store wearing jeans and t-shirts and loaded into two black SUVs with dark tinted windows. They didn't have any decals or stickers on the back of them, but both had California rental car plates. *Could just be hikers heading out to the trailheads into the National Forest.* Yeah, and they could be dumb enough to hike in the expensive sneakers he'd seen on their feet.

Deli nodded his head as he turned on his ignition and backed up to follow them. The traffic was fairly heavy for a Sunday morning and he blended in with the rest of the residents going about their business. He held his position a couple cars back from the SUVs, watching them follow Caroline's truck out of town.

He didn't have a reason to be suspicious of the vehicles, but his gut said they weren't ordinary tourists. He paused at a stop sign and let another car get in front of him as he scanned the road ahead for Caroline's truck. She'd stopped at the next stop sign, her blinker on to turn left across traffic. The SUVs sat two cars behind her.

It's probably nothing. But he never ignored his gut, and he flipped his turn signal on as he and another car pulled in behind them to make the left.

Caroline turned and headed up the road. Another car followed her and the SUVs had to wait their turn to cross traffic. He reached under his passenger seat and pulled out a locked gun safe. He didn't like to carry while on vacation, but he had the necessary permits just in case. *This is just one of those cases.* He unlocked and opened the safe as he waited for the traffic to move.

The Glock 9 remained where he'd left it and all the magazines sat full. He shot a look out the windshield as the first SUV made the turn, but the second had to wait. He inched forward before he loaded a magazine, but he didn't chamber a round. Not yet. He might not need it.

Deli shut the gun safe and returned it to the floor just as the second SUV and the car in front of him made the left turn. He wasn't quick enough and had to wait for three other cars to pass him before he could follow. He set the Glock on the seat beside him and turned the wheel, accelerating slowly to keep from looking suspicious.

The road ascended higher into the forest and he'd lost sight of both Caroline's truck and the SUVs, but he kept his speed just above the speed limit. His Jeep was a bit too visible to blend in. He just hoped he was wrong about what the SUVs intended.

But my gut's never wrong...

****

Caroline took a deep breath for the hundredth time, telling herself she'd made the right decision. *A woman needs a man like a zebra needs a frying pan.* She didn't need a man to make her life better, but she would hear the chief out. And he deserved to have some real vacation, not waste time making sure her life was easier.

Chief Rubenovich wasn't part of her world anyway. He'd only come to Cascade Breaks for R&R, not to stay. And certainly not to fight her battles for her. Not that she had a battle to fight, at least not at the moment. The cartel's thugs probably wouldn't be back for a few days, and she'd be ready for them.

Despite her little pep talk, she kept her eyes open for anyone she didn't recognize on the road. *Oh yeah, like I'm going to notice a cartel thug versus a tourist.* But she kept her gaze moving as a chill ran up her neck. She shot a look at Trace, but the dog sat with her own gaze swiveling around.

Movement in the rearview mirror caught her attention and she frowned. Two matching black SUVs a lot like the one she'd shot at the day before roared up the road behind her. She thought they'd stay back and follow her, but they sped up, closing on her back bumper with frightening speed.

"What the hell are they doing?"

She split her attention between the road and the encroaching SUVs, slowly increasing her speed to keep ahead of them. But the vehicles weren't slowing up and she couldn't increase her speed without endangering herself on the winding mountain road. The asphalt would enter the trees and stretch into a gentle curve where the trunks would be close to the edge.

Caroline swallowed hard and kept her speed high enough to stay just ahead of the nearest SUV as they entered the forest. Ponderosa mixed with fir and spruce produced cool shade when the weather grew hot, but now they only made the road harder to see with the sharp contrast between light and shadow.

"Okay, we'll be okay. We just have to get around this curve and we can find a place to get off to the side of the road. They'll roar past and we can turn around and get back to town." She didn't know why she was talking aloud. Trace wouldn't answer, but the sound of her voice brought her a little comfort in the face of her pursuers.

She shot a look at her cell phone in the holder on the dash, wondering if she could call the sheriff, when the first SUV made its move. The imposing vehicle accelerated and slammed into her back bumper, shoving her toward the edge of the road and the trees speeding past. Trace barked as Caroline yelled her outrage, but she held onto the wheel and turned into her skid, keeping her grip on the road.

"Holy fuck!" She pressed her old truck to go faster before they hit her again. *If I can just get to the wide spot around the next curve...*

But the SUVs didn't give her the chance. As the first one bore down on her bumper, the second flew past and lined up beside her before it drifted closer and closer, intending to force her off the edge of the pavement.

"Oh, that's how you want to play, is it, you crazy bastards? Fine."

Caroline snarled at the encroaching SUV and floored the accelerator. The old Chevy leapt forward, for a moment outsprinting the SUV beside her until they hit the curve. She gritted her teeth and prayed no one would be coming the opposite direction as she shot around the turn before grabbing her emergency brake. *Please let me remember*

how Dad taught me to negotiate the forest service roads.
She spared a moment to glance at the second SUV coming
back before she returned her gaze to the front.

There it is.

"Hold on, Trace."

Her heart thundered as she yanked the wheel to the
right and jerked up on the emergency brake. The truck
fishtailed as it swung to the right onto the dirt and gravel
Forest Service road. The black SUVs shot past her, but she
didn't have time to watch them. Her truck couldn't find
purchase on the dirt and she had to turn into each skid as
she tried to slow down. She almost had it under control
when a large spruce came out of nowhere and she slammed
her foot on the brakes. The wheels locked and she skidded
into the huge trunk, her hood crumpling with impact.

Her head rocked forward, but her body was stopped by
the seatbelt across her chest before she slammed back into
her seat. Dazed by the double impacts, she tried to get her
mind in order to get out of the truck. Her chest hurt and her
neck screamed, but she forced herself to think. *Gotta move.*
But her eyes wouldn't focus.

A doggie whine sounded and she remembered Trace
had been seated beside her. She shifted her gaze and found
the blue heeler mix on the floor under the dash. She wore a
look of concern but otherwise appeared unhurt.

Gotta get out of the truck. They're coming.

Caroline unlatched her seatbelt and yanked the keys
from the ignition. No way would she leave those bastards a
way to get into her home. The release of the belt made her
gasp and pain reminded her she'd just hit a tree. She
groaned and shoved at the door, the hinge screaming a
protest against crumpled metal.

Before she launched herself out of the truck, she
scanned the dirt road behind her. No one had followed her.
Yet. I gotta move. She half-slid, half-lurched out of the
driver's seat, the impact of her feet on the ground jarring

her whole body. She suppressed her moan and looked at Trace.

"Trace, *here*. Hup."

The dog wormed her way onto the bench seat and leapt out of the truck.

"Damn, I wish I had your energy." Caroline staggered toward the pickup bed to cross the road into the trees behind them, but stopped when bullets tore through the dirt of the track. "Shit! Trace, *bleeben*!"

She ducked down behind the truck as bullets peppered the opposite quarter panel and flattened both tires on the side closest to the paved road. She crouched behind the wheel and held Trace in front of her to keep the dog from getting shot.

Oh my glory. Oh my glory. What am I going to do?

It took her a moment to realize she'd left her phone on the dash. *Smooth move, stupid.*

"Trace, *zits, bleeben*." She darted back toward the open truck door as more bullets ripped into the metal body. She poked her head into the cab, but she couldn't see her phone where she'd left it.

Shit.

Voices shouting at each other in Spanish carried before another blast of gunfire pounded the truck. Trace whined, her attention latched on Caroline.

"I know, Trace. *Bleeben*. Where the hell is the phone?" She scrabbled with her hands on the floorboards and managed to find the little plastic rectangle. "Got it. Oh hell." She slithered to the ground as the glass of her doors and windshield shattered from the hail of bullets.

She crawled toward Trace as the truck settled to the ground on its wheel rims when they blew out the other tires. She had no idea how many men shot at her, but she knew they had more ammo than she had minutes to survive. She checked the phone and swiped the screen, but it wouldn't light up. Had she run out of juice? Her fingers shook as she pressed and held the power button, but the phone remained inert.

The truck shook behind her as the bullets riddled its damaged sides. *Pretty soon they're going to come through.* She swallowed hard as she realized she couldn't call for help. *Sweet glory, what am I going to do?*

She wished she'd taken the Chief's offer to follow her home just to be safe. She ducked down as more bullets riddled the side of her truck and called Trace, holding the dog against her. She closed her eyes, knowing it wouldn't help, but she needed a moment to think. How would she get herself out of this one?

"We just have to hold on." For what? They'd get close enough to shoot her and that would be that.

After a few moments she realized the gunfire continued but they didn't seem to be firing at the truck anymore. *What the—* Caroline shoved the broken phone into her pocket and listened to the gun shots. They'd changed direction and the men shouted in what sounded like surprise and anger. She frowned. *What's going on?*

She crept to the back end of the truck and peered around the mangled tailgate. The men from the black SUVs were firing into the woods across the dirt road. One body lay on the ground in front of the decimated trunks as the men advanced toward it. *What are they doing?*

She rolled her back against her truck and shook her head. *It doesn't matter what they're doing. What am I gonna do?*

Before she could get her thoughts in order, a man appeared around the crumpled end of her truck and she took a breath to scream. He slid in beside her and covered her mouth, placing a finger at his own.

"Caroline, it's me." The hissed voice penetrated her panic and she swallowed her scream as she recognized Chief Rubenovich.

"Oh my glory, Chief." She swallowed hard against the

urge to burst into tears and throw her arms around him. *I can do that later.* "What are you doing here? How did you get here?"

"I followed them when they started following you." He looked her over with a curiously intense gaze. "Are you hurt?"

She shook her head, though her neck spasmed with the movement. "Not much. Just whiplash from the quick stop. So far we haven't been hit."

"Good." He nodded and some of the tension left his shoulders. "We gotta get out of here. We can't hold them all off. We're gonna sneak back through the trees on this side. It's not going to take them long to figure out I'm not back there. Once we get close to the clearing, we're going to head for my Jeep."

"Where's your Jeep?"

"It's parked along the highway across this road. It's gonna be a bit tricky to get there, but if you can run, we'll do it. Copy?"

Caroline nodded.

"Good. Come on. Trace, *foose.*" Chief Rubenovich motioned to the dog and met Caroline's gaze. "We've gotta get through these trees. Keep low and move as fast as you can. On the count of three." He held up one finger and peeked around the crumpled front of the truck.

She held her breath has he held up a second finger. *One more finger, and we have to move.* She'd never been so scared in her life, but she wouldn't stay pressed against the truck like a frightened rabbit. The shouting and gunfire slowed and she held her breath. Where were they?

Rubenovich held up the third finger and motioned her around him.

He wants me to go first? She swallowed her panic and scrambled to her feet, staying low as she crept around the tree against the truck's hood. She didn't see anyone, but she didn't want to attract their attention by making a sudden movement. Rubenovich moved into her line of sight, gesturing directions. She thought she understood them as they crept through the trees toward the highway, using the nearest SUV as cover from the men still scanning the trees across the dirt road.

They'd reached the far side of the SUV and crouched down when he held up his hand in a fist. She didn't know what it meant beyond *stop*, so she froze in place. Trace vibrated with tension, but held her position beside them.

"Okay, here's where shit gets tricky." Rubenovich's whisper made her jump. "We have to get across the open road to the trees on the other side then make it to my Jeep."

Sounded like a decent plan. "Where's the Jeep again?"

"On this side of the highway, but across the dirt road." He pointed to the open space in the forest before he took out a knife. "I'll run some interference and keep them distracted while you make a break across the road." He stabbed the nearest tire with his blade and the air hissed out slowly. "I'll be right back."

She nodded as he ducked back around the SUV and punctured the front two tires as well. She kept her eyes trained on the road and trees around them, but heard nothing but the hissing air. Where were the other men? Rubenovich returned to her side of the SUV and leaned close.

"The vehicle's been disabled, but the guys from it are approaching your truck. It's time to go."

He pointed toward the trees across the road. "Ready?"

She grabbed his arm. "Thank you for helping me?"

He flashed her a grin. "Of course. It's what I do. I took an oath to defend against all enemies, both foreign and domestic. I think these guys count as both."

She bit her bottom lip. "But I don't even know your first name."

He grimaced. "It's Eugene, but my friends call me Deli."

"Deli? Why?"

"Long story. I'll tell you when we are a little less busy." He pointed to the other SUV parked ahead of them. "When I say go, run to the SUV using it as cover to get into the woods. Once in the trees, head for the highway. The Jeep will be there and its unlocked. Get in the driver's seat. You can drive a stick, right?"

She scowled at him. "Of course, I can."

He grinned. "Good. Take Trace with you and start the Jeep. I'll be right behind you after I disable the other vehicle."

Her heart pounded in her chest as she measured the distance from their current position and the trees. *Not that far to the other SUV.* No, not far, but a lot of open space where a bullet could find her. She'd have to be fast and focused.

"Ready?" Deli handed her the keys.

"No, but I'm willing."

"Good. Go! Trace, *gay weeter!*"

Caroline sprinted for the other SUV with Trace beside her, ignoring the shouts from the men around her truck. She prayed they didn't see her in the open space between the vehicles, but she couldn't worry about it. Her heart pounded in her ears as she skidded in the dirt against the other black vehicle and looked back.

The men called to each other and while she couldn't understand everything they said, it became clear they'd figured out she was gone. Deli waved at her to keep going and she swallowed hard as she gathered her courage to move. *You can do this, Caro.* Yeah, but maybe not without getting shot.

"Trace, *here.*" She urged the dog with her as she ran, bent over into the cover of the trees. She normally would write the Forest Service about the overwhelming brush growing between the Ponderosa trunks, but today she was grateful it provided cover. She pushed her way behind a bigger trunk and looked back.

Deli made a dash between the vehicles, but the other men caught his movement and sprayed the area between the SUVs with a hail of bullets. He ducked behind the second SUV just as the road exploded with dust from the impacts. She heard him swear as he stabbed the nearest tire and looked up at her.

Go! He mouthed the word and waved frantically as he scrambled to the next tire.

She whimpered and ducked her head, but kept moving through the trees. The scent of Ponderosa bark and damaged wood hit her nose as she pushed through the brush. The highway appeared with a turquoise blue Jeep parked a few feet from the forest. She burst out of the trees and skidded around the front of the Jeep. Her feet slid on the gravel, but she grasped the door and herded Trace inside.

Start the car, start the car, start the car.

Bullets peppered the trees behind her as she followed the dog into the Jeep and shoved the key in the ignition. She twisted the key and shot a look toward the woods. Where was Deli? *Oh, please, let him be okay.*

The Jeep started with a rumble and she threw it in first gear, her foot on the clutch slammed to the floor as she waited. *Come on, Chief.* She watched the trees, her gut cramping with panic. She could hear the gunfire and the yelling, but she had no idea if he'd been hit. Seconds passed with agonizing slowness and she was ready to scream when he bolted out of the trees. He yanked the door open and roared, "GO!"

She peeled away from the scene, hoping he'd forgive her for making the engine work hard as she accelerated while shifting the gears. Her mind kept replaying the moment where the SUVs had forced her off the road and the gunfire started while she was stuck inside.

"Oh sweet glory, I couldn't—I couldn't help myself to

get away. If you hadn't come along, I'd be dead, and Daphne, and the dogs, and—"

Deli kept his attention on the road behind them. "Let's not worry about that now. You did survive, you did help yourself, and we're in this together, got me?"

She nodded, biting her lip. "What are we going to do?"

"Call in the cavalry." He swiped his phone and kept his weapon trained toward the rear window. "We can't do this alone. I'm callin' the team when we get to your place."

CHAPTER EIGHT

Deli didn't breathe much until they passed the Sentinels at the edge of Caroline's property. He kept his eyes scanning the road behind them, but the thugs hadn't followed them. *Thank glory for small favors.* He'd only been able to puncture two of the other SUV's tires, but hopefully that would keep them stationary long enough for him and Caroline to find a safe place to prepare for them.

Caroline skidded to a stop in front of her house and launched out of the Jeep. Trace whined in the back, her ears up and tense with the emotional energy in the cab, but she stayed with Deli. He slid out a little slower and let the dog out of the back before he checked for his gear. While he was armed, the Glock wouldn't be enough. *We're still gonna need backup.*

He leaned against the Jeep and kept his gaze on the road out while he looked up Ultimate Recon Inc. on his phone. It didn't take him long to find their contact information again and hit send.

"Ultimate Recon, may I help you?" The raspy, sultry voice on the other end belonged to the older woman he'd spoken to before.

"G'morning. I'm calling to speak with Master–er,

Cyrus Finch. Is he available?"

"I'm sorry, he's not at the moment, but I can send you to his voicemail to leave a message."

"Yeah, thanks." Deli scanned the road, listening with one ear to the conversation and the other on the forest around him. Had he heard an approaching car engine?

"One moment."

He listened hard until a familiar cowboy drawl came over the line in his ear. "Hey, you've reached the voicemail for Cyrus Finch. No point in pussy-footing around. Just tell me what you need and I'll get back to you." The tone sounded and Deli took a breath.

"Yeah, this is Chief Petty Officer Eugene Rubenovich again. Things just got a lot more serious with regards to that South American company we encountered a while back. If you can give me a call at this number, I'd appreciate it. Thanks."

Deli swiped the phone and called to Trace as he grabbed his gear. He needed to help Caroline get this place ready for an incursion. Something told him they hadn't seen the last of those thugs in the SUVs.

He'd need to move the Jeep behind the house to keep it out of sight from the road. Having transportation would be vital until the cavalry showed up. *If they showed up.* He didn't know Finch well enough to determine if they guy would help or not. He didn't expect Caroline to have the capital to pay a company like Ultimate Recon, Inc., and he couldn't require her to hire them. While it would be nice to have their backup, he only expected to get some intel out of them and deal with it as best they could. Alone.

Two is one. One is none.

The old survival adage rang in his head as he stepped through the doors of the house and scanned the room. Caroline held Daphne whose face showed the evidence of tears. Caroline herself had tears on her cheeks, but Deli was more concerned with the blood on her head.

"Let's get your head fixed up before those guys come by. Is the first aid kit in the bathroom?"

Daphne looked up and wiped her face. "Yeah. I'll get it." She rose and hurried down the hall while Deli settled into her chair to look at Caroline.

"Do I really have blood on my head?" She scowled.

"Yeah, but I think they're just cuts from windshield glass. Nothing a little cleaning up won't fix." He tilted her head a little before Daphne returned to the table with a washcloth, bandages, and ointment. "How are you feeling with the whiplash?"

Caroline groaned. "Like someone beat me with a baseball bat."

"You think the men who ran her off the road will come here?" Panic suffused Daphne's face as she ran hot water over the washcloth.

He didn't want to scare them, but that's what he'd do if his quarry got away. "It'll take them some time. I slashed all but two of the tires, so if each SUV has a spare, they'll get one vehicle running. I don't know if they can carry all the men they had, but I think it's safe to say they're not giving up on acquiring your property."

Caroline grimaced, but nodded. "I'm sorry you got caught in this, Chief."

He shook his head, his concern on her slurred words. "I wouldn't choose to be anywhere else. Let me clean those scratches."

Daphne brought him the washcloth and a bowl of warm water. He closed his lips on a whistle of dismay as he pushed Caroline's hair out of her face. She had a lot of little cuts, but most of them had stopped bleeding.

"All right, this is going to hurt like a bitch." He gave Caroline a half-smile. "Ready?"

"Not hardly, but let's get it done. I have to go take care of the dogs."

"Don't worry about the dogs. I'll do that." Daphne

shook her head. "You just get cleaned up. Have you called the sheriff?"

"Couldn't. My phone died. I'll call when Deli's done." Caroline closed her eyes.

His heart filled with warmth at her trust. "I'll put some ointment on the cuts and you should be good to go." He had to lock himself in his SEAL training to keep from allowing his worry and anger to override his focus. Those assholes had hurt his woman and he couldn't tolerate it.

Whoa. *His* woman?

He didn't give himself time to analyze the thought as he patched Caroline up and cleaned the table of the detritus.

"What are we going to do?" Daphne shot him a panicked look and Caroline reached for her hand.

"Give me the phone. I need to call the sheriff." She tried to smile, but pain tightened her lips. "I feel like I've been rolled in a rock tumbler. Even my hair hurts."

Daphne brought her the phone and she punched numbers before holding it to her ear. "Hi, this is Caroline Atherton. I want to report that my truck was shot at and run off the road on the highway." She paused as she listened to the speaker on the other end. "No, no, I'm okay. It's no longer an emergency. I just wanted to make sure Sheriff Tanner was aware." She listened again. "Really? An eight-car wreck on I-5? That's awful, Agatha." She pushed her hair behind her ear. "No, don't call them off the wreck. I'm safe at home and okay. The sheriff can come up here tomorrow morning to get my statement. Yeah, that's soon enough. Okay, thanks, Agatha." Caroline ended the call.

"Okay, the sheriff's office knows what happened, but there's a big wreck on the freeway and everyone is working on that."

"Oh, no. Was anyone killed?" Daphne rubbed Beryl's head.

"Agatha didn't know, but everyone's out helping there." Caroline scrubbed her face with her hands, only remembering that she had cuts after she smeared some ointment. "Oh, shit, I forgot." She wriggled gently in her chair. "Whiplash sucks. I hurt everywhere."

"Yeah, it does." Deli came back to the table and sat down. "Want me to make you some tea?"

"No, I think I'm just gonna go lie down and rest a little." She pushed up from the chair just as his phone rang.

"You do that and I'll check on you after I take this."

He stepped out the kitchen door overlooking the kennels while he answered the phone. "Rubenovich."

"Hey, Chief. This is Cyrus Finch. I got your messages. What's up?"

"Hey, Finch. I got a situation here and wondered if you could shed some light on it for me."

"This 'situation' you're referrin' to have to do with them folks from South America?"

"Yes, sir, that'd be them." Deli nodded even if the man couldn't see him. "I met a woman here—"

"Oh, now I think I understand." Finch sounded smug. "You found yourself some honey and want to keep the pot safe, yeah?"

"It's not like that." *Not yet, anyway.* "She's got a Columbian cartel on her ass, trying to forcefully remove her from her land. She's told them no, and they're not taking it well."

"Well, hell, that ain't good." Finch's voice sharpened. "What's going on?"

"They tried to run her off the road and kill her this morning. I got there just in time, but it was a close thing." Deli scowled at the kennels. "She runs a Military War Dog rehabilitation center up here in the Sierra Nevada outside of Cascade Breaks, California."

"What the hell do they want with a dog rehabilitation center?"

"Oh, they don't want the center. I suspect they want the land and its proximity to the freeway. Plus, they're close enough to town for supplies but have no close neighbors."

"Yeah, I can see why they'd like it. She's not bein' amenable to their offers?"

"Nope, and today they decided they were done negotiating."

"So, what can Ultimate Recon do for you, Chief?"

"I'm calling for intel. My gut says these people are the same folks you briefed us on a couple years back. They have a different name, now, but I'd bet it's the same scumbags."

"What name is this crew using?" Finch's voice hardened.

"Casa de Catequil."

"Cheeky bastards. House of the Thunder God. Yeah, that's them." He heard Finch tapping on a keyboard. "When the head of the cartel had an unfortunate accident, it took a while for the sharks to stop circling, but now they've got a brand new leader. Name's Dante del Fuego. He's a cagey bastard, too. More twitchy than Osama bin Laden. Doesn't sleep in the same place twice, always moving, and never repeats the moves in any particular order. Cagey."

"So, what brings him to up to California?"

"Near as we can discover, he's tryin' to set up way stations and supply routes from Mexico to Canada using Interstate-5. They get land so they can continue their drug and sex slave smuggling operation in peace and quiet. " Finch tapped some more. "You got a secure email you can read?"

Deli rattled off his email just before Daphne came out the back door. He raised his eyebrows and she shook her head.

"I'm going to get the dogs settled. Are we going to be okay?" She bit her lip.

He nodded, but she didn't look convinced as she continued on her way.

"That her, the woman you're talkin' about?" Finch's voice drew him back to the conversation.

"Nah, that's her niece. She was one of the women who visited that same 'resort' in Columbia."

Finch hissed a breath. "How's she holdin' up?"

"Better than some. She said she recognized me."

A short silence settled on the call. "Shit. What'd you say?"

"I told her I just got one of those faces before getting the hell out of there." He grimaced as he watched Daphne secure the dogs. "It sucked lying to her."

"Yeah, ain't that the truth? What you need to do is find a woman who knows what bein' a SEAL's all about. Then you don't gotta worry about it."

"Yeah." Deli shot a look over his shoulder at the house where Caroline recovered. "It's good advice." Too bad he probably wouldn't take it.

"Take a look at the intel I sent. If you think it's the same guys, call me back and Ultimate Recon will be on a plane tomorrow."

"Really? You'll send a team?"

"Fuck yeah. These mudfuckers are like cockroaches. You have to take them out little batches at a time because if you give 'em an inch, they scatter into the woodwork."

"I'll have your answer by this afternoon. Thanks, Finch." He paused and rubbed the back of his neck. "I don't know if she can pay you, not what you're worth, for sure."

"Yeah, well, I'm thinkin' the FBI and ATF can pick up the tab for this one. You're givin' us all the intel on the movements of the assholes they've been lookin' for." Finch chuckled. "In fact, we might just find out who they're makin' deals with up in our neck of the woods."

"What neck of the woods is that?"

"Issaquah, Washington."

Deli scowled. "You've seen activity up there from

these shitheads?"

"Yeah. Issaquah's on Interstate-90. It's a big ole pipeline of smuggling east to west."

"Shit. I'll take a look at that email ASAP and send you coordinates."

"Copy that. Talk to you soon."

"Roger that."

They ended the call and Deli swiped his phone, looking for the email Finch promised. He found it and scanned the attachments quickly. He didn't recognize any of the men photographed, but Caroline might. *I'll show these to her in a bit.* He didn't like the damage she'd sustained in the crash or the cuts on her face. Intellectually he knew she'd heal, but it pissed him off that it was needed.

His unease made him return to the house and head down the hallway to her bedroom. Caroline lay on her back, her pillows propping her up enough to keep an eye on the door. *Ever watchful, this woman.* He settled on the end of the bed and took in her room.

She hadn't hung much on the walls, but a comfortable armchair sat in the corner by the window with a lamp, a table covered in a pile of books, and soft-looking fleece blanket. He could imagine her sitting there on stormy days, sipping a cup of tea and reading while snuggled in the blanket.

"How are the dogs?" She caught his eyes with hers narrowed to slits.

He shrugged. "I think they're okay. Daphne went to check on them. How are you feeling?"

"Like someone jerked my neck and then bitch-slapped my entire torso."

He chuckled. "Good thing. Otherwise I'd have questioned your memory." She didn't laugh and he sobered. "Seems like we're both putting up with too much abuse lately. How about we take a more relaxed approach from now on?"

She grimaced. "Sounds like a plan. Sorry for ruining your R and R day."

He snorted. "It's all right. I was planning to do any hiking up here near your place anyway." He held up his hand when she opened her mouth. "I know, but I don't let stuff like this go. Not if I can help. So, to make up for me not hiking, how 'bout you tell me a story? Something easy to remember that's relaxing."

Caroline frowned. "What kind of story?"

"I dunno. Something from your past, maybe. Did you always live up here in the mountains?"

"No." She settled back on the pillows, her eyes barely open. "When I was a kid, my family had a place in Malibu, near the beach. This was when a regular family could afford to live there before it got ridiculously expensive."

"Wait, regular people could afford to live in California near the beach? I didn't think that existed." He moved closer to her on the bed. "You sure you're remembering right?"

"Shut up." She grinned a little and thumped him on the thigh. It didn't hurt, and he grinned with more than just humor. He wanted the connection with her. "Down the beach a ways was this house, built on the beach itself. I mean, it was literally out into the waves. The high tide mark was *above* the house by at least twenty feet. This thing was on stilts and would become an island when the tide was in."

"It had a natural moat?"

"Yeah. It was the craziest thing. I mean, can you imagine when a typhoon or some of the heavy spring storms came in? This thing was all wood and it would have to withstand the pounding of not only the waves, but the weather."

He shivered, remembering the rough seas he'd had to battle in BUD/S. The waves had dragged at him, and being the smallest guy in the crew, his legs had always gone out from under him first. He couldn't imagine living in a house that depended on the stilts' foundations remaining solid.

"My brothers and sister and I would walk by it all summer long, wondering when it would wash out to sea, and my dad who was a geologist said anyone who built on the bluffs, berm, or beach were either crazy or stupid, or both, because nothing was ever permanent on the California coastline." She gave him a nostalgic smile. "It was a crazy house, but it was magnificent in its own way, using nature to protect the residents. The surf was loud there, too, so it wouldn't ever have been quiet. But I admired the people crazy enough to live there. I guess that's why when my uncle offered me this place I was all too happy to take it. It's quiet and people pretty much leave me alone." She sighed. "Until now."

"Yeah, well, we're gonna fix that." Deli picked up one of her hands. "Are you sure you don't want some tea? I can get the kettle started."

Caroline waved her other hand. "No, I'm good right here for now." She took a deep breath and let it out slowly. "What about you? You got any stories to tell me?"

He huffed a laugh. "Yeah, plenty. But not many of them I can actually share."

"Oh, come on. Don't give me the SpecOps cop out." She grimaced. "What about a story from your past?"

"Hmm." He rubbed his chin and let his eyes unfocus as his mind mulled over her request. "So I grew up in New Jersey, and not the pretty part, either."

"There's a pretty part of New Jersey? That's news."

"Shut up." He grinned as he shook his head. "I grew up in Newark, but my folks ran a deli in Bayonne known for its kosher foods and bagels. Great place. Always smelled of smoked meat, spices, and fresh bread. But I had this uncle, my mother's youngest brother Eli, who used to travel up to Pennsylvania all the time and he'd tell me about the country up there. You know, wide open fields surrounded by rock walls or rail fences. Trees so tall and strong you could hang swings off their branches. Breezes so sweet you could smell the grass baking in the sun. And nights so dark the entire Milky Way was visible out your backdoor."

"Sounds fantastic."

"Yeah. It did to me, too. Growing up with car horns, fire escapes, loud neighbors, and light pollution, his stories seems like a fantasy world I couldn't touch. Every time he came back with a new story, I used to dream I was a kid, swinging on the lower branches of a big maple tree with the Milky Way filling the sky overhead." Deli grinned. "I used to think that's what paradise looked like."

"Used to?"

"Yeah. Until I came here and met you."

The words hung in the air, both sharp and bright, and comforting and soft. He hadn't meant to say them aloud. He hadn't even realized he'd felt that way until he remembered the story about his uncle. But Caroline, for all her hard determination, offered him the sanctuary he'd been searching for the last few months.

Caroline met his gaze, her expression wary. "What?"

Deli shook his head. "Nothing."

"No, no. Repeat what you said. I need to hear it again."

"It's nothing." He waved his hand and gave her his best impartial smile. "I should let you rest."

She frowned but nodded slowly. "All right. But I'd like some tea now."

"Yeah. Because tea makes everything better, right?"

"Right." She smiled and moved a little to get more comfortable in her bed. "How is Daphne doing? I know she gets stressed out when I'm down for the count."

"I think she's still out taking care of the dogs. I'll check on her after I start the kettle. Want me to help you under the covers?"

Despite the innocent statement, Caroline laughed. "I bet you say that to all the women."

At first, he didn't make the connection and he frowned, which made her laugh harder.

"It's usually women who say that to me, not that I need you to."

"Take a deep breath, Chief. I'm teasing." She sat up gingerly and set her feet on the floor so he could lift up the bedclothes.

His cheeks heated as he realized what he'd said to engender her teasing. "Oh, yeah." He chuckled and helped rearrange her pillows and blankets after she'd settled. "Too bad getting you into bed means resting, though I might come and hang out with you while you rest."

She opened her mouth to say something flippant but nodded instead. "I'd like that. Thank you."

"Good. You get some sleep, and I'll come in after a couple of mikes." He watched her settle back into the pillows. "Take a break, Caroline. I got your back."

She raised her eyebrows a moment, but nodded slowly. "Okay. Good."

She closed her eyes, exhaling slow and long. He clenched his jaw, fighting against the irrational fury. He couldn't stand to see her hurt. He wanted to hunt the bastards down and shoot them. Beating up on weaker people pissed him off. Too many thugs and bullies had looked at him that way, until he joined the Navy, and eventually the SEALs. But he stood up for others who couldn't do what he did, and he didn't tolerate continued harassment.

He shook his head. He'd take a look at the information Finch sent him and find a way to protect Caroline and the Last Chance Dog Sanctuary. But first he'd check on Daphne to be sure she was all right with this latest attack against her aunt.

CHAPTER NINE

Caroline abhorred pain, especially the kind that came and went in waves. Coupled with the frightening memories of the crash, irritation became a living thing. The only positive belonged to the hot man who'd come to rescue her and whom she periodically found in her room when she woke from her fitful naps. Chief Rubenovich made her heart pound with his chocolate eyes and sexy scruff.

Deli

Despite the excitement of being run off the road and the resulting injuries, having him there, talking to her with his northeastern accent as he got her more tea warmed her more than she wanted to admit.

He said I'm his version of paradise.

She'd never had someone value her so much. She'd heard lines from guys hoping to get either her land or fortune, but Deli didn't seem to want anything from her. His motivation appeared to be defense of her home and family. Which was odd given how little he knew her or Daphne or the dogs they cared for.

She'd woken up to see the late afternoon shadows creeping across the yard outside her window and watched the wind move the leaves on the trees. Summer had arrived with verdant green and she loved the mountains before the heat snuck up on them.

"Hey, you're awake. How you doin'?"

The New Jersey accent teased a smile from her and she turned her head to meet Deli's gaze as he stood in her doorway. Dark scruff edged his cheeks and the skin under his nose, framing his kissable lips. *I should not be thinking about that.* But despite the 'should nots,' she couldn't help but imagine what it'd be like to taste him.

"I'm okay, though everything still aches pretty good."

"Yeah, it might be that way for a while." He nodded as he stepped into the room and she couldn't help but admire how his clothes fit his body. He'd changed into a rust-colored t-shirt from Sedona, AZ, proclaiming the Red Dirt Shirt Co, and a pair of faded jeans that hugged his thighs. *So pretty.*

"Lucky me. How is Trace doing? Is she okay?"

"Yeah, I checked on her and she doesn't seem to be favoring anything. I think she'll be fine. She's a little shaken up, but Daphne brought her into the house to hang out with Beryl, so she's settling down." He shrugged. "Though she keeps looking toward your room so she might be worried about how you're feeling."

Horny. Okay, not something she wanted to say out loud.

"I should probably get up and reassure her." She started to rise, but he pressed a hand to her shoulder.

"Nah, she's okay. We're keeping an eye on her and giving her reassurance. You just rest. Do you want some tea?"

She shook her head and sat up anyway. "No, thanks. I need to use the bathroom after all the tea I drank earlier."

She slid her feet to the floor and pushed her body up, but swayed when her muscles protested. Deli caught her and braced her shoulder against his chest.

"Whoa, easy. I got you." He tilted his head to meet her

95

eyes. "You need any help?"

She frowned and shook her head. "No, thanks. I think I can manage."

"Okay. I'll just walk with you to the door, then you're on your own." He said it like a threat and she laughed.

"Oh, ow. Don't make me laugh. My ribs don't like it." She grimaced as she made her way to the master bath.

"I'll try not to, but I like when you laugh, so that might be a tall order." She caught his grin as she closed the bathroom door.

She shook her head. *Damn sexy man.* She used the bathroom and washed her hands, studying her face in the mirror. She caught the glints of silver in her hair from the lights and the crow's feet marching away from her eyes. Add to that the new scratches on her forehead and right cheek, and she resembled a hot mess. *But not the young kind.*

She returned to her bedroom to find it empty. Her stomach grumbled its matching state. *I need to eat.* She glanced down at her clothes and found them torn and stained from the excitement in the morning. *Was it just this morning?* Sighing, she headed for her closet to find clean clothes.

While the clothes didn't make her feel new, she did feel better and she headed for the kitchen to find something to eat. Before she reached the end of the hallway, she heard Daphne's laugh after something Deli said and she stopped. In the last two years, Daphne hadn't laughed that carefree or joyous.

Caroline paused to take in the scene. Beryl lay curled in a ball on her doggy bed near the back door while Trace sat beside Deli at the kitchen counter. Deli described some insane summer trip he and his brothers had taken to the Atlantic City where they almost lit the Boardwalk on fire from fireworks, and their parents threatened to send them to the Louisiana salt mines in punishment. Daphne laughed at his descriptions as she set a homemade pizza in the oven, her usual tension gone from her body.

I want more of this.

The thought came out of nowhere and settled into Caroline's heart. She wanted Daphne to be happy and at ease, laughing at something Deli said. She wanted the comfort of having her family alive and safe. And she wanted Deli to be there. Deli made Daphne feel safe, more so than Caroline ever had. Hell, having Deli around made Caroline feel safer, too.

"Hey, there she is." Deli slid off the kitchen stool and came to her, Trace trailing him with her butt wagging due to her lack of tail. "Are you hungry? Daphne just put a pizza in the oven."

She nodded. "Yeah. Starving." Trace brushed up against her and thrust her head into Caroline's hand. "Hey, Trace. What a good girl you are. I'm okay. Just a little banged up."

The blue heeler whined a little and pressed herself closer, her expression saying, *I'm worried about you.*

"I'll be okay, Trace. Good girl." Caroline kept her voice firm and gentle so the dog knew she would be okay. "What kind of pizza did you make?"

Deli took her hand and led her back to the kitchen, and she tried not to enjoy his touch. *He's just being helpful.* She shoved her inner romantic to the side and settled on one of the stools.

"It's an everything pizza." Daphne rolled her eyes as Deli grinned. "He basically made me empty the refrigerator onto it."

Caroline laughed before she clutched her ribs. "As long as there's no mustard or mayonnaise on it, I'll take some."

"Ew. No. No anchovies, either." Daphne wrinkled her nose.

"Oh, thank goodness." Caroline grinned. "So did the

sheriff call?"

"Nope, and it's been pretty quiet otherwise." Deli scratched Trace's head and the dog closed her eyes in an approximation of bliss.

I'd like Deli to scratch my head, too. Great, now she was envious of a dog.

"I'm glad to hear that. How are the dogs?"

The conversation turned to the sanctuary and the arrival of the dogfood delivery. Deli had helped them unload and everything was squared away. Daphne mentioned that Tallulah still hadn't shown signs of being close to delivery of the puppies, but Daphne suspected it would be soon.

The pizza came out of the oven and they shared a simple meal. At one point they turned on the news and saw the report on the eight-car wreck. Fortunately, there were no fatalities, but the cause appeared to be texting and driving. Caroline started to nod once her belly was full and Deli caught her before she slumped off the stool.

"I think it's time for you to get some more rest." He smiled as he helped her stand and let her lean on him.

He smells so good. Why haven't I noticed that before?

"Okay. Good night, Daphne. I'll see you in the morning." She let Deli lead her to the bedroom and crawled into the bed with a sigh. "I can't believe how much I want to sleep." *With you.* Yeah, like that was going to happen.

Deli blinked then grinned. "Yeah, me either. But I don't think that's a good idea given your bruised body. But I can lie next to you." Amusement rippled through his voice.

"What?"

"Sleeping with you. Right now, you need to heal. But I'll stay in here while you rest." His delicious lips curled into a smile.

"Oh my glory." The heat burned her cheeks as she closed her eyes. "I didn't mean to say that aloud."

"Really?" He settled onto the bed beside her. "At any other time, it would be a great idea."

"That's a typical guy thing to say."

"Oh, I'm anything but a 'typical guy,' though I have my moments." He chuckled. "But smart guys like me know it's all about female choice, and if an attractive woman says she's interested, the smart guys jump at the opportunity."

"Jump, huh?" She gave a tired smile. "Yeah, is that a metaphor?"

He laughed. "Not tonight, it's not. Get some rest, Caroline. We can revisit the 'jumping' later when you're better."

"Okay." That was fine with her. She settled into her bed and her imagination, enjoying the weight of his body beside her.

Deli's body heat and his scent followed her down into her dreams, wrapping her up in their comforts. Her mind served up an image of the meadow where they'd met the bear. In her dream, the sun painted the grass a golden green and wildflowers raised their bright faces toward the sky. She let the sun warm her back as she stretched her legs out in front of her on the blanket they'd spread on the ground.

"Are you hot, Deli?" She focused her gaze on his bronze shoulders. He'd lost his shirt somewhere, but she didn't mind.

"No, but you are." His brown eyes blazed with intense arousal as he took the hem of her shirt and lifted it over her head. "There, that's better."

Sunlight warmed her chest but his gaze warmed it even more. She hadn't worn a bra under her shirt and he growled his approval. She liked the sound so she shook her shoulders, making her breasts sway.

"Oh, you saucy minx. I love the shape of your breasts. So sexy." He cupped them in his warm, rough hands and she whimpered as his thumbs scraped over her sensitive nipples. "I need to taste these."

He pushed her to lay down on the blanket beneath them and settled over her to feast on her nipples. But instead of sucking the areola into his mouth, he stroked them with his tongue, tickling the sensitive skin. The slick heat of his tongue sent frissons of pleasure straight to her pussy and she moaned. Her logical mind tried to intervene with whispers that such a young, viral, well-trained man wouldn't want a washed-up old maid like her, but she banished it to the corner and told it to shut up. This was her time and reality could catch up later.

"Hey." He raised his head from her breasts and met her gaze. "Have I told you how fucking beautiful you are?"

"What? No." She shook her head. "Why would you say that?"

"Because you looked like you were wondering why I'd want you." He grasped her hand and scooted closer, resting her palm on the front of his jeans. A hard ridge of flesh pressed against the fly. "You're fucking beautiful, and not just because of your naked body."

She glanced down her body and found all her clothes gone. He still wore his jeans, but she kind of liked having something to take off him. It increased the suspense of what his cock and balls looked like. She returned her gaze to his.

"But I'm old. Older than you. You're more Daphne's age."

Deli snorted, a sexy smile curling his lips. "You're not that old, Caroline, and Daphne's a baby. Plus, she's way too innocent for me." He slid down her body without breaking eye-contact and pushed her legs apart. "I like a woman who has some experience and knows how to enjoy all the pleasure I want to give her."

He dipped his head and rubbed the flat of his tongue over her nether lips. Ticklish, erotic pleasure shot straight to her brain and she whimpered as she threw her head back. *Sweet glory, that feels amazing.* He seemed to take her response for encouragement and settled in to savor her slick folds.

It had been so long since she'd enjoyed the attentions of a man and she'd forgotten the illicit pleasure of his mouth on her pussy. Wet, ticklish heat touched every fold and sparked arousal in her clit. She moaned and wriggled her hips, trying to get closer to his delicious mouth.

"Damn, you're so sweet, Caroline." He growled the words before he dove back in. His growl continued against her sensitive flesh, sending tremors through her whole body.

He lapped at her folds, sucking and humming, pleasure in the sounds as much in the sensations. Instead of sucking her clit into his mouth, he rubbed his tongue against it in a swirling motion and sparkles lit up the insides of her eyelids.

Sweet glory, don't stop.

She tightened her hands in the blanket as his masculine scent filled her nose and the heat from his body warmed more than her legs. *I want him. And I want him to stay.*

It seemed like an odd thing to think when she'd only known him thirty-six hours, but her heart agreed. *Must be from all the excitement.* But it felt like more than that. She started to analyze her emotional connection to Deli, but her attention shattered when he slid a finger into her wet pussy.

"Oh, sweet glory!"

He hummed as he thrust his finger into her sheath with measured strokes, stoking the fire of her arousal while he licked her labia. She whimpered and writhed, trying to move faster, but he held her hip with one hand as he thrust with the other. When he added a second finger, stretching her, she cried out as her orgasm surged.

"You're so damn sweet and wet." He shoved his fingers deep and curled their tips into her g-spot. "Come for me, gorgeous."

His words were all the encouragement she needed and

her orgasm shot through her body as he thrust his fingers at a steady pace. Hot, boiling pleasure coupled with his tongue on her nether lips flooded through her and sent her into a delirious spin of colored lights and ecstasy. Deli hummed his approval of her release as he lapped up all her cum. She settled back onto the blanket with a satisfied smile.

"You look like a cat who just ate the canary."

He smirked as he licked the last of her cream from his fingers. "Not the canary, but definitely the cream." He licked his lips as he crawled up her body, his jeans miraculously missing. "But now I want your pussy. Will you let me pleasure you some more?"

"Bring it on, Chief." She wiggled her hips as he settled between them, his chest hair brushing her breasts. "I can take everything you got for me."

Deli grinned as he grasped his cock and placed it at her slit, rubbing her folds with the pre-cum on the tip. She shivered as the hot, smooth skin slid over hers.

"How do you want it, Caroline?" His hot dark gaze held hers as he pushed into her body. "Hard and fast? Or deep and slow?"

He pulled back, dragging his cock along her inner walls until only the head remained then reversed and shoved back in until his balls rested against her ass. He stretched and filled her completely, the hot, hard intrusion making her eyes roll back in her head.

"What's it to be?"

She shook her head. "I don't care as long as there's more. Please, Deli, give me more."

He chuckled. "Yes, ma'am."

The muscles of his chest and arms bunched as he braced himself over her, moving only his hips. Despite the intensity in his eyes as he held her gaze, he moved in the same measured rhythm he'd used with his fingers in her pussy. And damn if it didn't spark her arousal again. *Oh, glory, I want him so much.*

"Damn, you're so tight, Caroline." His body flexed and she whimpered at the pleasure he gave. "I've wanted you since the moment I saw you in that meadow with Trace."

The words were pretty, but her logical mind warned her they might be fantastical. She shoved the logical side away.

If this is my fantasy, I want to live it to the fullest.

"Oh, glory, Deli. Move just like that." She grasped his hips as he rocked them, dragging his cock between her nether lips. "Oh, yes."

The delicious friction of his hard shaft against her clit made her see stars as she closed her eyes, but he stopped and she jerked them open again.

"What are you doing?"

He smirked. "I want you to look at me when you come, Caroline."

"Why?" She met his molten chocolate gaze.

"Because." He slid his cock into her pussy. "I want to see when the pleasure I give you takes over."

He rolled his hips, driving his dick against the walls of her sheath. Her arousal surged as he refused to look away and his eyes filled her vision. She wanted this man and this moment to last forever. He rocked her world and her body, and she wanted more.

I want his heart.

It was a ridiculous wish but staring into his eyes as her orgasm broke over her solidified the wish in her heart. This was the man she'd looked for as a younger woman when she'd dreamed of happily-ever-afters and knights in shining armor. Pleasure suffused her body, but her gaze and her mind remained fixed on Eugene, rocking his cock in her pussy until his own release took him.

"Oh yeah, take my cock, beautiful. Take it all."

He threw his head back and thrust the last few strokes into her hard, and she fell into the best pleasure she'd had in a long time. This was what she wanted from now on. The question was how to keep him.

****

Deli scrolled through the documents from Finch on his phone, reading the pattern of development to Casa de Catequil Cartel. They'd taken the Casita de la Sabiduria and shifted its operations from waiting for victims come to them to actively acquiring them for the illegal sex trade. But operations took money and connections. The Casa de Catequil needed the distribution lines from Mexico to Canada, and the coastal states had become a battle ground.

No wonder they want Caroline's place.

Her home and the acres of land around it would provide a perfect waystation for the cartel's trafficking of drugs and sex slaves. And from what he'd read, they were trying to make connections with the Seattle enclave of the Yakuza.

Shit, that would be bad.

At least Finch knew about it. But they'd have to find a way to shut down the Casa de Catequil before they ran Caroline off.

Not that she's running.

No, she lay sleeping in the bed next to him. He shot a look over at her as she moaned and his gut clenched. *Uh oh, is she in pain?* She stirred beside him, her body twisting a little under the covers. He stilled his breathing to watch, trying to determine how much pain disturbed her sleep.

"Sweet glory...don't stop."

He blinked. Her voice had been slurred from sleep, but he didn't think she sounded unhappy. In fact, if he was a betting man, he'd say she was going to—

"Oh, oh. Oh." Her breath caught and she stiffened before relaxing into a boneless lump on the bed.

Holy shit, did she just come? He stared at her, wishing

he could make her do that. *Hell, I'd like to make love with her.*

Caroline moaned again, rocking her hips and he couldn't help but watch. Her wet dream must have been fantastic and he'd give much to be inside her head with her.

"Please, Deli, give me more."

Damn, it sounds like I'm already there.

She writhed in the bed and he set his phone aside so he could watch. He wanted to wrap her up in his arms and feel her move against him, but he didn't want to wake her from her dream. She moved slowly, her hips rocking, and his cock hardened in his pants. Her moans made him rub the hard ridge under his fly, and he groaned as she gasped and stiffened again.

Fuck, I must've made her come in the dream. If only he could do that in real life. She'd been interested before she slept, and evidently, she still was from that demonstration.

He slid off the bed and adjusted his wayward cock while she settled back into sleep. *I'm gonna have to take a cold shower after that.* He shot one more look at Caroline, now sleeping peacefully, before heading to the bathroom.

****

It took him a lot longer to settle down after his shower, but when he finally got his body under control—Caroline's sexually satisfied scent hadn't helped—Deli managed to drift off to sleep. He'd set his alarm to wake up in a couple of hours and hoped he could catch a few z's before he had to face her after her dream.

Whump! Whump-whump! Whump!

Deli sat up and froze, listening hard. A rhythmic thumping came from somewhere near the house. *Holy shit, are those Casa de Catequil bastards actually using some sort of battering ram?*

He slid his feet to the floor and shot a look at Caroline. She slept soundly and didn't need to wake for another twenty minutes according to the clock. He didn't bother to put on his shoes, but grabbed his Glock and thumbed off the safety as he padded through the house.

Why aren't the dogs barking?

He paused at the end of the hallway before it opened into the living room. A light beside the couch and another over the kitchen table glowed in the late evening darkness, but otherwise the house remained still. He scanned the room for movement, while he listened for the thumping. It had stopped while he crept down the hall. But after a few breaths, it started up again.

He followed the sounds, keeping to what shadows were left in the room. He paused again at the door to the covered porch outside, rising on his toes to peek through the window. Someone moved with strength and grace through the space beyond, but he couldn't clearly see who. Grasping the doorknob, he cracked the door and focused on the person inside.

Only one light burned in the far corner of an open-air porch with outdoor carpet on the floor. White holiday lights hung around the edges of the porch allowing soft illumination. To the left of the door, he caught sight of a large red punching bag. The rhythmic thumps came from the strikes of the assailant's fists.

He could only see the person's back, but the shoulders were petite and not much higher than his own. He pushed the door open a little wider and found Beryl, Daphne's boxer, lying against the wall of the kennels beside the gate. The dog raised her head to stare at him, but otherwise seemed calm.

Deli thumbed on the safety of his Glock and shoved it into the waistband at his back, throwing his shirt over it before he pushed out onto the porch.

He watched Daphne take on the punching bag with

Judo moves, and from what he could tell, she had good form and skill. A knife dummy made of smooth wood stood to his immediate left with arms that could be folded up for easy storage. He hadn't seen it before tonight and wondered where it had come from.

He shifted to the side so she'd catch sight of him before he said anything. He didn't want to surprise her, though given her abilities, he might end up being the one surprised.

"Nice moves. How long have you been taking Judo?" He leaned against the door, well out of her way.

Daphne shot him a quick look before returning to her assault on the bag. "Pretty much since I got back from my…trip." She shook her head as she punched the bag again. "I figured I needed to be better prepared."

She landed some more punches and kicks that made his balls ache just from watching.

"Knowing how to disable an opponent and get away won't do any good if you're drugged." Hadn't Rimshot's woman learned that the hard way?

"I know." Daphne slammed the bag a few more times before she paused and turned to him. "But I'm done being a victim. I can't do anything about drugs, but maybe these skills will help keep me from getting drugged in the first place." She shrugged. "It makes me feel better, anyway. What are you doing out here? How's Caroline?"

Deli gestured to the bag. "I heard the thumping and came to check it out. And Caroline's sleeping." He didn't mention the sexy dream. He tilted his head as Daphne headed for the knife dummy. "Does she know you do this?"

Daphne shook her head as she picked up a hard resin "knife" and took her stance. "No, and I don't want her to. She has enough to worry about. This would stress her more than necessary, so please don't tell her."

He raised his eyebrows. "You don't think she'll want to know that you can defend yourself?"

"I think she won't understand my need to do this. She's a healer, not a fighter, and this kind of skillset might make her think I'm going to seek out my attackers."

He nodded. "Are you?"

"No, I don't even know who they are. I was drugged, remember?" She shot him a look that said she knew he remembered her very well, but she returned her attention to the dummy without pushing it.

"Right. But you said your aunt's a healer. How do you know that?"

Daphne shrugged before she took some shots at the dummy. "She set up this sanctuary for the Military War Dogs. She believes in second chances and that everyone can be reached with love and patience." She stopped a moment to meet his gaze with a wisdom he hadn't expected. "She almost always knows what's wrong. She's good with people. She's an expert with dogs."

"Has she always had this skill?"

Daphne nodded as she stabbed her assailant a few times. "Yeah, even when I was little. She's had this talent to read people since she was a kid, you know? She could figure out where the hurts were."

He snorted. "Without them telling her? Wow. Why didn't she become a doctor?"

She shrugged again. "I don't know. I think it's because she doesn't trust people very much, but she definitely trusts dogs. She knows exactly what each dog needs when it comes here. Including Sergeant Trace. She's a kind of medicine woman, but not a fighter."

Deli tilted his head. "I don't think that's the case. She's been holding off those thugs and protecting you."

"But she only does that because she has to. And I don't want her to become a fighter like that." Daphne paused and fixed him with a hard stare. "That's your job."

She turned back to her workout without another word, pounding the knife dummy with various shots. He watched her for a while, thinking on her words and he had to agree. Caroline was strong and a fighter in her own way, but she wasn't meant to be a warrior who took the fight to the aggressors.

Deli retreated back into the house and found Sergeant Trace seated a few feet inside the door, ears up and waiting.

"How'd you get in here? Aren't you supposed to be in your kennel?"

The dog tilted her head and looked at him like he was the one out of place. *Yeah, I wish I was back in bed with Caroline.*

"Come on, Trace. Let's get you back in your kennel. *Foose.*" He started to reach for her collar when the dog got to her feet and pointed her nose back toward the exercise room he'd just left. He nodded. "It's just Daphne with Beryl, training."

The dog snorted as if to say, *I know, jackass.* But she shot him a look then returned her gaze to the door. He rolled his eyes and moved to take her collar.

"Come on, I'll show you. Hup."

The dog moved to stand beside him as he pushed open the door to the exercise room. Daphne had her back to them and kept thumping the dummy. But Trace's gaze focused to Daphne's left, out the side toward the hills above the house. She rumbled a low growl and Beryl came to her feet, her body tense.

Deli dropped his hand to Trace's back and felt her stiff awareness. *Shit, she's telling me something's out there.*

"Daphne, I'm gonna turn off the light."

"What? Why?" She turned to look at him like he'd lost his mind.

He flipped off the light, but kept his gaze focused on the grounds outside. He almost missed the red laser light appearing on her side but he launched himself into her, taking her down to the floor as a rifle shot cracked across the mountain.

Daphne squealed in pain and fear as the porch filled with gunfire.

"Shit! Are you hit?"

She whimpered and shook her head.

"Good. Get back into the house and stay low." He pushed her toward the door. "Turn off..."

Another laser dot found Daphne's leg and he swore. "Fuck! Get inside now."

She scrambled for the door as more shots rang out. *The mudfuckers have NVGs.* He scurried after her, holding the door open as Beryl and Trace ducked in with them.

"Stay low, but turn on the lights. I don't want them using the NVGs."

"The what?" Daphne's tear stained gaze met his.

"Night vision goggles. I want them to use their regular vision."

"Oh my glory, what's going on?" Caroline stumbled out of the hallway, her face white.

"Get down, Caroline." Deli darted over to her and pulled her low. "You need to stay down."

"What? Why?" He got her to crouch with him, but regretted the wince as her muscles pulled against the bruises from the seat belt.

"They're up on the hill." Daphne hunched down over Beryl. "They're shooting at us."

Another barrage of bullets hit the house and Caroline squeaked as she ducked.

"Just stay low and away from windows. And draw the shades if you can, but leave the lights on." Deli scrambled to the door and dug into a basket on the floor, searching for the dog vests he'd seen stored there.

"What are you going to do?" Caroline crawled along the floor, switching on lamps as she went.

"Trace and I are gonna go hunting."

CHAPTER TEN

Deli missed his tactical gear as soon as he stepped out the front door. Trace stuck with him as he crouched low and ran for the trees along the driveway. There seemed to be only a couple of shooters, both on the hill above the house. *That evens the odds.* Between him and Trace, they should be able to take out the would-be snipers.

All he had with him was his Glock and the dog, but if he got the jump on one of the shooters, he'd have a whole new set of weapons to use.

"Trace, *zooch.*"

The whispered command hit the dog's ears and she shifted into reconnoiter mode. A new feeling of purpose and excitement flooded through his system and he settled into the focus he'd been missing for the last few months. *It's a helluva Monday morning wake-up call.*

Trace put her nose to the ground and headed up into the trees west of the shooters' positions. He didn't have NVGs, but his eyes had adjusted to the predawn darkness as he followed the heeler. They made steady time through the silent trunks and his soft-soled hiking shoes made little sound, in contrast to the gunshots that continued.

Damn, the mudfuckers don't seem to care about bein' quiet.

That worked for him. He picked his way up through the underbrush until he judged he'd gone higher than the snipers' nests. He paused to listen, motioning Trace to stop.

The breeze rustled the canopy overhead and the Ponderosas creaked a little in answer, but the men had stopped shooting.

"*Zooch.*"

The dog headed off downslope a little, her footsteps just as quiet as his. Damn, he missed working with a well-trained MWD. Their path brought them to a granite outcropping no more than a couple feet high, but it provided a good vantage point above the house.

And a straight shot into the covered porch.

He scowled as he waited to make out the shape of the man on the rock. The guy hadn't heard him or Trace, and he kept scanning the brightly lit house below for movement. The women had taken his advice and left the lights on, but stayed away from the windows.

Deli eased closer to the granite, motioning Trace to stay behind him. He debated whether to incapacitate the Tango or to kill him as the man turned and caught sight of him. Deli leapt at him, ducking the swing of the rifle as he squeezed off a couple of rounds.

Decision made.

Deli dropped low and slammed into the man's midriff, knocking him against the rock. The guy grunted and let off more bullets into the brush. The roar of the automatic rifle rattled Deli's ears, but he grabbed the guy's gun hand and twisted it out of his grip.

Deli slammed his elbow into the guy's chin, but he lurched his head and rolled away. Deli turned to follow as the guy rolled to his feet with a large K-bar knife in his hand.

Oh, good. I was missing mine.

The sniper came at him with a low snarl but Deli used the rifle to block his swing as he pivoted into the strike. He dropped the rifle and grabbed the guy's arm, using his momentum to flip him over his shoulder while overextending the guy's wrist. He yanked the knife out of his weakened hand and wrapped his arm around the guy's throat.

Go to sleep. Go to sleep. Go to sleep.

He tightened his arm until the man hung limp from lack of breath. Deli dropped him and scrounged around to for something to tie his hands with. Fortunately, the guy had brought a bag full of supplies, duct tape being the most useful.

Gracias, hermano.

Deli pulled the tape out and went to work on the sniper's hands, feet, and an extra strip over the mouth. Though the fight had been mostly silent, the gunshots had echoed through the pre-dawn woods and he figured the other sniper would come looking. Deli collected the weapons off the unconscious man and waved at Trace to come to him. The dog picked her way to his side then turned her head to stare laterally across the hillside.

A radio crackled nearby and a voice speaking in Spanish asked for a response. *He ain't comin', buddy. How 'bout you come to me?* Deli faded back into the shadow of the rocks and hunkered down to wait.

Pretty soon another guy dressed in dark clothes, toting an AK-47 and a radio, slipped through the trees. He was marginally quieter than the first guy, but he seemed to think he was the baddest guy on the hill.

"Miguel!" The whispered name bounced off the silent trunks.

Deli waited for him to come into the small clearing, signaling Trace. He needed her to distract the guy long enough to incapacitate him.

"Miguel!"

Come on, asshole. Step into the clearing.

It took him a few more seconds to spot the body lying in the detritus. His head came up, searching for his unconscious partner's assailant. Deli suppressed the urge to grin and took a deep breath, settling the surge of

113

excitement. *Patience, patience.*

At last, the other sniper moved forward, releasing his rifle and crouching beside the body. Deli signaled to Trace and the dog launched herself at the bastard without a sound. She latched onto his arm and he shrieked, jerking back onto his ass.

Deli followed after Trace, planning to get the guy into a headlock and incapacitate him. But the sniper saw him at the last moment and pulled a pistol, whether to hit Trace or him, Deli wasn't sure. He grabbed the guy's gun arm and yanked it away, slamming his other hand against the overextended elbow.

The sniper grunted and the pistol went off, but he managed to fold his arm to get the muzzle in position to shoot Deli. Deli twisted and used his leverage to move the muzzle just enough that the next shot went into the guy's head. The sound made his ears ring, but the sniper dropped to the ground, the back side of his head missing.

Fuck, he was using armor-piercing rounds.

Deli stepped back and scowled. They'd stepped up the game. They were coming in hot and Caroline and Daphne were marked for death. *That ain't gonna happen if I have anything to say about it.*

"Trace, *poost.*" The dog opened her jaws and sat back from the body, her gaze on Deli. "Good, girl."

He scrounged the second body for weapons and radio. He didn't regret killing the one guy and leaving him with his unconscious friend—they'd endangered the women he protected—but he wasn't about to leave anything others could use to continue the assault. He took the time to move the unconscious guy up close to one of the smaller saplings and used more tape to secure him there. His head lolled against his chest, but Deli smiled with satisfaction. That'd hold him until the cops could come get him.

And they kindly offered me their keys. Having the radios would give him a clue about which frequency the tangoes communicated on and he'd offer that info to Finch and his crew when they arrived.

The sky had just started to grow light and give him a sense of how close the mudfuckers had gotten to the house. Finch would have to set up a perimeter. He glanced down at the body. He'd rather bury it, but the local sheriff's department might want to take a look. *And it will scare the hell out of the other guy if he wakes up.* He made sure the dead guy wasn't visible from the house and slung the guns over his shoulders.

"Trace, *zooch.*"

The dog jumped to her feet and put her nose to the ground, sniffing around the bodies before heading along the hillside. Deli followed her to the second sniper's nest and found his brass coating the needles from the pines above. He nodded and urged Trace on, backtracking their path through the forest.

They followed a wildlife trail winding through the trees until it came back to the small bridge crossing the creek bed in Caroline's driveway. The snipers' truck sat parked off the road in a wide spot against the hill.

Chevy Silverado. Nice.

They'd left the navy blue truck unlocked and the extended cab provided a nifty place to stash the weapons. *And all their other supplies.* They had food, more weapons, and camping gear in the back. Plus the truck.

Suitable replacement for Caroline's.

He whistled for Trace and she leapt into the cab, settling into the front passenger seat. He shoved the key in the ignition and the vehicle rumbled to life. Loud rock music blared from the radio and he turned it off, shaking his head.

"Sorry about that, Trace. I'm surprised we didn't hear the bastards coming." He put the truck in gear, backed up, and steered toward Caroline's house. "We're definitely gonna have to call in the cavalry now. They stepped this shit up and we're gonna have to shut them down."

Trace growled in agreement and he grinned. The Casa de Catequil assholes had just started a fight they were going to lose.

****

Caroline looked up at the sound of a truck rumbling up the driveway and held her breath. Panic surged as she crawled to the front window to look out. Her chest hurt from the bruising, but she didn't let her it stop her as she peered over the sill.

"Who is it?" Daphne's voice reached her from across the room. She crouched behind the island wrapped around Beryl.

"I don't know. I saw a truck but I can't tell who's driving it." *Sweet glory, I hope Deli's okay.*

"Do you think the chief got the guys? They've stopped shooting."

"I don't know, but I'm glad they've stopped." *I hope he got them and isn't dead.*

When he said he was going hunting, she suddenly understood what kind of warrior he was. He'd been dressed in his black hiking gear and it made him hard to see when he'd disappeared out the door with Trace. She'd almost called him back, but like a whisper, he was gone without a sound, and she'd been left to hope neither him nor the dog would get hurt.

She cocked her head, listening for whoever was in the truck, but all she could hear was the pounding of her heart. *They're gonna be okay.* She had to believe that, but scrambled to reach the rifle resting beside the door. "Someone's here in a truck I've never seen before. It's not Deli's. Glory, I hope he's okay."

Daphne shot her a surprised look and Caroline grimaced. She didn't know what she was more afraid of:

116

Her and Daphne and the dogs getting killed by the cartel's thugs, or Deli getting killed by them. *Glory, I don't think I could handle losing him.* Which was stupid. He wasn't her boyfriend or her lover or even an old friend. She barely knew him. But she wanted to know him a helluva lot better and she couldn't do that if he got dead.

She glanced out the window again and swallowed hard. The dark pickup with an extended cab slid through the early dawn light and disappeared behind the barn. She wondered if the asshole behind the wheel hoped to surprise them by coming in the back. She swore under her breath and hurried toward the door to the covered porch, cocking the rifle. She'd shoot anyone who came through.

Deep breaths. Be calm. Be ready.

The words helped her settle, but her heart still hammered at her ribs when someone rattled the doorknob.

"Daphne? It's Chief Rubenovich. Open up."

A dog's whine sounded after that and Caroline let out her breath before lowering the rifle.

"Open the door for him."

"Are you sure it's him?" Daphne poked her head up over the island.

"Yeah, pretty sure. But I have the rifle if it's not."

Daphne nodded before she hurried to the door. She peeked through the curtain over the inset window and her shoulders slumped in relief.

"It's him and Trace." She opened the door to reveal Deli with the blue heeler.

Both of whom had blood on them.

"Oh, my sweet glory. You're bleeding!" Caroline uncocked the rifle and set it down before she rushed forward to inspect him. "Where's it coming from?" She grasped his shoulders, needing to feel his body in one piece. She managed to resist the urge to run her hands over his chest and belly, but only just.

"I'm all right, Caroline. So is Trace. The blood's not

117

ours." He dropped a large bag on the floor with a heavy clank.

"Not yours?" She frowned as she visually checked him over. "Whose is it, then?"

His gaze moved over to Daphne before he returned it to hers. "One of the snipers'. The other guy's unconscious."

"Snipers? Plural?" Her gut sank to below her knees and took her balance with it.

"Whoa! Come and sit down before you fall." Deli moved with predatory grace and pulled her against his chest. "Let's get you to a chair. How are your bruises?"

"I'm fine. You're really not hurt? And there were really more than one sniper outside?"

"Yes and yes." He lowered her into a nearby chair and crouched in front of her, studying her face. "I shut them down and I got you a new truck out of the deal."

"A new truck?" Caroline shook her head, wishing the world would slow down just for a moment. "What are you talking about?"

"The snipers aren't going to need it and they owed you a replacement." His cute smirk warmed her heart but the new situation of having snipers on her hill pushed her beyond her stamina.

"Sweet glory, what are we going to do?"

"Hey, it's going to be fine. I've already called in the cavalry." He took her hands. "My buddy at Ultimate Recon, Inc. is on his way down here with his team. They've been working with the FBI and ATF to take down the Casa de Catequil Cartel for a while now. Protecting you and the Last Chance Dog Sanctuary is definitely something they're willing to do, especially because it gives them a chance to root out the cartel."

"But I can't pay them. I can support me and the dogs, but this isn't something I can afford. Oh glory, what am I going to do?" The panic overwhelmed her usual stoicism and tears started in her eyes.

"Hey, breathe for me, Caroline. Breathe."

Deli's New Jersey accent washed over her as he squeezed her hands but she shook her head. How would it be fine? There were men shooting at her and she had nowhere else to go. This was her sanctuary and her home. She couldn't just pack up and leave.

"Caroline! Focus on me." Deli tugged on her arms and she raised her gaze to his. "That's it. Breathe with me. In and out, real slow. That's it."

She didn't want to have to breathe slow. She wanted to be safe, in her home, with Daphne and her dogs. She wanted the world to make sense and be calm again. And she wanted to stop being afraid that someone she loved would get hurt or killed.

Deli could get hurt or killed. He's a member of the US military and SpecOps to boot.

"Oh, glory."

The sob broke loose before she could stop it and unleashed the tears she'd held back. She didn't know what she'd do if she lost everything, and Deli counted as part of everything.

I need him.

Suddenly she was wrapped in a warm embrace, hard muscles smelling of sweat, sandalwood, and the coppery tinge of blood. She ignored the last and poured her heart out into the chest of the man who held her like he'd never let her go. *Damn, I'm getting sappy.* But she didn't want him to let go. She didn't want him to leave. He'd managed to sneak his way past her defenses and score some prime real estate in her heart.

"I got you. It's okay. We're safe and that's how we'll stay. Deep breaths, Caroline."

His smooth, confident voice just about undid her and she released all her pent up fear and frustration. She had to protect her dogs and her niece, and she didn't know how anymore. She didn't have the strength, the training, or the knowledge.

"I can't do this."

"Yes, you can. But you're not alone. I got you."

He squeezed gently, holding her against his chest. He wasn't tall, but there was nothing little about Chief Rubenovich. He had a big heart, giant determination, and a huge presence. A presence she wanted in her life. Because right now she needed his strength and determination to see her through.

Please don't leave me.

It was an unreasonable request, one he couldn't fulfill while remaining an active chief petty officer. He'd be deployed without warning and if he was SpecOps, he wouldn't be able to tell her where he was going or why. All she could have was right now. She couldn't ask for more even if he wanted to give it to her.

And I'm way too old for him.

The dream notwithstanding, she had to be at least ten years his senior, and hot men like him wouldn't be interested in a woman who had crow's feet around her eyes and silver strands in her hair.

"Breathe, Caroline. Come on. I need you to breathe."

Had she stopped? She forced herself to inhale and settle into his arms a little more. This was all she could have, but she wanted to remember it forever to give her comfort when he left. Because he would and she'd be alone with the cartel coming after her.

"I can't."

"I can do a lot of things to help you, but not if you stop breathing." His breath moved her hair above her ear and she realized he held her close enough to kiss. "Breathe for me, beautiful. If it helps, follow my breaths."

He breathed loudly for her to track and she tried to follow him, forcing her lungs to fill when they wanted to shut down. Her heart pounded in her chest and her stomach turned over, queasy, but she focused on his heat and her breathing evened out.

"Good. Daphne, can you make some tea, please?"

He maneuvered Caroline to the couch and dropped them both into it. But his arms never loosened and his breathing never changed.

"Breathe with me, beautiful. You're safe and I'm with you."

"Don't leave me." She hadn't meant to voice the plea, but it had slipped past her lips.

"I'm not going anywhere. Me an' Trace. We got your back." He squeezed her. "I won't leave until I know you're okay."

Tears slid down her cheeks and she shook her head. She'd never be okay. Just because they defeated this batch of thugs didn't meant the cartel wouldn't still come after her. And Deli couldn't stay forever. She'd be on her own to fight them off again.

But she couldn't say any of that. It wasn't fair to ask it of him. *Hell, none of this is fair, and that's just life, isn't it?*

The thought made her want to cry harder, but she was done having her pity party. Crying wouldn't change a thing and she needed to pull herself together so he would feel okay when it was time for him to leave. She pushed the grief away, but she remained in Deli's arms, not willing to give up what little comfort he could offer.

"Better?"

She nodded against his chest. At least he couldn't see her lying.

"Good." He squeezed her before he pushed her back to look in her eyes. "I have some good news. I told you that Ultimate Recon is bringing a team down here, right?"

She nodded again as she wiped her face. "Yes, you said."

"Right, well, because they're already trying to ferret out where the hell these thugs are running, the FBI has agreed to foot the bill for their services." He pushed her wayward hair behind her ears. "You don't have to spend a thing for this and we'll get rid of the Casa de Catequil's thugs. Win-win for everyone."

"Except the cartel." Daphne held out a mug of tea with a smirk. "I like it."

Caroline liked it, too, but she met Deli's gaze as she wrapped her hands around the mug. "You're sure this is okay? That your friends at this place—"

"Ultimate Recon."

"Yes, Ultimate Recon, are good with this? I'm serious, Deli. I really can't pay them."

"I know you're serious, and yeah, I'm sure. Finch sounded downright thrilled to have a crack at these assholes." He shut his mouth and a surprisingly adorable blush colored his cheeks. "Sorry. Rat bastards."

She grinned in spite of the news. "Either works." Then she sobered. "But you're okay after this morning?"

"Yeah, yeah, I'm good."

No question in my mind about that.

"I am gonna take a shower, though." He glanced down at himself and grimaced. "And maybe run some laundry. Trace will probably need a bath."

Daphne snorted. "She's needed a bath for a while now."

"Heh, yeah. And call the sheriff again. He definitely needs to get up here today. One of the snipers is still alive, though tied up and unconscious. The sheriff will want to collect him and the body, and meet with the Ultimate Recon guys. I'm pretty sure he'll want to know what's been going on in his jurisdiction." He paused, touching her elbow. "You gonna be okay for a bit?"

She nodded, the lie easier when she didn't have to use her voice.

"Okay. I won't be long." He trotted toward the bedroom hallway.

Daphne sighed. "You're not okay, are you?"

Caroline shrugged, still holding back the tears. "I'm going to call the sheriff and tell him about this new development after yesterday's car chase." No, she wasn't okay, but sometimes that was just the way things were.

CHAPTER ELEVEN

They say before you start a war, you better know what you're fighting for.

Deli stepped into the hot water spray and sighed. Not only did it feel good to get clean, but he suspected Caroline wasn't as fine as she said. And that damn near ripped out his heart. He'd only been with her for forty-eight hours, but she'd stormed the fortress of his heart and crashed through the locked doors.

What was it about her? He reached for the shampoo and squirted some into his hands. Maybe it was her determination to keep her home and land out of the hands of the Casa de Catequil Cartel. Maybe it was her infinite gentleness with the Military War Dogs she rehabilitated. Maybe it was her fierce persistence to make sure her family and friends had a place of safety in a world so bent on harm.

Maybe it's all of those. He scrubbed his head hard. He didn't want any of the dead sniper's blood left on him anywhere.

Caroline had captured his heart without his say-so, and he wouldn't be able to walk away without helping.

Because I love her.

The words made him start and some of the shampoo got in his eyes. He cursed and shoved his face under the spray, rinsing them. How the hell had that happened? He was an active duty Navy SEAL. He didn't have the luxury of hanging out longer than his leave. Hell, he could be called back to base at any moment, leaving her in a predicament without his help.

Please, Universe, let me stay at least until the guys from Ultimate Recon get here.

He couldn't leave Caroline and Daphne, and their dogs, unprotected. It would undermine one of his core reasons for becoming a SEAL. He'd done it to protect the 'little guy,' somewhat literally. At 5'8', he was the shortest member of the Bravo Squad, but his lack of height had only been a problem for others. He'd been his BUD/S class's Steve Rogers, a scrapper and a wrestler, using his body in ways the bigger guys couldn't.

He filled the puff with body wash and scrubbed his body with thick suds, chuckling at the memories. It was the first time he realized size didn't matter. He attended to his cock and balls as he shook his head. He'd never had any complaints when it came to the use of his anatomy, whether in war or in sex.

It didn't matter now, either. He didn't need to be huge to do his job, he just needed heart. He knew what he was fighting for, or rather, for whom. Caroline was his heart, and he'd make sure it was better defended than his original one.

He finished his shower and toweled off, listening for arrivals of any kind. He hoped Caroline had called the sheriff, though he wasn't looking forward to explaining the dead guy in the rocks above the house. It was a clean kill, though he had no corroborating witnesses or evidence, and dead men didn't talk much.

He pulled on clean clothes and headed back out to the living room. Daphne stood in the kitchen, peeling potatoes.

"What are you doing and where's Caroline?"

"She's out repairing the windows around the porch before she works with the dogs." She put the potato down and chopped it into chunks. "I'm making stew for when this herd of people is supposed to show up."

"Did she call the sheriff again?"

Daphne nodded. "Yeah. Agatha said she'd make sure to send everyone up here ASAP." She chopped a little harder. "You do know Caroline's not okay, right?"

"What? Did something happen while I was in the shower?" Deli froze.

"No, nothing happened then. But she's not cut out for this. I told you she's not that kind of fighter." She fixed him with narrowed eyes. "She's a healer and a nurturer." She moved on to chopping carrots.

"I know."

"No, you don't know." She put the knife down and leaned forward, her expression frustrated. "Caroline's good with dogs, not humans. She doesn't take people in, especially not men she meets at the feed store/bar. She's never trusted a man in her home. Until you."

"She doesn't date?" He stuffed his feet into his shoes.

"Oh, she dates. She just doesn't bring them here." Daphne chopped more carrots. "I think she wants to protect me after my bad time in South America." She shrugged with a grimace. "I appreciate it, but it's not really fair to her." She raised her gaze to his. "You're the first guy she's brought to our house and trusted enough to be around me. But I can tell you she's not okay with what's going on. She's scared of what's going to happen when you leave."

"I'm not going to leave—"

"You're active military, aren't you?" She pointed the knife at him.

"Yeah, active Navy." He nodded.

"You're only on leave for so long and then you're back to whatever war effort needs you. And she'll be alone to face the consequences of whatever these bastards are going to throw at us." Daphne went back to chopping, this time onions. "Here's the thing I'm getting at. You're going to leave. Try not to rip her heart out when you go."

Daphne's words shook him to his core. *Rip out her heart?* How could he do that? She hadn't said anything about love or connection or even friendship. Hell, they'd just met a couple days earlier, and he hadn't thought it'd gone all that well. Okay, she'd had that wet dream featuring him, but that was lust, not a relationship.

And despite it, he'd already started falling for her without hope of reciprocation. *The only easy day was yesterday and I just made today a helluva lot harder.*

He shook his head. "I don't think you have to worry about that, Daphne. Caroline doesn't feel that way about me."

She stopped what she was doing to shoot him a dry look. "You're kidding, right?"

"Uh...no?"

"Oh my glory. She wouldn't have come over when you were covered in blood to hug you. No way in hell. She hates blood, both the sight and smell of it. But she threw herself into your arms. She might not have said anything, but she's definitely into you."

"I...okay. I'll go check on her." He'd never been so uncertain about anything in his life, but Daphne had just thrown him a curveball.

"Good." She went back to making the stew and he took himself out to the kennels, definitely dismissed.

Damn, she'd make a good CO.

He found Caroline taking one of the hounds through her training exercises. The hound looked like a big, happy mutt until Caroline gave the order. The dog immediately stood straight and attentive, the floppy ears up to listen and the eyes never leaving her body language.

She took the dog through a series of moves that

outwardly didn't appear to be anything special – sit, stay, come, wait, protect, down. But each time the dog did what she wanted, Caroline gave her a treat and praise. The dog responded by acting on the commands faster the next time she asked. The hound worshipped Caroline and jumped at the chance to please her.

Deli watched, enthralled with her gentleness, and yet her command of the animal with her. She was the alpha of the pack, and the dog knew it, but she also engendered devotion and adoration from the hound. Deli was right there with the dog.

When she finished running the hound through her paces, she called a halt, removed the harness, and threw a ball. The dog bounded after the bright orange sphere with abandon, and Deli laughed.

Caroline turned her head and gave him a tired smile. "I didn't know you'd come in. How was your shower?"

"Good enough, I guess." He shrugged.

She stopped, her brows coming down. "Is there something wrong? No water pressure or something?"

"No..." He trailed off, wondering if he should take a risk on Daphne's assessment of Caronline's motivation. "Just kinda lonely. Needed someone to scrub my back."

Her eyebrows went up. "You can't scrub your back?"

"Nope. Arms are too short." He grinned. It wasn't true, but if it got her to laugh, he'd say just about anything.

She did laugh as the hound ran up with the ball in her mouth. "Good girl, Henley. Drop."

The dog obediently released the ball and Caroline threw it again before she tilted her head toward him.

"Next time, let me know, and I'll give you a scrub brush."

"Aww. I was kinda hopin' you'd volunteer to get my hard-to-reach spots." He was only half-joking, but he didn't want to push if Daphne was completely wrong about Caroline's feelings. "Actually, I wanted to ask you how you were feeling. Is your body feeling better?"

"Yeah, not as achy this morning." She turned her back as the hound returned.

He waited for her to say something more, but she kept her attention on the dog. Her energy remained calm, but something was off. The hound noticed too, because she brushed past Caroline before sitting in front of her with a wagging tail.

"Good girl." She ruffled to dog's ears before taking the ball and throwing it again.

Could she really be feeling more for him than simple generosity? They'd had an adventurous couple of days, but that didn't equate to something more than basic kindness. Did it?

Fuck, I have no idea how to ask.

Especially since he'd already given her his heart. *And haven't told her.* Yeah, he was winning points left and right. And pretty soon the sheriff and the guys from Ultimate Recon would be there, taking up space and creating a distraction.

How the hell could he ask how she was feeling without sounding presumptuous? *Tell her how you're feeling, jackass.*

"How come you're just throwing the ball to her?" Okay, not what he'd been thinking of saying, but at least it might get her talking.

"She's been training for a while today so it's always good to remind her it's okay to play, too." Caroline threw the ball again.

"Do you ever take time to play, Caroline?"

Her shoulders stiffened and he smothered a groan. *Nothing like making her defensive.* But it was a legitimate question. She rehabilitated dogs, trained them to help others, took care of Daphne, and did all the work. When did she ever let herself relax and play?

She shook her head. "I don't have time to play. There's

too much going on."

He recalled the conversation he'd had with Farkas, of finding and acknowledging the emotions before they blew up on him. He'd been trying to do that, but he hadn't found anything to focus on beyond them. But now he realized he had something he wanted to do and someone with whom he wanted to do it. He wanted to protect Caroline and Daphne, and he wanted to work with them to rehabilitate the Military War Dogs. Because like him, the dogs needed something to do and someone to wait on them.

"You know, before I came out here on R and R, a buddy of mine told me to take some time to play and relax. Because I was just like you. There was no time and too much going on to settle down." He stepped closer to her, trying to keep his own energy mellow and comforting. "And you're right. There is a lot going on with the Casa de Catequil Cartel coming after your home, Daphne, and the dogs. But like my buddy reminded me, sometimes you just have to let it go and let others take up the slack."

She rounded on him. "You think I should let it go when someone is trying to take everything I've built and love? You think I should just stand back and go, 'whatever, it's fine'?" Caroline's eyes filled with tears. "You don't understand. This is just a weekend jaunt for you and you can go back to your life of saving the world, while my world collapses around me. You're going to leave, and move on, but I can't do that. This is my home. This is my world. This is what I have to fight for."

"I have nothing to go back to."

"What?" She blinked, her anger giving way to surprise. "What are you talking about?"

Deli took a deep breath. "I came out here to get my head on straight about what I'm doing and where I'm going with my life. Yeah, I'm in the Navy, but my enlistment comes up in about seven months and I got nothin'. I don't really want to reenlist, but I don't know what to do if I don't. I don't have a life to step into after the Navy. I came here to find one because I'm runnin' out of time to tell 'em if I want to separate." He paused, staring into her eyes and hoping universe would catch him when he took the plunge. "And I think I have."

"You have?"

"Yeah…I want to come back here, to the Last Chance Dog Sanctuary, and help you work with the dogs. And I want to be with you." He licked his lips as panic surged, but he pushed through it. "I want to stay with you, help you fight for this world right here, back you up when the shit hits the fan. I'd like to join your world. I got enough leave that I could separate early. If you'll have me."

"But…but we hardly know each other." She shook her head, her brows low over her eyes. "You've only been here a couple of days. How do you know you'll like it here? How do you know you'll like me?"

"That's just a question of time. I already know you a little and I already like being here with you. I want more of that. And I want to know I have someplace to go when my time in the Navy is up." He took another step closer. "How 'bout it, Caroline? We found each other. Give me a chance at least."

"We found each other because of a dog and a bear."

"I'll have to thank the bear, then." He smirked as he stepped into her space.

"I'm serious, Chief. You barely know me."

"So am I, Caroline, and I know enough. One thing I know for sure: when an opportunity like this comes up, jump at it before it disappears for good. I'm a SEAL. I don't let shit like that go by."

She shook her head. "But I'm old. Older than you. Wouldn't you want someone younger?"

"No." He cupped her face in his hands as they stood eye-to-eye. "I want you."

And he tilted his head to press his lips to hers.

****

He wants me!

Wait, he wanted her? Was he sure? This didn't make any sense. But her mind threw its metaphorical hands in the air as he deepened the kiss and she let herself fall into the pleasure. And damn, Deli knew how to kiss.

She hadn't ever received such a wonderful kiss and she wrapped her arms around his chest to make sure she didn't miss a moment of it. She tilted her head and opened her mouth to enjoy his tongue sliding over hers. *Sweet glory, I want kisses like this every day.*

Pleasure zinged through her body, making the cream flow in her pussy. She tried to get closer to Deli and the hard ridge of his arousal. *I guess he does really want me.* She moaned as its hard length rubbed her mound, igniting more desire.

He pulled back, his chest rising and falling against her breasts. They both panted and held each other's gaze, and she wondered if he'd take it further. *Please take it further.*

"Please, sir, may I have some more?"

Deli blinked, then threw his head back and laughed. "Yes, ma'am."

But before he could make good on his promise, Daphne cleared her throat and Henley forced herself between them, drooling around the ball as her tail beat against their legs.

"Sorry to interrupt, but the sheriff is here."

Chagrin surged through Caroline and she felt the heat in her cheeks. "Uh, yeah, okay. Let me put Henley back in her kennel and I'll be right in."

"Okay. I made some coffee if you want a cup." Daphne raised her eyebrows at Deli, an odd smile curling her lips. "I'll give one to Sheriff Tanner while he waits."

"Thanks." She took a step back from Deli, her heart

still pounding. "I, uh, better get Henley back in her kennel."

"Wait." He caught her hand. "I meant what I said and when there's more time, I'd like to pick up where we left off." He slid his thumb over the back of her hand. "And I'd like to talk more about coming back here when my tour of duty is done. Are you good with that?"

She nodded, suddenly sure of one thing. "Yes, I want to talk more for sure."

"What about the kissing?"

"Uh-huh, yup. More." She'd lost coherency when she thought about his lips on hers.

He laughed and let her go. "All right then. I'll go in and talk to the Sheriff while you put Henley away. Where's Trace?"

"She should be in her kennel, but knowing her, she's figured out the latch and is staging a coup." Caroline rolled her eyes and Deli laughed. "I'll check on her when I get Henley situated."

"Roger that."

She nodded and guided Henley back to the kennels. The other dogs barked and wagged their tails when she went by, and their happy greetings soothed some of her excitement. *Or is it anxiety?* Something was off when it came to her interaction with Chief Rubenovich. *Deli.* She wanted him, no question, but did they have what it took to go long term?

And he has to go back to being a SEAL. He belonged to a group of operatives who went into the worst parts of the world. Some never came back. *I can't think of that.* Right now, he was here with her and Daphne, doing his best to protect their home from cartel thugs. *And he wants to come back when his tour is up.* Why the hell would he want to do that?

Normally, she'd obsess on the question, worry it like a dog with rawhide, until it was nothing but tatters. But this time she didn't have the energy. She'd take it at face-value

SIOBHAN MUIR

and just go with it. *He wants to come back here and I want him to do that, too.* There were plenty of reasons why he shouldn't, but she'd already sacrificed to help others. For once, she wanted to have someone just for her. And Deli was that someone.

It seemed so alien to decide she wanted something more for herself. She'd always helped others, making sure they'd gotten what they needed. She'd often set aside her wants and desires as too expensive and wasteful. And she could follow that trend now. She could tell Deli not to worry about it and send him on his way.

But that's what I always do.

She had an opportunity to do something different. *Even if my timing sucks.* She had thugs trying to take her home and he'd be going back to the Navy. But what was that line the SEALs liked to say? *The only easy day was yesterday.* She nodded sharply and headed for the house. Time to get started on today.

She found Sheriff Tanner standing at parade rest with his arms crossed over his chest in her kitchen, listening to Daphne. Her niece described the many visits they had from the Casa de Catequil Cartel over the last few months and the sheriff scowled.

"Why didn't you come into the station and report it?"

"And tell you what, Sheriff?" Caroline poured some coffee into her favorite mug and tilted her head to fix him with her gaze. "Until yesterday, they hadn't done anything overtly violent. They'd always come to ask me to sell or offer me more money. It wasn't until I told them to get the hell off my land that they stepped up their game."

"How do you mean 'stepped up their game'?"

"They ran her off the road yeste'day. Shot up her truck with automatic weapons and gave her whiplash and those scratches on her face." Deli reported everything in an even voice like it was a usual day in the field.

Maybe it is for him.

134

"Didn't you get the message from Agatha? You were busy with the eight-car wreck on I-5 when I called." Caroline raised her eyebrows. "And this morning they came back and started shooting at the house. We called you immediately."

"You had people shooting at the house this morning?"

"Yup. I can show you the bullet holes and the bodies." Deli accepted a cup of coffee from Caroline.

Sheriff Tanner straightened. "Bodies?"

"Yes, sir. I did some recon and found the snipers. I tried to convince them to come quietly, but they declined."

"Did you kill 'em?" The sheriff scowled and Caroline's belly cramped.

"I tried not to. One's unconscious, but the other ended up shootin' himself while I tried to disarm him." Deli didn't try to play it off as amusing. "I can show you where the bodies are and the weapons they were using."

"They're still out there?"

Deli nodded. "I figured you'd want to know about them. Also, I've called Ultimate Recon, Inc, a protection service who've had a lot of experience with the Casa de Catequil Cartel. I believe they're coordinating with the FBI and ATF. They're going to help diffuse the threat to Caroline."

"They're comin' here? With the FBI? Why the hell didn't you tell me?"

Caroline sighed and held up her hands. "Gentlemen, take a breath. We're telling you now, Sheriff, and I'd much rather get the FBI and Ultimate Recon involved since they have dealt with these people before. I don't really want you or your deputies killed by the cartel."

"I suspect Ultimate Recon will contact you the moment they get into town, if not before. I understand they work with local law enforcement whenever they have to face something like this." Deli moved over to the bag beside the couch. "I collected the snipers' weapons.

Forensics should verify these were the weapons used to target the house."

The sheriff looked skeptical until Deli unzipped the bag. Caroline had never seen so many automatic weapons in one place at one time. *Holy shit, that's what they used to come after me?* Her knees gave out and she staggered to the kitchen counter.

"Caroline!" Daphne jumped to her side, pressing her body against the counter. "Are you all right?"

She shook her head. "They ran me off the road yesterday, and now they come to my home and spray it with bullets."

"Tell me about yesterday. We got a call about some abandoned vehicles on a Forest Service road off the highway. We checked and found your truck and an SUV with bullet holes in them. No people and no bullet casings."

"Damn, they policed their brass." Deli nodded with surprised admiration. "As we said earlier, two black SUVs with tinted windows chased her up the highway and forced her off the road. Then came after her with automatic weapons."

The sheriff took out a notebook. "You say that like you were there, Chief Rubenovich."

"I was. I pulled her out during the firefight. I needed to get her somewhere safe so she could call you." Deli shrugged.

"Why didn't you call during the incident?"

Caroline shook her head. "The phone was damaged in the crash and wouldn't work. I called as soon as we got home, but you were busy with the crash on the freeway." She raised her gaze to the sheriff. "Look, Sheriff, I hired Ultimate Recon to protect me and my home after that. I'll make sure they coordinate with you, but unless you can stop international terrorists with automatic weapons, I feel this is the best course of action."

Sheriff Tanner frowned. "I've known you a lot of

years, Caroline. I've never seen you this reactionary."

"This isn't reactionary, Nate." She met his gaze with her own. "This is well thought out and considered. Be honest with me. Could you really protect me and Cascade Breaks from men who use automatic weapons?"

Nate Tanner was a handsome man with straight teeth, chiseled jaw, deep dimples and smile lines, and silver in the chin portion of his blond goatee. He liked wearing a cowboy hat and he had a bit of a drawl when he spoke. His rich hazel eyes had enough crow's feet to make him look wise and experienced. Most of the ladies, both old and young, flirted and swooned around him. Despite that, the lawman remained unhitched, though he'd made a move on Caroline a few times. She'd turned him down each time. She could usually count on him to be level-headed and have all the angles thoroughly covered.

But he had an ego like every other man in an authoritative position, and he didn't like to admit he couldn't do something.

"You could always come into town."

She dropped her chin. "I'm not abandoning my home and my dogs. And you shouldn't be expected to try to take these guys down on your own. While I am part of the town, I live far enough out that it's not feasible for you to cover everything. You're going to need help and I've hired someone to take the burden of my protection off your shoulders."

"I never asked you to do that."

"No, you didn't. You needed to know what's happening around here and what you should prepare for, but when it comes to this, I need better protection." She shook her head, still sickened by the firepower Deli had confiscated off the snipers. "I'll make sure the guys from Ultimate Recon contact you if you're not still here when they arrive."

"Who talked you into this, Caroline? Was it him?"

Tanner threw a derisive thumb at Deli, but the SEAL didn't even bristle. "You've known him for, what, three seconds and he's suddenly an authority? He's been causing trouble since he got here."

"No, he has not." She raised her chin. "He protected me from five men bent on assault. Don't you snort at me. Women know when men are about to take liberties where there are none. Just because it's never happened to you doesn't mean it doesn't happen to us. And he saved me from getting gunned down in my truck on my drive home."

"You should've reported it while it was happening."

"I told you, my phone was dead, but I called as soon as I got home. And now Chief Rubenovich has saved me from some snipers."

"So he says." Tanner crossed his arms over his chest.

She marched past him to the door to the covered porch and yanked it open. "See for yourself."

He shot a scowl at Deli but dutifully followed her onto the porch. Bullet holes riddled the walls and the punching bag hanging from the ceiling. Nate said nothing, but his shoulders tightened and his gaze sharpened.

"Is this the only area they fired at?"

"No." Daphne stood at the door. "They fired into the house, too. Chief Rubenovich realized they must be using night vision goggles when they kept firing at us as we scrambled away from the porch." She shook her head. "He had us turn on all the lights and stay down so they'd have to use their regular vision to hit us."

"You got proof of these NVGs?" Tanner shot a look at Deli.

"In the bag, Sheriff."

He grimaced as he pulled out his phone and snapped pictures of the bullet holes. His gaze sharpened as he followed the lines of holes back toward the kitchen. Caroline scowled at all the damage. *Those mudfucking bastards tried to kill me and destroy my home.* Rage surged and she beat back the urge to scream. This was her home and her land. She wouldn't be driven off it just because some assholes wanted it.

She shook her head and returned to the kitchen, determined to do what needed to be done to protect her home, whether Sheriff Tanner liked it or not. *Okay, but first, tea.* That was something she could control. Even if no one else wanted some, she did, and she could make it happen.

By the time the pot of tea finished brewing, Tanner and Deli had returned to the house. Tanner had a notebook full of notes and a deeper scowl. Deli had retreated into affable blankness and she wondered what Tanner had said to him. The only other time she'd seen that expression on Deli's face was when he took on the five would-be assailants at the feed store. *That can't be good.*

"Let me take a look at the bag of tricks before we go collect the bodies." Nate moved over to the bag Deli had left on the floor and pulled out a pair of latex gloves before he unzipped it.

Deli's phone rang and he pulled it out of his pocket to glance at it. "Excuse me while I take this." He gave no other explanation as he stepped out the front door.

"Are you sure you trust him, Caroline?" Nate still pawed through the bag of weapons and gear without looking at her.

"Are you questioning my state of mind or my experience, Nate?"

"I beg your pardon?" He stood and looked at her with raised eyebrows.

"Damn straight you should." She crossed her arms over her chest. "If I was a man, living up here and doing what I do, with the evidence I've provided and the experiences I've had, would you ask me that same damn question?"

"He's a stranger, Caroline. Hell yeah, I'd ask you the

same question if you were a man."

"And if I was a man and said, yeah, I trust him because he's saved my ass several times since he's been here, would you take my word for it? Or would you keep checking to see if I'd made my mind up about him?" She shook her head. "He's US Navy, on R and R, and he's chosen to stand with me. I'd say that makes him at least an asset."

"According to him, he's killed a man on your property."

She dropped her chin. "You've looked through the gear and seen the bullet holes. They were trying to kill us. And no, he wasn't the one shooting at the house. He was here when the shots were fired. None of that gear is his."

"How do you know that? This could have been stashed up in the hills for him to bring down to you. He could've had partners that he took out to make it look like he's legit." Nate shot a look at the front porch before returning his gaze to hers. "He could've set this all up." He shook his head. "Do you even know anything about this company he says is coming in, this Ultimate Recon? This could be an elaborate scam to get your land."

"If you're done constructing conspiracy theories, Sheriff, I'll take you up to the spot where the snipers' bodies are." Deli's dry voice cracked through the room. Caroline shot a look at him, her chagrin heating her face.

"Yeah, let's do that." Tanner nodded and headed for the door.

Deli let his gaze linger on her face, but she couldn't read his expression. *Oh, glory, what he must think of me.* But she could understand the sheriff's perspective. He was just now hearing about the attempts to take her land and Chief Rubenovich had appeared out of nowhere when Trace kept the bear at bay.

Could Deli have set this all up as an elaborate ruse? Maybe, but he'd been nothing but helpful and protective.

He'd taken out the five guys at the feed store and she'd brought him home, but he'd also followed her when the guys in the SUVs attacked her truck. *And Trace trusts him.* The blue heeler had a good sense of people and she'd responded to Deli's commands the moment she saw him.

"Daphne, Chief Rubenovich was here when the shots started, right? They woke me up and he was still here, right?"

Daphne shot her a look of disgust. "Yes, he was. He was the one who told me to turn all the lights on so they couldn't use the night vision goggles and he pulled you to the floor. Don't tell me you're believing what Sheriff Tanner is suggesting."

"No, but I want to make sure I didn't dream this."

"Caroline, look at me."

She blinked, surprise flooding through her at Daphne's frank and firm tone.

"I know Chief Rubenovich, even if he can't admit he knows me." She strode into the kitchen and poured herself some coffee. "He's a damn hero and he's not here to take your home or hurt you. I can tell you he puts himself in harm's way because that's the kind man he is. I'm sure he's used to having a team of other guys with him, but he still took out those snipers to make sure you, me, Beryl, and the other dogs were safe. Sheriff Tanner doesn't know shit and he hasn't been here. Rubenovich has been here with us the whole time. Who are you gonna believe?"

When she put it that way, the sheriff's suspicions looked pretty stupid. "Do you think Rubenovich could've set this up beforehand?"

"No." Daphne's flat tone brooked no argument.

Caroline nodded. Yeah, she didn't believe that either. "I just hope the guys he called are legit."

"They are."

Caroline raised her eyebrows. "How do you know that?"

Daphne shrugged and brought her laptop over to the kitchen. "I looked them up. They're a real company who provides real protection. Here's their website." She opened the internet browser on her laptop. "They're made up of members from four of the five military branches. They do everything from protection to forensic accounting and undercover work. They're even highly rated by the Better Business Bureau. Chief Rubenovich wasn't making them up."

Caroline perused the site. The more she read, the more grateful she became that Deli knew these guys. She'd faced more then her fair share of challenges in her life, but the Casa de Catequil Cartel was more than she could do on her own. Deli said he'd called in the cavalry.

I guess we'll find out if it's true soon enough.

CHAPTER TWELVE

The sheriff has a thing for Caroline.

Deli kept his blank expression in place the whole time the sheriff went over all the evidence and examined the bodies. The older man seemed to be looking for proof of Deli's complicity in the efforts of the cartel, but at least he was thorough in his preliminary investigation. He called for the local ME to come get the body and had his deputies collect the unconscious man. The forensics crew arrived to bag and tag everything.

On their way up, the deputies called in with more info on the abandoned SUV full of bullet holes. When he heard, the sheriff shot a look at Deli.

"Your handiwork?"

Deli shook his head. "Just the flat tires. I didn't have an automatic weapon on me at the time."

Tanner nodded but his expression tightened in annoyance. Deli hid a smile. *You're not gonna pin this one on me.* And he wasn't going to get Deli out of Caroline's life. Deli suspected the sheriff was used to having the attention of all the women in his jurisdiction swoon over him. He was a tall, charismatic, handsome man in a position of authority. He didn't seem to like it much that

Caroline wasn't "yessiring" him after everything he said.

Tanner hung up his phone. "All right. Sounds like you've been dealing with these guys for a couple of days. Anything else you want to tell me about them?"

Deli shook his head. "I don't know half as much about them as Cyrus Finch, lead investigator from Ultimate Recon, Inc. They should be here in…" He glanced at his phone. "About forty-five minutes. He'll be able to brief you in full."

"So, what are you really doing here at the Last Chance Dog Sanctuary, Chief?"

"I'm on R and R leave from the Navy. I came up to Cascade Breaks to go hiking and ran into Caroline while she was out walking one of her dogs in the National Forest."

"And how did you get to her place?"

Deli shrugged as they returned to the yard from the sniper's nest on the hill. "I dissuaded some men from assaulting her at the Cascade Breaks Feed Store & Bar and sustained a concussion. I'm sure your deputies told you. Caroline took me to her place to recover. In the morning, she returned me to my Jeep at the feed store's parking lot."

"But you're back."

"Yes, sir, I am."

Tanner scowled. "How did you come to be back here again?"

"I noticed the two big black SUVs with tinted windows following her out of the parking lot."

Tanner snorted. "This is California. Everyone here has a big SUV with tinted windows."

Deli nodded. "That's why I planned to do my hiking for the day up the same road. If they were just hikers, she'd get home safely and I'd be on my way. But instead, they forced her off the road and started shooting at her."

"Why didn't you report it then?"

Deli shrugged. "She was injured and needed to get to

safety. My concern was for her welfare. Besides, you were tied up with the wreck on I-5. We're reported it as soon we got back to the house. This morning, the snipers tried to take out her home. No one deliberately tried to keep you in the dark, Sheriff. Caroline initially thought she could dissuade them on her own. She didn't even want my help."

"And she just took your help without protest?" The sheriff raised an eyebrow.

"Oh, hell no. The only reason she accepted was because she was injured. I reminded her to call you." He held up a hand to stop the sheriff's response. "Look, you might not know what happened to her niece Daphne, but I have it on good authority the Casa de Catequil Cartel is the same one who kidnapped her about two years ago. They're known for their drug and gun running, and sex and human trafficking. Now they want Caroline's place. Strategically, it would make for a good, out-of-the way safehouse along their route up north. The guys from Ultimate Recon know this cartel real well and have been working with the FBI to dismantle their supply lines through the western US."

"And how do you know all this, Chief?"

I was there rescuing Daphne, Jaime Hensen, and the others out of their cages.

"I talked to the guys at Ultimate Recon, how else?"

The sheriff looked like he wanted to talk more, but the ME's van arrived along with police SUVs. *The Sheriff's right. They do have tinted windows.* Deli stuffed his grin down deep and ducked back into the house. Daphne continued her stew preparation and an almost-full pot of coffee sat on the counter.

"Ohh, can I have some of that?"

Daphne laughed and nodded. "Yeah, help yourself. I'd say you deserve it given all the things you've done this morning before the sun was even up." She pulled a cup out of the cupboard. "What did the sheriff say?"

Deli shrugged as he poured the coffee. "Want some of

this?"

"No, I have some already, thanks." She nodded to her mug.

Deli nodded and put the carafe back. "He's naturally suspicious of me and my motives. Considering I took down two men with deadly force, I'd say he has legitimate concerns."

"And it doesn't help that he's sweet on Caroline, either."

Deli raised his eyebrows. "How do you know that?"

She shrugged one shoulder as she added onions to the stew. "I don't for sure, but he's the most eligible bachelor in this town and he kinda expects all the women to fawn over him. Caroline is one of the few who doesn't and he seemed okay with that until he saw you with her. I'd say it's kinda a case of he didn't want her until there was competition."

Deli rolled his eyes as he added cream to his coffee. "He does understand that it comes down to female choice, doesn't he? Caroline's completely capable of making her own decision on who she wants around her."

"You're just saying that because she chose you." Daphne smirked as she slid some red peppers into the stew.

Deli laughed. "No, but I'm pretty pleased it turned out to be in my favor." He checked his phone as it chimed with an incoming text. "Where is she, anyway?"

"She's taking a shower."

He thanked his lucky stars he'd turned away to look at his phone before his cock gave him away. The idea of Caroline in the shower with the water sluicing over her curves definitely gave him a better jumpstart than the coffee. *Focus, jackass, before you give Daphne a view of your boner.* He checked the phone.

Just hit the scene at the dirt road. GPS puts us five mikes out.

The text from Finch made him smile. **Roger that.**

Cops and ME have come to retrieve the bodies. See you in five.

Copy that.

Deli breathed a sigh of relief. It might not be the men of Bravo Squad, SEAL Team 9, but it felt good to have real backup.

He didn't bother to reply to the last text as he watched the front yard. Soon two silver SUVs—*Again with the tinted windows*—pulled up beside the ME's van. The man who slid out of the driver's seat of the first SUV stood damn near a foot taller than Deli with silver hair at his temples. He walked with loose, easy moves, giving the appearance of being relaxed. But Deli knew better.

"Senior Chief, good to see you again." He held out his hand to shake and noticed a wedding band on the other man's fourth finger. "Did you get hitched when I wasn't looking?"

Finch grinned. "Yeah. I went on vacation and met a Marine. She had me hogtied faster than I could say, yes, ma'am."

Deli laughed. "You look good, I gotta say that. Seems like retirement suits you."

Finch nodded as two other men and a woman joined him. "This is my crew from Ultimate Recon. Brian Tanaka, Marine sniper retired. Elias Reece, Army Ranger retired. And Alissa McAvoy, Air Force, retired."

"Thanks for coming. The sheriff of Cascade Breaks is up helping with the removal of the two snipers I took out this morning." Deli shrugged at the surprised looks in the crew. "I incapacitated one and the other was self-defense when he chose not to come quietly."

Finch snorted, but nodded. "Roger that. Okay, we'll run point with the local LEOs and introduce them to our FBI liaison, who should be arriving any minute."

Reece made a sound resembling a derisive laugh. "If he can find the roads. I don't think the guy's ever been outside a city."

"Dude, give him a break. He had to find this place on your directions, Reece." McAvoy shook her head. "I couldn't have found it with those instructions."

"That's because you're dependent on Google Maps, McAvoy." Reece rolled his eyes. "Some of us know how to read real maps and a compass."

"That's enough showing off, you two." Finch clapped his hands. "Reece, go move the vehicles behind the barn. Is it okay if we set up in there?" His gaze rested on Deli.

"I think so, but I'll have to check with the owner of the sanctuary, Caroline Atherton." He gestured toward the house. "Do you want to meet with her first or the Sheriff?"

"Let's meet Ms. Atherton first so we can get set up. By then, maybe our FBI contact will be here." Finch followed Deli to the porch. "Anything I need to know going in?"

"Not about her." Deli didn't bother to hide his amusement.

Finch stopped, his eyebrows raised. "Someone else?"

Deli sighed. "The sheriff has a thing for Caroline and doesn't like it that she's called in reinforcements from outside."

"Aw hell, are we looking at a Wyatt Earp kind of guy?" Finch grimaced.

"Not quite. Seems level-headed, but still thinks if she'd reported this to him the moment it started he would've been able to stop it." Deli pushed open the door. "And he didn't like it that I've protected her instead."

"Rubenovich, are you honing in on the man's woman?" Finch smirked.

"No, sir, he's honing in on mine."

****

Caroline heard the last little bit of conversation as Deli stepped inside with a tall, handsome man with a cowboy drawl. *No, sir, he's honing in on mine.* His woman. She knew she should protest she was anyone's anything, but the way Deli said it made her heart swell and her nipples grow tight. She'd never been into alpha men who thought of women as their possessions, and military men in particular. But Deli's words warmed her all over and gave her the oddest sense of home.

"Hey, Caroline, I'd like you to meet Cyrus Finch, owner and CEO of Ultimate Recon, Inc." Deli stood back so Finch could offer his hand.

"Nice to meet you, ma'am. I understand you have a problem with some out-of-towners not takin' no for an answer." Finch had an easy way about him with a mellow voice that had a bit of the "aw-shucks" cowpoke style. But his hazel eyes took in details most people probably wouldn't have noticed and she felt rather exposed.

"Thank you for taking the case, Mr. Finch." She shook his hand and tried not to shiver. "I can really use the help. If it hadn't been for Chief Rubenovich here, I'd be dead already."

"Well, now, that sounds like a good story, and when we clear up this mess, I'd like to hear it." His lips curled into a smile. "But in the meantime, I have a crew to get settled and wanted to get your permission to set up in the barn. Would that be all right?"

"Oh, of course. Yes. The barn has some old stalls that have been modified as sleeping spaces if you need them. And there should be room to park your vehicles inside." She knew she was babbling, but she couldn't stop her nervousness. Finch had an intensity that set her teeth on edge. "My niece Daphne's making a stew so there should be plenty to share for supper when it comes around."

"That sounds fine, ma'am. I'm gonna go talk to the sheriff and get the scuttlebutt on what all he needs from us to help stop these guys. I'll get my crew to set up and have them come by to introduce themselves. That all right with you?"

"Uh, yes, of course. How many in your crew, Mr. Finch?" She mentally tried to figure out if she had enough towels and beds for his people.

"There are four of us, three men and a woman, and an FBI agent should be stoppin' by anytime now. He works with us on the task force assigned to the Casa de Catequil Cartel." Finch gave her a disarming smile. "I'll just get the sheriff squared away with our involvement. If you see a guy in a dark suit and tie, have him come look for me and the sheriff."

"Right, okay. Thanks." She had no idea what she was thanking him for, but she couldn't think straight with him in the room.

He nodded and ducked back out the door, and Caroline let her breath out in a long sigh.

"Good glory, he's intense."

Deli laughed. "Aw, he isn't too bad. Just wait until you meet his sniper."

"He brought a sniper?" Caroline swallowed hard. "This is going to be a bloodbath, isn't it?"

Deli shook his head and took her hands. "Not if they can help it. Their goal is to catch and incapacitate, but they'll kill if they have to stop them permanently. From what Finch said on the phone, the FBI wants to know supply lines and regional managers. They wanna catch the whole damn chain."

"Have you met the FBI agent yet?"

"No, but he should be here soon."

Daphne stepped inside the house with Beryl, her face flushed and her eyes bright. "Caroline, there's a man here claiming to be from the FBI. I, uh, I said he should talk to you."

Another man stepped from behind Daphne and gave a professional smile. "Special Agent Rick Sandoval, FBI. Can I ask you a few questions?"

Caroline took his hand to shake, pleased when he didn't try to crush the daylights out of her fingers. She studied his dark eyes and black hair cut in a classic style while Daphne hovered in the background, her attention on Sandoval.

"Welcome, Agent Sandoval. What can I do for the FBI?"

"Actually, ma'am, I think it's what the FBI can do for you. I understand you've had some run-ins with the Casa de Catequil Cartel?"

Caroline nodded. "Yes, they've been harassing me for a few weeks now."

"Why didn't you report it before?" He brought out a small tablet and started taking notes.

"I didn't know who they were at first. The man came well-dressed and well-spoken and acted like a realtor with interests in some sort of resort idea." She shrugged. "They didn't get nasty until my no remained firm."

"How did it start?"

"To be honest, I think it started when my niece Daphne was kidnapped and abducted about two years ago. I won't go into the whole story because I don't know it all, but that's how we knew about them." Caroline shot a look at Daphne, but she had her gaze locked on Sandoval. "I don't know if they're targeting us because of that or we just got lucky, but about three months ago this guy in a white suit and fancy black SUV started coming by asking if I'd be interested in selling my home to him."

"Do you remember his name?" Sandoval kept writing.

"Carlos Antigua."

Sandoval raised an eyebrow. "Seriously?"

She shrugged as she strode over to a basket she kept beside the wall phone. "Here's his card. He said he was a real estate agent for a big company in L.A. that was looking to set up a resort here. He gave me the usual spiel about jobs and money blah blah blah, and said I'd be paid handsomely for my land."

"Did he actually use the word 'handsomely'?" Deli raised his eyebrows.

"Yup. I thanked him, but politely declined. He said he'd give me time to think about it."

Sandoval took the card and scowled at the picture on it. "This guy was the one who approached you?"

Caroline nodded.

"His real name is Carlos Santo Domingo, and he's one of the lead bosses in the California branch of the Casa de Catequil Cartel." He held up the card. "Can I take this as evidence?"

"Sure. I've turned down his "offer" enough times now. I don't need it."

"Okay. What happened next?"

"He came back the next week and doubled the offer, but I turned him down again, saying no, I was just fine where I was and I wasn't going to leave." She rubbed her arms as her gut tightened. "Then just a couple days ago he came back and I'd had enough. I greeted him with a rifle and told him to get off my land, I wasn't selling."

"Did you shoot him?" Sandoval's eyes widened.

"No. I shot a stump and told him if he came back, I'd tag his truck with a little redneck decoration. He hasn't been back since." She shook her head. "But yesterday, two big black SUVs ran me off the road and guys with automatic weapons shot at me. Gave me whiplash and destroyed my truck. If Chief Rubenovich hadn't been following me back to my place, I'd be dead."

"That true, Chief?" Sandoval slid his gaze over to Deli.

"Yes, sir. Every word. I noticed them peeling off to follow her when she brought me down to get my Jeep at the feed store and something didn't sit right." He shrugged. "So, I followed them and helped her escape when they tried to shut her down."

"Did you know who they were?"

"I had an idea they were from the cartel, but I needed better intel, so I called the guys at Ultimate Recon, Inc. to confirm. I've worked with Finch before and I know he knows his shit."

Sandoval grimaced at the use of the expletive, but he nodded. "Did anything else happen before Ultimate Recon arrived this morning?"

"Yeah. Two snipers decided it would be a good way to make us not wake up by using their automatic weapons, old AK-47s, to shoot at Daphne and me this morning on the covered porch." He moved to the bag full of the snipers' gear still resting beside the couch. "They had NVGs and scopes. I had Daphne turn on all the lights to render them useless and stay out of sight while I went to neutralize them."

"Are they alive?" Sandoval raised an eyebrow.

"One is. The ME should be bringing the other down off the hill here soon."

"You killed him?" Sandoval scowled.

"No, sir, I defended myself after incapacitating the first one. The guy chose not to make it easy. In the end, he lost."

"Aren't you on leave, Chief?" Sandoval's expression slipped into the patented FBI stoicism.

"Yes, sir." Deli matched the agent's stoicism with his own. "But I swore an oath to protect this country from enemies both foreign and domestic, and these are foreign enemies threatening me and people I care about. Just because I'm not on duty at the moment doesn't change the nature of my oath. But since I am on leave, I had Ms. Atherton call in Ultimate Recon."

"And you took this gear off the dead men?"

"I took it off the foreign snipers, only one of which is dead. The covered porch is riddled with bullet holes if you'd like to check my story." Deli's voice remained calm, but anger sparked in his gaze.

Before anyone could say anything more, the front door

opened and a woman dressed in a suit and silk shirt poked her head in. "Hey Sandoval, you gotta come out here and take a look at this."

"What is it, Murphy?" Sandoval didn't take his eyes off Deli.

"Found the cartel's guys' truck. They were loaded for bear." Agent Murphy nodded to Caroline. "Were you aware that they'd parked on your property, ma'am?"

Caroline shook her head. "No."

"They didn't. The were parked on the access road about a quarter of a mile up." Deli nodded. "I moved the truck behind the barn in case any more Tangos came looking. I didn't open any compartments or check their gear beyond what I took off them."

Sandoval blinked. "You took their truck but didn't check it?"

"Nope. I left it for the FBI to search." Deli cracked a grin and Sandoval grunted with what sounded like annoyance. "Besides, once you guys do your work on it, I figure the Casa de Catequil Cartel owes Caroline a truck and that's an awfully nice one the dead guy won't be needing."

"That's not how this works, Chief."

"Sure, it is. You'd take the truck, go over it with a fine-toothed comb, and then auction that sucker off. Caroline needs a new truck. These assholes provided one and you guys don't need to have one more vehicle on your books. Why not benefit the victim of these attacks? It won't take any more paperwork than you're already saddling yourself with."

Sandoval growled, but Murphy knocked on the door. "Just come and take a look, Sandoval. I think this might be the break we're looking for."

Sandoval narrowed his eyes, but nodded. "Be right there." He tucked his tablet back into his inside jacket pocket. "Thanks for your information, Ms. Atherton. Is there any way we could convince you to come into protective custody?"

"No. This is my home and I'm needed here to take care of my dogs."

Sandoval nodded. "Yeah, I figured you were going to say that. Thank you again." He shot a look at Deli. "I'll get back to you on the truck." He turned and strode out the door.

Deli whipped out his phone.

"What are you doing?"

"Texting Finch. I suspect he can acquire that truck through more official means and I'm just putting in a requisition request for you."

Caroline crossed her arms over her chest. "You're assuming I want that truck."

He raised his head and his eyebrows. "It's a nice truck and you need a new one. The cartel owes you."

She shook her head. "And somewhere in their records they have the VIN number of that vehicle. I'd rather the FBI or whoever just gives me the money that comes from the sale of the truck so I can buy my own."

"I think that can be arranged."

I don't think I want to know how. She grimaced and headed for the kettle only to realize she'd already poured herself a cup of tea. *Shit-oh-dear, I'm losing my mind here.* And if she wasn't careful, she'd lose a lot more than that.

CHAPTER THIRTEEN

It took the better part of the day for the police, FBI, and Ultimate Recon to investigate and clear the scene. *Scene, as if this is some sort of TV drama.* By the time the forensic techs had "bagged and tagged" everything, it was dinner time and Caroline just wanted to eat a quiet supper with her Kindle.

Murphy and Sandoval, the two FBI agents, had settled down once they coordinated with the Ultimate Recon guys, and left to make their own reports. They promised to return the next day and said they'd be keeping an eye on things in town. Sheriff Tanner hadn't liked sharing jurisdiction with any of the newcomers, but he grudgingly agreed he was outmanned and outgunned. Now that Ultimate Recon and the FBI were on the case, he said his priority was the town of Cascade Breaks and he'd use his manpower there.

But he'd pulled Caroline aside and bent close to her ear when the others were occupied with Daphne's animated story about the time she'd hiked half the Pacific Coast Trail.

"I know you're surrounded by these yahoos who think they know everything about what's goin' on, but if you need me, don't hesitate to call, okay?" Nate handed her his card. "I'll be here in a heartbeat." He'd gazed at her with such earnest tenderness she had to fight the urge to laugh.

"Thanks, Sheriff."

"It's Nate, and you're welcome." His smile warmed as he squeezed her hand. "You take care, now."

He'd resumed his stoic sheriff face and waved to the others, taking his leave. She'd rubbed the back of her neck and wondered why another man's interest always set off a competition in men who'd never really noticed a woman before. She shook her head, thinking of something her mother's oldest sister once said. *Some men just don't want a woman unless another man does, darlin'. It don't make no sense, but it's like they need the competition to see her value.*

"That's stupid."

Her aunt had agreed and told her to steer clear of men like that.

"Roger that, Aunt Elsie."

"Sorry?" Deli appeared at her shoulder, his eyebrows up.

"Nothing. Are you ready for dinner? I'm starving."

"Good luck. Between Finch and his crew, we'll be lucky to lick the bowls." Deli grinned. "What did the sheriff say before he left?"

She narrowed her eyes. "Do I detect a thread of jealousy in your tone, Chief?"

"No, ma'am, just wanted to make sure he didn't come on to you while in his official capacity as a law officer." He kept his expression carefully blank, but she read more in the blankness than he hid.

She nodded, biting back a smile. "Sheriff Tanner has asked me out a time or two in the past, but I turned him down. He gets plenty of female attention in town. I'm not sure why he has to play white knight now, but I'm not up for the role of his damsel. Besides, while a cowboy is a nice hero to have around, I'd rather have a Navy SEAL. They're often far more creative."

"Hooyah, ma'am." Deli grinned and some of the tension flowed out of his shoulders. But he tilted his head and lost his smile. "How are you holding up?"

"My chest hurts from the seatbelt, but my neck and shoulders are like rocks and hurt more." She tilted her head from side to side, hoping to stretch the muscles out.

"Tell you what. Let's make sure you're fed and the dogs have been seen to, and I'll work on those shoulders."

She sighed. "That sounds like a plan. What were you saying about licking the bowls?"

It turned out that while the Ultimate Recon crew hadn't eaten all the stew, there wasn't much left, so Deli volunteered to make fajitas with some of the steaks she had in the freezer. It was fun to watch him putter around the kitchen preparing the food. She sat with a cup of tea in front of her, watching as he worked and carried on conversations with Finch and Alissa McAvoy.

The retired airman had snark and humor Caroline appreciated, and she didn't let the men get away with anything. The two men on Finch's crew were doing actual recon while Alissa set up her networks and prepared her drones.

"Wow, you're really taking this surveillance seriously." Daphne stood behind Alissa and watched her fingers fly over the keyboard.

"I know I am." Caroline nodded, grateful for the professional company. "These guys won't take no for an answer and they're apparently willing to kill for our place. I want them permanently deterred from coming back."

"Are you going to kill them?" Daphne's question came out in a calm, mildly curious tone.

"Only if we have to, Ms. Phelps." Finch scraped his bowl with a spoon. "Our goal is to dismantle their supply lines and close off their routes through the US. But some of these people would rather die than get caught so we don't

158

always get our wish." He licked the spoon. "Damn fine stew you made. My wife will be glad to know I'm eating well."

Daphne smiled, but it looked strained. *Seems like his intensity is getting to her, too.* Caroline bit her lips together to hide her smile.

"How did you meet her, Finch?" Deli set the meat on the grill with a delicious hiss. "You never mentioned that."

"Heh. I was on vacation, actually." He shot Deli a wink and the SEAL had the grace to blush. "I was supposed to be relaxin' in northern Arizona, but I fell asleep on her shoulder on the train ride. She agreed to have dinner with me and we got to talkin' about what she was doin' now that she'd retired from the Marines."

Caroline choked on her tea. "She was a Marine?"

"Yes, ma'am. Master Sergeant, retired. And you know us Navy guys. We always need help from the Marines." He grinned as Deli snorted. "Or that's what the Marines will tell you after we've saved their asses a few times, makin' 'em look good."

"Hooyah, Senior Chief." Deli bumped knuckles with Finch before he turned the meat.

Caroline laughed. "You were in the Navy, too, Finch?"

"Yup. I actually got to meet Chief Rubenovich here a little over two years ago. We had a joint training session together." Finch's affable smile held all his secrets. "But I actually had first-hand experience with the Casa de Catequil Cartel when they threatened to move in on my wife's mother. They tried the same tactics there as they are here, which is why I recognized their MO. They first offered to over pay her for her place, then threatened to kill her, and even set a bomb in her oven. They were tryin' to run guns along I-40 when we did our best to stop them. Got ATF and the FBI involved."

"And that's how you met your wife?" Caroline shook her head. "That's some meet-cute you had there."

"Beg your pardon, ma'am?" Finch shot her a blank look.

"Meet-cute. It's a term in filmmaking that refers to when the hero and heroine meet for the first time." She tilted her head with a smile. "I saw it in a documentary about screenwriters."

"Oh, heh, yeah, well, I did fall asleep on her shoulder and woke up to her lookin' down on me, so yeah, it might've been kinda cute." Finch grinned. "I bet there's a pretty good story on how Chief Rubenovich had the good graces to meet you, Ms. Atherton."

"You're defending my home, Mr. Finch. You can call me Caroline."

"Fair enough. Since we're gonna be informal, you can call me Cyrus. So, how did you and Rubenovich meet?"

"Food's done." Deli announced it like it would save him from the retelling of their meet-cute.

"You mean when he tried to steal my dog?"

"What?" Cyrus shot Deli a wide-eyed stare. "Seriously? You tried to take her dog?"

"No." Deli rolled his eyes as he served the meat in a bowl and set it beside the tortillas. "I just wanted to know where she'd gotten an MWD. I knew Sergeant Trace from before I joined the SEALs."

"Oh, so you stole *his* dog." Cyrus shot her a smug grin.

"I think that sounds about right." Deli nodded.

"No, he's just trying to get out of responsibility for trying to take her away from me." Caroline crossed her arms over her chest. "Trace is retired from the Navy, and has some issues with PTSD. She was brought to me for rehabilitation and recovery, but she's proven to be an excellent member of our pack and we've decided to keep her." She shot a look at Deli. "*Not* his dog."

Cyrus laughed but Deli only served up the food so they could eat. Despite being able to serve herself, Deli made sure she had meat and tortillas as well as cheese on her plate before he grabbed his own.

"How long you been doin' this, Caroline?" Cyrus waved at the house as if to take in the barn and the kennels.

She frowned as she chowed down. "It'll be fifteen years in August."

"Wow. Have you rehabilitated lots of dogs?"

"Oh yes, she's done amazing work." Daphne nodded as she settled beside Caroline. "She's even trained a few service dogs, some of which went to some notable clients."

"Who are confidential." Caroline shook her head. "But the Military War Dogs have been the greatest joy to work with. Most of them still want to serve, they just can't be in war anymore. They make excellent guard dogs with the right handler."

"Do you just give your dogs to anyone?" Alissa raised her eyebrows.

"No. Not only do I need to see how the dog interacts with the person who wants her, I need to see credentials that they're able to care for and protect the dogs. Some people have tried getting a service dog and I've turned them away."

"Really?" Deli wore surprise on his face.

"Yup. You should've seen the rich guy who lived near Mt. Shasta." Daphne rolled her eyes. "He wanted a guard/companion dog to help him maintain his reputation as a badass."

"He wanted a guard dog for his estate, Daphne."

"He could've gotten a dog at the local shelter for that." Daphne shook her head. "Anyway, he came here in his Maserati, complaining about the ruts in our gravel road. When we took him to meet the dogs in their kennels, most of them bared their teeth at him, and the rest just stayed back. We turned him away and he threw a shit-fit."

"What did he do?" Alissa leaned forward with interest.

"First, he tried to blacklist us as being frauds. Then he ran an active campaign to get our permits revoked."

Caroline scowled as she shook her head. "Too bad he brought too much attention to himself. He was arrested two months later for child pornography and sex trafficking."

"Holy shit. No wonder the dogs wanted nothing to do with him." Cyrus nodded, his expression full of admiration.

"Yeah, they know who they're willing to be with and who should be put in their own cage." Caroline wiped her mouth and shot Deli a smile. "That was a great meal, Chief. But you're still not taking Trace with you."

"Well then, I'll just have to come back here so I can be with my dog."

Time stopped and the silence stretched. Deli met her gaze and his amused smile never slipped. *Holy shit, he's serious.* He'd said he wanted to come back and work with her and the dogs, but she hadn't expected him to really mean it. It seemed like something men said when they wanted a little nookie. Oh, she believed he felt that way at the moment he said it, but she didn't think he'd admit it in front of everyone here.

"You thinkin' of retirin' from the Navy, Chief?" Cyrus sipped his glass of water as he raised an eyebrow.

Deli shrugged as he shook his head. "I don't have twenty yet, but I am thinking of separating early, if I have something to look forward to. I can't keep doing this forever, and I'd like to get out before my body quits on me."

No one mentioned the possibility that he'd be killed on any given mission.

"This isn't the first time I've been thinking about it, but I've been trying to figure out what I'd do after." His gaze rested on Caroline's, the stoic mask in place.

He's giving me a chance to tell him to jump off a cliff.

"Well, if Caroline doesn't snap you up, I'll have a job opening for you." Cyrus shrugged, his amiable smile in place. "Our workload has been gettin' heavier going after the Casa de Catequil Cartel with the FBI and ATF. Plus our usual work load of investigations and providin' security for folks. We could always use a good SEAL."

Deli raised his eyebrows at her a moment before he turned his head and nodded. "I'll definitely give it some thought, Cyrus. It's hard to switch gears after my current service."

"Roger that." Cyrus nodded and wiped his mouth. "But Caroline's right. Damn good meal and I'm gonna get my surveillance on. Thanks again for feedin' us, ma'am." He nodded to Daphne, who blushed.

"Will you need any linens or blankets tonight, Cyrus?" Caroline began clearing the plates.

"No, ma'am. I think we're set. Thank you." He and Alissa prepared to head out to the barn. "But if you don't mind, I'd like to borrow the Chief here for just a bit."

"Sure. Daphne and I need to feed the dogs, anyway."

Cyrus nodded and headed for the door with Alissa. The airman's gaze skipped between Caroline and Deli before she followed Cyrus with a little smile. *Yeesh, I know what the scuttlebutt in the barn will be about tonight.* She shook her head and loaded the dishes into the dishwasher as Deli grasped her arm and squeezed gently before releasing her.

"Be back in a bit to finish our discussion, yeah?"

"What discussion?" She blinked a few times, trying to sift through all the conversations she'd had with him since the threat to her home showed up.

"The one we had over Henley." He winked and disappeared out the front door.

"Sounds like you've hooked a Navy SEAL, Aunt Caroline. Well done." Daphne grinned.

Yeah, but what would she do with him?

****

Deli stepped into the barn and found it completely transformed into a technological headquarters. The concrete floor had been swept clean and the old crates and equipment had been set up as tables and shelves. They'd hung canvas tarps over the windows so nothing could be seen from outside and used a few more as "table cloths" to keep the equipment from collecting dust. The four stalls in the back had been cleaned out and used as "bedrooms" for the Ultimate Recon crew.

Not that anyone's going to get much sleep while this is going on.

"Looks good. Like a real field HQ." Deli nodded to Cyrus and his sniper, Brian Tanaka, as they discussed field positions over a topo map.

"We do what we can." Cyrus pointed at the rise above the house where the other snipers had nested. "You can use their spots, which were here and here, but there may be a better vantage point from here." He pointed at the granite outcrop that curled around the house to the southwest. "It's harder to hike to, but that might be to our advantage."

Tanaka nodded. "I can see that. From the satellite photos, it looks like it has pretty good cover, too. But I won't be able to get down very fast."

Cyrus waved his hand. "Don't worry about that. It's better if you have the higher ground in a place where no one can cherry-pick you off."

"Roger that. Want me to get set up there now?"

"Nah. Hit the rack and get some sleep. I figure we have a few days until the cartel realizes their men ain't comin' back. They'll want to wait for the hubbub to die down, hoping we think the threat is done." Cyrus stood up and shot Deli a grin. "Seems like our Weekend Warrior here gave us a couple days to prepare."

Deli snorted. "There's no 'weekend' about it. But you're welcome."

Tanaka's lips curled in a smile before he focused back on Cyrus. "I'll be up early to recon a good perch."

"Good. Reece is out there right now and he'll have

some additional intel for you."

"Roger that. Night, boss."

Tanaka disappeared into the aisle between the stalls and Cyrus turned to Deli. "Want some coffee? One thing Reece requires even of his field HQ is a damn good cuppa joe."

Deli grinned. "You know, I can't fault him for that. Most of the places we got sent, good coffee is the first casualty."

"Copy that." Cyrus's fervent answer made Deli laugh. "He gets this stuff from Alaska or some shit. But damn if the man doesn't have good taste." Cyrus handed him a cup.

"Thanks. So what do you need, Senior Chief?"

"You know you can call me by my name, right?"

Deli shrugged. "Still active Navy and it's habit."

"Yeah, well, you ain't gonna be active Navy forever and it's your future I thought I'd talk to you about."

"What did you have in mind?" Deli rested his hip against the bumper of the Ultimate Recon's SUV as he sipped his coffee.

"As I mentioned, the workload for Ultimate Recon is gettin' bigger and bigger, and we almost don't have enough personnel to cover everything. While I have a damn good woman in the home office fielding calls and directin' traffic, I'm the CEO and I should be there to do the hirin', firin', and directin'. And my wife would prefer I didn't travel quite so much." Cyrus smirked. "Or rather do any travelin' with her."

Deli chuckled. "Yeah, I can see how she might feel that way."

"Yeah, so I'm always on the lookout for good people to fill in the ranks as we expand." Cyrus nodded his head toward Deli. "If you're lookin' for somethin' to do after the Navy kicks your sorry ass out, I'm pretty sure we can find a place for you."

Deli nodded, but took a few breaths before he said

anything. "I appreciate the offer, Se–Cyrus, but I think I need to come back here to be with Caroline. I used to work with the K9 units before I joined the SEALs and after working with Trace again, I realized I've missed it. The idea of rehabilitating MWDs so they can be used again really appeals to me."

"Hmm, yeah, I wouldn't want to get between a man and his dog." Cyrus winked.

"Shut up." Deli laughed as he shook his head. "Thanks for the opportunity, but I wanna come back here, I think."

"All right, I can read the terrain as good as any other SEAL, but think on this a bit." Cyrus rubbed his chin before he rose. "I could always use a guy who knows how to handle dogs. Right now, we don't have any K9 units at all. Eventually, we're gonna need at least one. And a dog. What if you come here after you retire, get your certification as a dog handler and trainer up to date, and work for me when I need a K9 unit? That'd be the best of both worlds, don't ya think?"

"You mean, have me on retainer whenever you need a dog?"

"Yeah, exactly like that."

Deli blinked. He'd never considered what he'd do after he left the SEALs, but mostly that had to do with not knowing how to use the skillset he'd acquired. When he'd seen Trace again and got to know Caroline, he thought he could be a dog trainer and therapist. But Cyrus's offer combined his skills with the need to work with dogs, and brought everything together in a neat bowline knot.

He rubbed his chin as he thought over the options. "Are you seriously offering me a job?"

"Yup. We're beefing up our ranks and I'm always lookin' for anyone from the Teams." Then he squinted as he tilted his head. "I mean, you're not DEVGRU, but you're okay."

Deli barked a laugh. "Shut up. All right, Cyrus, let me

give your offer some thought and I'll have an answer for you by the time we're done here. Or my leave ends. Whichever comes first."

"Roger that. When does your leave end?"

Deli set his coffee mug down and stood. "Need to be back in Coronado by 0800 on Saturday."

"Shit-oh-dear, son, that ain't much time."

"Nope. But at least you won't have to wait long for an answer."

Cyrus shook his head. "That's not what I meant. I was talking about convincin' Caroline that you want more than a fly-by-night hookup."

"Why would you say that?"

"Shee-it. I might be a good ole boy from Texas, but I recognize when a man has found his heart's rest."

"I'm pretty sure that's the Navy for me."

"Maybe it was before, but I think you found it with a good woman in the mountains surrounded by some slobbery mutts." He grinned. "Don't walk away until you've considered all the angles on this one, Chief. You could either win big, or lose bigger."

"Copy that. Have a good night, Cyrus."

"Always."

Deli let himself out into the mountain night and stopped to take in the stars. The temperatures dramatically cooled once the sun went down and he let the stress release with the heat of his body. He scanned the darkness, watching for the telltale signs of a sniper or scout. He didn't see anything, but the birds had quieted and so had the crickets.

Predator nearby.

He slowed his breathing and listened as he retreated to put his back against the dark side of the barn. Something large approached from the hill. He didn't have any weapons on him, but he could use his stealth to take down an intruder.

"Comin' in on your two o'clock." The voice floated out of the darkness and a piece of shadow moved into his direct line of sight.

The man stood only about three inches taller than Deli, but he had shoulders like a linebacker. He also had light blond hair and some of the bluest eyes Deli had ever seen. They held intelligence, intensity, and humor as he stepped into the light from the house.

Deli recognized Elias Reece, retired Army Ranger, whom Cyrus had introduced earlier.

"Thanks for the warning. I wouldn't have known you were there except for the crickets." He held out a hand to shake and Reece's bigger palm engulfed it.

"Those damn crickets. I try to reason with 'em, but they just shut up anyway." Reece grinned before he nodded at the barn. "The boss inside?"

Deli nodded. "Yup. Everyone's bedded down. You on watch tonight?"

"Nope. It's McAvoy's night." He smirked as he leaned closer. "She might be Chair Force, but I gotta say, her cameras and drones make surveillance easier."

Deli laughed. "I won't tell her a thing."

"Roger that. I'm gonna hit the rack. Night."

"Night."

Deli watched him go before he continued his own path to the house. He wanted more time to think on what Cyrus had offered him and how it jived with his own initial plans, but he didn't want to stand exposed outside. He still had at least four more months of being shot at during work. He didn't really want it on his vacation.

Where I'm in the middle of a turf war.

And where he'd met the most amazing woman in his life. He let himself in the house and closed the blinds on the front windows. He debated leaving the porch light on, but decided it might be wiser not to give the cartel's thugs any extra help.

And McAvoy has the sensors and drones to keep an eye on things.

They wouldn't be surprised again.

He locked the door and closed the blinds before checking on the door to the porch. Everything seemed secure and he nodded to Daphne on the couch as he headed for the bedrooms.

"Where are you going?" The arched brow conveyed her surprise at his audacity.

"I need to talk to Caroline before I turn in."

"Uh-uh." She snorted and shook her head. "Just try not to make too much noise while you're 'talking.' I would like to get some sleep tonight."

He wanted to smirk and say something like, "I'm a SEAL. You'll never hear me coming," but he didn't think it was appropriate. *Too many double entendres in that line.* Instead, he shot her a dry look.

"Good night, Daphne."

"Mm-hm, to you, too, Chief."

He curbed the urge to grin as he headed back to Caroline's room. He found her dressed in soft knit shorts and an overly large t-shirt with the words, "In my house, if you don't like dogs…You can sleep OUTSIDE" written down the front.

"Permission to come in, ma'am?" He waved at her t-shirt. "And for what it's worth, I do like dogs."

She shot him a blank look before she glanced down. "Oh! Good. Yes, you can come in." She watched him as he settled on the foot of her bed. "Everything okay with the Ultimate Recon guys?"

"Yeah, they're fine. Your barn gives them a good place to set up. They got everything covered." He tilted his head. "How are you doing?"

She shrugged, tucking a lock of hair behind her ear. "Good, tonight. I feel safer with everyone here. Not so alone."

He nodded. "Yeah, it's good to have a team to back you up."

"Speaking of team, your time to go back to yours must be coming up soon, isn't it?"

He grimaced. "Yeah, I have to be back in Coronado at 0800 on Saturday morning."

She shot a look at the calendar hanging on the wall beside the door. "Oh. That's soon."

"Yeah, it is." He ran a hand over the back of his head, trying to find a way to tell her what he wanted without making too many assumptions. "But I want to talk to you about the future before I go. I, uh, might be presumptuous in asking this, but do you think you'd be okay if I came back here to work with you, Daphne, and Trace, on rehabilitating the dogs? It'll give me a reason to start the discharge process."

She tilted her head, her brows lowering a little. "Didn't Cyrus offer you a place in Ultimate Recon when you retire from the Teams?"

Deli nodded. "He did, and that's a damn good offer. But I wasn't going to say anything until I checked with you. I need to know I have more than just war to come back to."

"But isn't that what you SpecOps guys always need? Some sort of adventure and thrill with the element of danger to make you feel satisfied with life?" She didn't smile, her question as serious as the threat she faced with the cartel.

He dipped his head in acknowledgment. "Yeah, there's an element of that in every special operator. But once they've done it and survived the Teams, not every specialist needs more. I'd rather work on helping people and animals heal than fight more. So what do you say? Will you let me come back here to work with you and the dogs?"

She tipped her head and narrowed her eyes. "Is that the only reason you want to come back here? For something to do?"

"No, ma'am." He leaned forward and captured her hands. "I want to come back here to be with you."

CHAPTER FOURTEEN

I want to come back here to be with you.

The words echoed in her head as she met his chocolate-brown gaze. He didn't look away while he held her hands. His expression remained calm as he waited for her response, while her heart thundered in her chest ahead of the excitement.

He wants to be with me.

"But you barely know me." That was a stupid thing to say, but her old fears of being too old, too rundown, too independent for a man like him came roaring back.

He didn't smile or scoff, but nodded at her words. "I recognize that, and to folks who aren't in the Teams, I'm sure it seems real fast. But here's my thinkin' so you know where I'm coming from." He took a deep breath. "I haven't known you long, but what I've seen of you in that time tells me you're worth knowing. I might not know all your quirks—how you take your coffee, if you like the bed made, what your morning routine is—but I know I want to take the time to learn them. I also know that you're the kind of person who doesn't just tuck tail and run when a problem comes up. You work at it to find a solution. I suspect you'd do that with a relationship, too, and since I'm the kind of guy who isn't about to give up, I think we'd be pretty good together." He gave her his sexy smile. "I'd like the chance to see if we could be good together without the threat of armed conflict hanging over our heads. What do you think, Caroline?"

"What if you don't like my morning routine? Or my need to be as independent as possible?"

"Your independent streak is something I like most about you." He lost his smile. "What about you? What if you don't like my need to have shit organized? Or the few random times I have nightmares from my memories?"

"Do you have PTSD nightmares a lot?"

He shrugged. "No, not very often. But it would definitely help to have a dog around for that. The question is, could you handle me being here each day?"

She knew the answer before she spit out the word. "Yes."

His eyebrows went up. "Really?"

"Yes, sir." Now that she admitted it, she'd take it and run with it. "Yes, I want you to come back here and work at the Last Chance Dog Sanctuary. Yes, I want you to have my back, or whatever you say in the Teams. Yes, I'll hold your hand when you have PTSD nightmares or I'll make sure you have a dog to take you through them. And yes, please come back here to stay with me and keep me safe."

She hadn't meant to say the last, but it was true. He made her feel safe just by being there. She hadn't told anyone, but she'd never been so glad to be followed by a guy as when he came to her rescue on the road home. They'd been outgunned and outmatched, but he'd taken on the challenge as if it was the most natural thing in the world. She'd been relieved and so grateful he'd ignored her insistence to stay away.

"I'll always do my best to keep you safe, Caroline." He brought his hands to her face and rubbed her cheeks with his thumbs. "Always." He leaned forward and brushed his lips over hers.

Excitement, pleasure, and desperate need broke over her in a rush and she gasped, allowing his tongue to sweep into her mouth. She moaned at the slick heat and tilted her head to get closer. The man was a skilled kisser and she fell into his kiss with abandon.

His growl of approval set her body alight and her pussy grew slick with arousal as he deepened the kiss. His tongue swept along hers before he pulled back and pressed his lips over her jaw and down her neck to her shoulder. She leaned into his caresses as his hands slid down her back and grasped her ass.

When his lips reached her collar, he lifted his head and met her gaze. "I want to make love with you, Caroline."

"Wh–what?" She couldn't quite make sense of the words through the pleasure swamping her mind.

He reached out to grasp her hand and pulled it to his groin. A large, hard ridge of heat between his legs pressed against her palm.

"I want to make love with you. See what you do to me?"

"No."

He blinked. "What?"

"No, I can't see what I do to you. But I can feel it." She gave him an impish smile as she squeezed his cock beneath his clothes. "Come show me what I do to you. I've been dying to see your hard SEAL's body since you came in from your run yesterday morning."

A smirk curled his lips as his cock flexed under her hand. "Yes, ma'am."

He stood up and whipped his shirt over his head, exposing bronzed skin and perfect coppery nipples. Dark hair covered his pecs and belly, creating a dark line between his abs arrowing straight down to his groin. Caroline couldn't help whimpering as her gaze rested on his hands at his waistband. But he stopped.

She blinked and looked up. "What's wrong?"

"Nothin'. I just enjoyed seeing you lick your lips and whimper as you waited for me to take off my pants." He grinned.

"Don't tease me, Chief." She growled as she raised her chin. "I might not be a SEAL, but I know a thing or two about torture." She tilted her head and ran her hands over her breasts, moaning under her breath.

"Fuck." His eyes turned damn near black as the pupils expanded with his arousal. "Where the hell did you learn to tease like that?"

She raised her eyebrows as she settled back on the bed, her hands massaging her breasts until her nipples grew taut.

"Are you kidding? It's in the Confident Girl's Guide to Great Sex. We all get one at puberty." She winked. "What? Didn't you get a guidebook at puberty?"

He threw back his head and laughed, but unzipped his jeans and pushed them over his hips. "No, ma'am. We did not. But I've picked up a few tips and tricks along the way." He paused and tilted his head as he spread his hands to the sides. "So what do you think? All you'd been hoping for?"

The skin on his legs was the same color as his chest until his upper thighs where it lightened around his groin. He had scars on his legs and torso, some that appeared to have been bullet holes, and a few bruises left from the assholes at the feed store. But the glorious thatch of dark hair around his cock and balls had her gaze zeroed in.

"Oh, glory, yes you are."

He chuckled as he crawled onto the bed, his hard cock hanging below his flat belly. "I think it's time for you to get undressed for bed, young lady." He knelt between her legs and slid his hands up the outside of her thighs to grasp her waistband. "Let me help you with that."

He tugged her knit shorts down her legs, letting his fingers trail along her skin. The light touches sent sparks of pleasure zinging through her and cream wet her pussy lips. He took his time, pulling each leg of her pants over her ankles with attentive care before replacing her feet on the bed. Then he settled onto the coverlet with his shoulders between her thighs.

"Much better, ma'am."

She loved it when he got all military formal with her. There was something about the way he said it that had her heart fluttering with excitement.

"Now, if it's all right with you, I'd like to taste this pussy I can smell, and show you some of the tricks I learned without the benefit of a guide book."

She threw her head back to laugh, but it ended in a gasp as his mouth settled over her core. The slow, lazy slide of his tongue between her folds made her whimper and writhe, but Deli held her hips still. He peeled her nether lips apart and stroked between them, laving them with a sweet, sensual massage that stole her breath.

He hummed against her sensitive flesh, the vibration better than any of her electronic toys. She shivered as he slid his tongue around her clit and flicked it with teasing motions. Her arousal began to build with each flick of his tongue, and the humming pushed it higher. She fisted the sheets as she closed her eyes.

Sparks danced against the backs of her eyelids with each swipe of his clever tongue. She wanted to grab his head and press his mouth harder against her folds. But he slid one hand up her side and caressed the curve of her breast under the shirt, and her thoughts splintered. The tickling graze of his fingers on her skin combined with the slick heat of his tongue ramped up her arousal.

Oh glory, I want more.

"Don't worry, Caroline, there's more comin'." His rumbled voice flooded over her and she looked down her body to meet his gaze. "I promise."

She hadn't meant to say it aloud, but the look in his

eyes as he dipped his head sent her erotic ecstasy surging. She wanted his touch more than she'd wanted anything in a long time and the reality far outstripped her fantasies.

His weapon-roughened hands skimmed her sides down to her hips where they caressed in lazy circles as he sucked on her slick folds. One hand massaged her mound while the other trailed under her buttock and up to her inner thigh. He used the tips of his nails to lightly score her skin, making her shiver.

"Glory, I love to watching you take my touches. It's so fuckin' sexy." His voice had grown as rough as coarse sandpaper and part of her wanted to preen at his obvious arousal. "I need to see more."

He dipped his head and pulled her clit into his mouth as he thrust a finger into her slick sheath. Caroline arched her back and wailed at the erotic intrusion, pleasure surging. He sucked harder and curled his finger inside her as he pressed down with his other hand. The resulting pressure made her rock hard against his thrusting finger, and when he pulled back, he added a second, stretching her pussy around their combined girth.

"Oh, glory, Deli. Yes, please. Suck on my clit. Glory!"

"Yes, ma'am."

He growled the words before he tongued her clit and thrust harder with his fingers. She clutched his head, riding his face to generate as much friction as she could. Her breaths came in whimpers as the pleasure built beyond her control.

"Oh, oh, oooohhhh!"

Her orgasm burst over her, dragging her consciousness into a field of bright stars and sparkles. Pleasure cocooned her in a warm blanket against the fears and worries, and sent her spinning among the sparkling lights of ecstasy. She allowed herself to ride it until it released her back onto her bed with a grinning man between her legs.

"Yes, ma'am. You are welcome."

His evident satisfaction made her laugh as he wiped his mouth and licked his lips. But instead of crawling up her body as she'd expected, he rolled off the bed and grabbed the pants he'd shucked earlier. His cock stood up stiffly from the nest of dark hair, and her pussy clenched with the need to feel him despite the recent release.

"What are you doing?"

Deli smiled as he held up two foil packets. "Makin' sure we're not makin' babies quite yet."

"Quite yet? You planning on something in the future?"

He met her gaze with determined intensity. "Always."

The way he said it made her heart swell. *I want him to be part of my future.* If they managed to survive the days ahead. The cartel wasn't about to give up and Deli had to return to his Team in the SEALs. He still had just over seven months of service left on his term and the kinds of things the SEALs were sent to do weren't easy or safe. Her smile fell and his gaze sharpened on her face.

"What's wrong, dearest?"

It was the first time he'd called her an endearment, but he'd magically chosen the best word to use. She bit her lip and shook her head as he settled onto the bed beside her.

"Hey, talk to me. Where did you go?"

"Somewhere stupid and hypothetical. I shouldn't have." She shook her head. "Kiss me to empty my thoughts."

But he shook his head. "Tell me what you were thinking. Maybe I can ease your mind."

"It's stupid."

"I can't make it better if I don't know what it is. I'm a damn good operator and sometimes I can outthink someone, but that's in the field on mission. With you, I'd rather not guess." He stroked her face with those callused fingers and met her gaze. "Come on, talk to me."

"I'm afraid." She admitted it with her heart in her throat. What would he say to that?

"Of what? Of me?"

She shook her head again. "No, of what might be. Or not be. Or whatever. See? I told you it was stupid."

He frowned, his expression thoughtful. "Are you worried about what's goin' on with the cartel?"

"That, and what will happen to you in the next few months when you go back to your Team. What if you're hurt or killed or something awful like that?" She clamped her mouth shut, pretty sure she'd just brought bad juju to him for even thinking it.

"I'm not gonna bullshit you, Caroline. None of us have a line on the future and you know bein' a SEAL is hazardous." He gave her a warm smile and stroked her cheek with his thumb. "But I'll tell you this, we're gonna take down the cartel's thugs and make sure you're safe before I go back to the Teams. And if you're here waitin' for me, that gives me more reasons to make sure I come home alive."

"Did you need other reasons?"

He nodded. "Lately, yeah. I needed to know someone cared if I made it home."

****

He hadn't meant to drop that on her, but he meant it from the very depths of his soul. He needed someone to be there when he stepped off base. Looking into her whiskey-golden eyes, he only wanted her to be waiting on him. *Her and Trace.* He'd come to northern California to clear his head and find his balance so he could make a decision about the future. And here she lay, her golden-brown hair in a silken halo around her head.

"I need to know you care if I make it home."

Caroline searched his eyes as she lay beside him and he prayed to whoever listened that she wanted the same. After a few moments of silence, she sat up and pulled her t-

179

shirt off, dropping it beside the bed. Then she crawled over him, letting her breasts hang above his chest as she straddled his hips. His cock approved of the move and swelled into fullness.

"I care if you make it home, Deli. I want you to make it home alive and well, and I'll do my best to be there when you step off your ship. Or whatever SEALs do when they come home."

She reached down and grasped his shaft, sliding the hard flesh in her palm. He moaned and arched his hips up into her grip as the pleasure built in his balls. He'd held out against her moans as he'd feasted on her succulent pussy, but having her hands on him shot his control to hell.

"I'm going to be there, Eugene, so you know someone is hoping you made it home safe."

She stood his cock up and reached past him to grasp one of the foil packets. "But first, I want to ride you until you lose that famous SEAL control and give yourself to me."

Holy fuck, that's hot. He'd never had a woman take him in hand, quite literally, and fuck him senseless. But he was ready for any new experience she wanted to give him, including a relationship longer than a one-night-stand.

Caroline tore open the foil package and held his cock up, but paused and met his gaze. He damn near held his breath as he waited to see what she would do. When she leaned forward and slid her mouth over the head, his vision whited out with the hot, slick pleasure engulfing him.

"Oh holy hell, Caroline."

He threw his head back and hissed as she licked around the head and down the shaft, humming her pleasure. Between the softness of her lips and the low vibration, his balls threatened to empty before he was ready. He caught her shoulders and shifted her up, his cock popping out of her mouth hard enough to make him moan.

"I don't have the stamina to hold out. I've wanted you

too long for that."

A sultry smirk curled her lips before she licked them and he groaned. But she moved away and slid the condom down over his shaft without protest.

"Permission to come aboard, Chief."

"Oh, fuck yeah, granted."

She held his dick up to her sheath and the heat from her seeped through the condom. He whimpered a little before she sank down on him and his vision whited out again. *Fuck yeah, she's perfect.* Better than his fantasies. Better than the nameless, faceless women he'd fucked after missions before. She fit him perfectly as she settled onto him, her pussy lips kissing his balls.

"Oh, glory, Deli. You feel so damn good." She wriggled her hips as if to get more of him into her, but she already had all of him. "Better than I imagined."

Her words both surprised and pleased him. "You imagined fucking me?"

She whimpered as she wiggled her hips on his cock. "Oh yeah."

"Ride me, Caroline. Let me see those tits bounce as you take your pleasure from me."

That seemed to be the right thing to say because she lifted herself off his shaft and sank back down in a smooth slide. Her tight pussy dragged on his cock, reluctantly releasing it from its snug heat. But the hot vice returned with pleasure so intense, he wouldn't last long.

He raised his gaze to her breasts, full, round with perfect, large rosy nipples, and couldn't resist running his hands up her sides to cup them as she rode his dick. She gasped when he massaged the aureolas, flicking the nipples with this thumbs. They tightened into hard nubs and he pulled her down so he could taste them.

"Oh glory, yes, Deli."

She grasped his head and held it to her breasts, still rocking her hips. Each time her clit raked his cock, it sent more arousal flooding through him. He growled as he sucked on her nipples, laving them with his tongue before gently nipping. She gasped and bore down harder on his cock, whimpering her pleasure.

He looked up, enjoying the flush to her face and the way she bit her lower lip, her focus on bringing herself pleasure on his hard shaft. He loved that. She didn't fool around and she'd make herself come using his cock. It was beautiful and arousing at the same time.

"That's it, dearest. Fuck me hard. Ride my cock."

She opened her whiskey-colored eyes and met his gaze as she rocked harder, moaning with each thrust. He matched her, grasping her hips and pumping into her tight sheath. His arousal threatened to break over him and he reached between her legs to flick her clit with his thumb.

"Oh my glory, I'm going to come."

"Do it, my sexy woman. Come for me. Oh fuck, yeah."

He ground his cock deep into her pussy and it clamped down around him like a velvet vice. His orgasm broke over him as she wailed, rocking her hips in jerky motions as if she couldn't quite keep the rhythm during her release. But what amazed him most was how long she came. The lovely euphoria swelled around him, allowing his mind to float free and watch his woman take her pleasure. And it lasted longer than he expected.

Damn that's sexy.

At last she shuddered to a stop and collapsed on his chest. He expected her to lie there like a warm, soft blanket on top of him, but she nuzzled into the hair on his chest with a contented moan.

"Thank you." The whispered gratitude made him chuckle.

"Actually, I was gonna thank you, but I'm happy to say you're welcome."

She snorted softly and pushed herself up to look him in the eyes. "You're welcome." And squeezed her inner muscles around his shaft.

He closed his eyes and moaned. "Damn, woman, you tryin' to get me hard again so soon?"

She kissed the edge of his mouth. "What if I am?"

He opened his eyes and met her gaze. "Give me a chance to get rid of this condom and clean up a bit, and I'll be ready for round two."

"Are you sure you're up for that? It's been a long day, what with you taking out two snipers this morning." She slid to the side and he grasped the edges of the condom to keep it from slipping off.

"Yes, ma'am. I'm up for anything you care to throw at me. SEALs never give up until the mission's complete."

"Well, then, I'd like to test your stamina, Chief. See how far you can go." She grinned as she watched him get up. He'd never been so turned on so fast in his life.

"Hooyah, ma'am." He'd go as far as it took to give her pleasure and secure her heart.

The only easy day was yesterday. Hell yeah, but this would be the best difficult day ever.

CHAPTER FIFTEEN

Deli sighed and rubbed his face with his hands before rolling his head on his shoulders to loosen the muscles. Between him, Finch, Tanaka, Reece and McAvoy, they'd been taking watches to make sure no one got the jump on them. Finch had even handed out earpieces to everyone, including Sandoval and Murphy, and Deli shoved his more securely in his ear. *I need more coffee.* But the cartel had been suspiciously silent over the last two days.

He poured out three cups of coffee from the pot, rinsed it, and filled the coffee maker back up again. They'd been going through so much liquid black gold, they'd had to make a few runs to the local warehouse store for supplies. Caroline's jaw had dropped when she saw how much food they'd brought back to the house, including her brand of dog food, but Deli thought it only an average amount for a SpecOps squad.

In addition to taking watch shifts, Caroline had been on puppy watch. Her rottweiler bitch had whelped puppies in the middle of the night, and everyone had been lending a hand. They had nine new squealing charges and an exhausted mama, and no one had gotten much sleep.

Deli handed out the mugs to Caroline and Daphne as

he settled at the table. "How's Tallulah doing?"

"Good this morning. All the puppies are nursing strongly, so I think we'll have seven new dogs to train when they're old enough." Daphne sighed as she sipped her coffee. "Two will go to the owner of the papa dog, but the rest are ours."

"You bred her on purpose?" He raised his eyebrows.

Caroline nodded. "Yeah. Both Tallulah and the male had great confirmation lines, and sweeter personalities with high intelligence. Those traits are great for guide dogs, service dogs, and family dogs. We're hoping the pups will get the same qualities."

"Will you breed Tallulah again?" He stretched his shoulders, trying to work out the stiffness.

"Maybe in a year or so. We don't want her to be a puppy mill. She's actually a great service dog herself." Caroline nodded at Daphne. "Daphne is actually her handler and they're suited for each other. If she didn't have Beryl, she'd be paired with Tallulah."

"Sounds like she's a great dog."

"She is." Caroline smiled and its warmth shot straight to his dick.

Damn, she's gorgeous. He loved the way the laugh lines showed up around her mouth. It made him want to kiss them until she moaned.

Okay, jackass, start thinking with another part of your body.

Fortunately, Finch picked that moment to come in with FBI Agents Sandoval and Murphy. Finch scowled at the dripping coffee pot, but set out another mug for when it finished. Sandoval and Murphy held to-go cups from the local coffee shop in Cascade Breaks.

"Good morning." Caroline stood up. "Take my spot and sit down a moment. Coffee's brewing and I can make some tea if you've already had enough caffeine."

Sandoval snorted and shook his head, but took

Caroline's seat. Murphy settled beside Daphne on the other side.

"Hey, tea makes everything better." Deli lifted his chin as he shot a wink at Caroline.

"That's right." She grinned as she put the kettle on.

"So anything new going on in town?" Deli aimed his question at Murphy. She hadn't quite written him off like Sandoval had.

She shook her head. "Nothing yet. The sheriff said he'd had an increase in tourist traffic, but no one screamed 'foreign thug' to him. His words, not mine. We contacted our intel crew and there's been chatter about a new resort along the I-5 corridor, which is cartel-speak for safe house or way station, but nothing specific about Cascade Breaks or any place nearby."

"Satellite imagery hasn't been very helpful, either." Sandoval grimaced. "I would've expected these guys to congregate somewhere until they're ready to take you down now that they know someone took out their snipers. But we've got zero activity to suggest they're getting ready for an offensive."

Deli snorted. "My gut says they're comin'. The question is when."

Finch nodded. "Oh yeah, they're definitely comin'. My gut's screamin' at me. But they're bein' cagey about it. McAvoy hasn't caught any movement with her drones yet, either. I think they're hopin' we'll relax our guard and then come in for the kill. Either that, or they're going to do a sledgehammer attack, hopin' to kill everyone and pick up the pieces afterwards."

"Fuck. The last thing we need up here is a shootout at the OK corral." Sandoval glowered then blushed. "Beg your pardon, ma'am." He nodded to Daphne. "Didn't mean to be so crass."

She smiled at him and waved it away. "It doesn't bother me, Agent Sandoval." Still she stood up. "I need to take Beryl for a walk anyway." She held up her hand as all the men at the table opened their mouths. "I know, I know. I'll stay within the yard and sight of everyone. I'll be safe and aware. I promise."

"How about I go with you? It would just make me feel better." Sandoval scooted his chair back. "Just let me use the bathroom first and I'll join you."

"Okay." She smiled, a bright twinkle in her eyes. "I'll wait for you outside."

Caroline raised her eyebrows as Daphne headed out the front door with Beryl at her side. No one said anything until the bathroom door shut behind Sandoval. Then Finch grunted with amusement.

"I think Sandoval's smitten."

Murphy grinned and nodded. "Yeah, I kinda noticed that myself over the last couple of days." She shrugged. "He's been keeping it professional, but yeah, I noticed."

"What surprises me is Daphne's interest in Sandoval." Caroline smiled wistfully. "After her abduction two years ago, she hasn't shown interest in anyone. It's nice to see."

Deli opened his mouth to say something when the sounds of squealing tires on gravel reached them just as their phones began pinging with texts and calls.

"Finch."

"They're here. Fuck, they came outta nowhere and grabbed Daphne!" McAvoy's voice came through clearly as Deli and Finch raced toward the door. Sandoval charged out of the bathroom behind them.

Deli yanked the front door open and shot through, pulling his Glock and aiming at the back of the nondescript gray van speeding away. He shot out the back windows and tried to hit the tires, but his shots went wide.

"Tanaka! Gray van, heading out. Take out the wheels." Finch shouted the words as he sprinted down the driveway. "California tag. Alpha romeo zero niner zero eight three! Fuck. They have Daphne."

"Sandoval, stay here with Caroline. Keep the house secure!"

"Dammit!" The FBI agent skidded to a halt. "Shit. I found Beryl. I'll keep the dog and the house safe."

"Roger that!"

Deli shoved his weapon back into the holster as he raced down the driveway after Finch. He settled into search-and-destroy mode as he focused on catching up to the van. Two loud shots cracked through the breezy air, followed by a loud crash.

"Target vehicle down." Tanaka's voice sounded calm. Another shot rang out. "Tango one down. Three others and hostage out of sight and on foot. Hostage appears unconscious."

Fuck. "Any sign of injury on her?" Deli pushed his body faster.

"Negative."

Relief cascaded through him. Hopefully that meant Daphne was still alive and they had a chance to recover her. *If they don't kill her before we get there.* He followed Finch, the other man relaying commands through the radio.

"Sandoval, Murphy, stay at the house. We got the van covered. Reece, converge on target. Tanaka, keep birdseye."

"Copy that."

"Roger that."

"Roger." The FBI agent sounded furious, but at least he wasn't planning to play hero with the former SpecOps guys headed into the fray.

Not former yet.

"McAvoy, keep scanning the area. Tell us where they're headed."

"Copy that. Intel soon coming."

Deli caught sight of a drone zipping above the tree canopy as they came around a bend in the road. They paused and Finch gestured for Deli to take the left flank, using the cover in the gully beside the roadbed to disguise his movements. Deli nodded and darted across the road, listening for movement.

Nothing came to his ears as he caught Finch's motion on the other side of the road. "Target vehicle appears vacant."

"Confirmed. No heat signatures inside." McAvoy's voice sounded over the coms.

"Moving in. Reece, report."

"Approaching target vehicle from your twelve, Finch. No movement detected."

Deli crept through the brush toward the van's rear tire. "Approaching from left flank. No movement, no sound."

The back windows stared like hollow eyes of a corpse eaten by ravens as he approached the doors. Finch met him at the right corner, Sig Sauer at the ready. Deli pulled his Glock as Finch counted down from three.

Deli took the rear position as Finch yanked open the doors. The stench of blood and sweat hit his nose as light flooded inside. The cargo van only held four things. Two empty weapons crates against the wall toward the gully, a discarded dirty rag, and a dead body.

The man slumped over the driver's seat, a pool of blood filling the footwell. The driver's door was yanked open and Reece hissed. "One Tango down. Deceased."

"Copy that." Finch shook his head. "I have a blood trail."

Deli backed up and glanced at the ground. Dark splotches marred the dirt and leaves along with some scuff marks leading down into the gully.

"Copy that. Have a confirmed trail here." He waved to Finch, motioning to the brush off the road. "Path leads south on a heading of 185 degrees."

Finch raised his eyebrows, but didn't ask how Deli knew. Hell, Deli didn't know how he knew, but his internal compass had never been wrong. He'd never gotten lost. He could read any map and sense the degrees of the compass on the ground, rain or shine, night or day. Even under water or underground, his compass needle sense had been true.

"Copy that. Deploying drones in a vector along 185 degrees south from target vehicle."

"Roger that. Ground team moving out." Finch gestured he'd take point, Deli following, and Reece bringing up the rear.

They headed down the embankment and followed the signs of several people crashing through the underbrush. Broken branches, crushed leaves, and blood spatters gave them a fairly easy trail to follow. Deli, Finch, and Reece had the advantage of silence and mobility.

Deli had expected the woods to make it easy to see anyone moving through, but the summer foliage disguised movement with fluttering leaves in the breeze. Despite the wind, the rest of the forest stood in silence. *The animals and birds sense predators.* The question was, were they sensing Finch's team or the tangoes?

Up ahead, Finch froze and clenched his fist beside his head. They stopped and crouched with him as he motioned he'd found the tangoes. Finch turned and gestured to Deli to keep on this heading. To Reece, he signaled to take the right and he'd take the left. He held up his hand with four fingers and they nodded. *Four tangoes.* Fine. They had even odds. The problem would be Daphne.

They fanned out, Finch and Reece disappearing into the trees. Deli resumed hunting on the path ahead, listening to the way the tangoes moved. They were going slower than expected and their voices held anger and fear.

"Targets in sight." Reece's voice whispered in Deli's ear. "Three with automatic weapons, one badly wounded, favoring his left side. Hostage unconscious, but appears whole."

Deli snarled inwardly but forced his focus ahead. He found a break in the underbrush, keeping low and quiet until Reece and Finch got in position.

"Roger that. Try for non-kill shots."

Non-kill shots? Was he fucking kidding? Deli's snarl grew louder in his head, but he kept it behind his lips. They'd threatened Caroline and her home, disturbed the service dogs, and abducted Daphne. And Finch wanted them alive?

"Say again," Deli whispered.

"I say again, non-lethal force. We need them for questioning."

Deli ground his teeth. "Roger that."

He pushed ahead a few steps, but kept his Glock pointed forward. "In position."

"Roger that. Almost there." Finch's voice held excitement.

You can take the man out of the SEALs, but not the SEAL out of the man. Deli grinned.

"Reece in position." The former Army Ranger couldn't have been more than a few feet to Deli's right, but he never heard him move.

"Roger that." Finch took a breath. "In position. On the count of three. Three, two, one. Go!"

Deli surged to his feet and shot the guy crouched over Daphne through the thigh. He went down howling as the others spun toward him. Reece's first shot took one of the uninjured through the shoulder and his second hit the injured tango, who did nothing but jerk and cry out. The fourth guy sprayed bullets in an arch around their clearing, screaming in Spanish. Deli dove to the ground, sighted along the top of his Glock and nailed the bastard between the eyes. He dropped like a discarded doll.

"Report!" Finch's voice sounded oddly strained.

"Clear." Reece appeared beside the guy Deli had hit in the thigh, pistolwhipping his head. "Targets down. One crawling to you, Rubenovich."

"Copy that." Deli rose from his crouch and the sighted

on the guy with the bullet hole in his shoulder. "*Alto, o esta muerte.*" Not the most elegant phrase but it got the job done. "Clear. Target secure." He kicked the AK-47 away from the guy's hands and kept him in his sights until Reece could join him and ziptie the thug's hands behind him.

"Finch, all clear?" Deli headed to check on the two other tangoes, collecting the automatics as he went. "Finch?"

"Yeah. Comin' to you." Finch stepped out of the brush, holding his arm as pain whitened out his eyes.

"Fuck. How bad is it?" Deli set the weapons aside, well out of reach of the tangoes, and headed to Finch.

"Shoulder. Lucky bastard. Through-and-through. Nothing vital. How's the hostage?"

Deli holstered his Glock and shoved his shoulder under Finch's left armpit. "I haven't checked. Two tangoes dead, two wounded and secured."

"Shots fired! Shots fired!" McAvoy's urgent voice shouted through the coms.

"All clear, McAvoy." Finch frowned.

"No, sir. Shots fired at the house! It's a fuckin' assault."

"Dammit all to hell. This was a diversion." Deli's gut sank. "I gotta get back to the house."

"Rubenovich!"

Deli turned and caught one of the AK-47's Reece tossed at him. "Take that and the extra magazines. You're gonna need 'em."

"Thanks."

"And watch your six."

Deli nodded. "Roger that." He darted off into the trees, following the line back to Caroline's house. "Tanaka, comin' to you."

"Roger that. And Chief?" The sniper's voice held strain.

"Yeah?"

"Fuckin' hurry."

****

Caroline wanted to scream, but it would only freak out the FBI agents and wouldn't save Daphne from the cartel's thugs. Instead, she busied herself with cleaning up the breakfast dishes and starting the dishwasher.

It's going to be fine. Deli and Finch will find her. It's going to be okay.

She tried to believe her own inner thoughts and calm her racing heart, but it only served to make her more nervous. *Deep breaths, Caroline.* She wanted to go check on Tallulah, but she didn't want to stress out the rottweiler mama. Instead, she came over to the dogbed beside the couch and settled on the floor with Beryl. The boxer shook with stress and turned her sad brown eyes up to Caroline with entreaty.

"I know, darlin'. I'm with you. She'll be okay. We'll all be okay. Your mama will be home soon and you can comfort her." Caroline stroked the dog and hugged her to her side.

When Sandoval had brought the boxer inside, Caroline had thought she was injured. But upon inspection, she found the dog only shivering from fear. Not that she blamed Beryl. She'd been trained for comfort, not defense.

That's Trace's job.

She caught her breath and shot a look toward the kennels. "I need to get Trace."

"What?" Sandoval scowled. "What are you talking about?"

"Beryl couldn't protect Daphne because she's trained for comfort. Trace is trained to defend her pack. We're going to need Trace." Caroline rolled to her feet and headed toward the covered porch.

"You can't go out there. It's too exposed." Murphy got

to her feet.

"Then watch my back. I need to have my dog with me."

Caroline didn't wait and the agents cursed behind her. She paused at the porch door and glanced over her shoulder. Murphy had her weapon out and pointed at the ceiling.

"Ready?"

"This is stupid, but yeah."

Caroline didn't bother to correct her as she yanked the door open and darted through the covered porch to the kennels. She unlocked the second door and ran straight to the Aussie cattle dog.

"*Here*, Trace. Hup."

The heeler darted out of her kennel, her ears up and her attention on potential threats. Caroline didn't waste time, but reversed course and headed for the house. Murphy stood at the back door, her expression tight as she scanned the hillside beyond the porch.

"Get in here. Now." Murphy's gaze shifted away from the kennels.

Caroline bolted for the doorway with Trace at her side as bullets sprayed the walls behind her. She yelped and ducked through the door before Murphy slammed it behind them.

"Fuck. Shots fired. Multiple threats incoming." Murphy reported everything as she swung Caroline to the floor and pointed to the kitchen. "Stay down and away from the window."

She didn't have to be told twice as the window above the sink shattered in a spray of glass. Beryl yelped and flattened herself beside the couch. Trace whimpered and stuck close to Caroline as she crouched and skittered into the kitchen.

"I know, Trace. I'll keep you safe." She had no idea how she'd accomplish such a thing, but she'd be damned before everyone she loved was hurt by these bastards.

Murphy let off four shots through the broken window before she ducked down beside Caroline.

"How many, Murphy?" Sandoval stared out the window next to the front door.

"Two that I could see. One's down." She shook her head. "But I wouldn't count on just those two."

"Oh, sweet glory. Did Deli and Finch get Daphne?" Caroline caught the look the agents shared between them. "What?"

"They found Daphne, but she's unconscious."

Caroline's gut sank. "Is she hurt?"

"I don't know." Sandoval's expression turned stoic. "We won't know until this is over." He pressed a finger to his ear. "McAvoy says Chief Rubenovich is coming back to help."

More bullets sprayed the front windows, shattering them into slivers of glass and Sandoval ducked down.

"Fuck!"

Caroline's sentiments exactly. She tried to keep her body low, covering Trace who whined and flattened her ears. *This is going to remind her too much of her work.* She stroked the dog, whispering that it would be all right in hopes of finding some calm. Beryl whimpered from the couch and Caroline wondered if she could get to the other dog.

A heavier boom echoed over the automatic weapons fire and a few more single shots, closer, made Sandoval peek over the edge of the window. Murphy scrambled across the floor to join him.

"Looks like Finch's sniper is taking out a few of them and McAvoy surprised them from the barn."

"How many are out there?" Caroline held Trace tighter as Beryl whined again.

"Three down in the front, at least one in the back, and three more standing and shooting." Murphy ducked as more bullets pelted the front door.

Another heavy boom cracked the air and the shooting stopped.

"Two more gunmen down." Sandoval narrowed his eyes. "Murphy, I don't trust this shit. Keep an eye out at the back. I'm pretty sure they're planning to storm both doors."

"Roger that." She nodded before she scuttled back to the porch door. "I don't see any movement out the covered porch, but the kennels and the wall restrict my view."

Beryl whined and Caroline couldn't stay still anymore. She patted Trace and told her to stay as she rolled onto her hands and knees. She carefully avoided glass and other broken items as she picked her way to the couch. Beryl kept her head buried under the couch ruffle, her body shaking.

"Hey, Beryl. Come on out, honey. I got you."

The dog simply shook and whined, and anger surged in Caroline's chest. How could these assholes scare her dogs like this? She tugged on Beryl's collar, hoping to convince the dog to come out. But then the silence got to her and she looked around.

"What's going on? Why have the stopped shooting?"

"I dunno." Murphy glanced out the window in the door to the porch. "The guys back here are gone."

Sandoval narrowed his eyes and peeked over the windowsill out the front. "Oh fuck."

"What?" Caroline felt her stomach drop into her shoes.

"They have Chief Rubenovich."

"What?" Caroline froze.

This can't be happening. She looked at Sandoval, hoping he was joking, but his face said he didn't find anything humorous. *But Deli's a SEAL.* SEALs didn't get caught. They were the masters of war and stealth.

"Señora Atherton. Come out or I shoot your little man."

She knew that voice. It belonged to the guy who'd

visited in his ridiculous white suits. *Carlos Antigua. Or Santo Domingo, whatever*. She looked at Sandoval.

"That's Carlos. That's the guy who kept coming back here." She whispered it and Sandoval's expression hardened. "What am I going to do?"

"Sit tight." He pressed his ear. "Tanaka. Do you have a shot?" He listened for a moment. "If I go out there, will that give you enough time to move?" He scowled at the answer. "Fuck."

"What about Trace?" Caroline tugged his sleeve.

"Trace?"

"Yes. She's an MWD. She knows how to handle this kind of situation. And she'll protect Rubenovich." Caroline looked at the dog who'd raised her head at her name. "Trace. *Here*."

"No way. She'd get us all shot."

Caroline shook her head. "No. All you have to do is distract Carlos long enough. Trace will slip past you and go for him, giving the chief time to do his thing. Trust me."

Sandoval raised an eyebrow.

"Rubenovich trained with her. She's a Military War Dog. They both know what to do." Caroline raised her chin, waiting for him to understand. *Think it through, Sandoval*.

"I'm waiting, Señora Atherton, and I don't like to wait." Carlos's voice slithered through the broken windows.

"Please, Agent Sandoval." Caroline beseeched him. For once she knew better than him, but she didn't know if his ego would let him believe it. "I know what to do."

Sandoval growled. "All right. Here's what we're gonna do. Tanaka, McAvoy, listen up 'cause I only have time to say this once."

CHAPTER SIXTEEN

"Señora Atherton. Come out or I shoot your little man."

Deli struggled against the two bigger thugs holding him and ground his teeth. He'd stumbled into their damn ambush and been overpowered. Usually he was quicker and smarter, but he'd been too intent on getting back to the house that he didn't pay attention and they caught him. This was the only time being the smaller guy sucked.

"Tanaka. Do you have a shot?" Agent Sandoval's voice came through his earpiece and Deli fought not to react. No one had noticed the little earbud and he had no intention of alerting them to it.

"Negative. There are too many guns on the Chief. And I don't have time to take out all of them before Santo Domingo shoots him."

"If I go out there, will that give you enough time to move?"

"Negative. I can't get down in time. You're gonna need a diversion or more guns."

"Fuck."

Deli concurred. He could help with a diversion, but he didn't have any body armor which meant a good chance of dying from lead poisoning. He scanned Santo Domingo, looking for weak points. He didn't appear to be wearing body armor either, and that could be an advantage. Unfortunately, he held a big damn cannon in his hands. It looked to be a Colt .45, with a pearl grip. *That would definitely make some holes.*

The thugs were overconfident and thought they had him subdued. Deli could definitely take them down if he didn't have Santo Domingo to deal with. Tanaka was right. He either needed a diversion or more guns.

"I'm waiting, Señora Atherton, and I don't like to wait." Carlos waved the pistol at Deli's face with a lazy grin.

The bastard is enjoying this.

"All right. Here's what we're gonna do. Tanaka, McAvoy, listen up 'cause I only have time to say this once." Sandoval's voice came through loud and clear. "I'm gonna step out the door and start talkin' to him to buy some time. I need everyone to pick a thug and don't miss when I give the signal. We have to take Carlos's attention off the chief. Caroline says she can get Trace to help distract Carlos, which might give Chief Rubenovich enough time to take him down. But we all have to work together or someone's gonna get shot and I don't want to sign anyone's death certificate. Copy?"

"Copy."

"Copy." McAvoy's softer voice held an undercurrent of excitement. "From my position, I have two thugs holding Rubenovich, Santo Domingo, and two more covering the porch entrance to the house."

"Copy that." Sandoval confirmed her words with sounds like he'd gotten to his feet. "Murphy has the northernmost thug out the porch side if you can sight the other, McAvoy."

"Copy that."

"Good. I'm going to go out the front to engage Santo

Domingo. Tanaka, can you shoot Santo Domingo without killing him?"

"Say again?" Tanaka's voice was quiet, but incredulity sat under the words.

"We need him alive. He's the best way for us to build a case that can be taken more seriously. Is there a way you can hit him without killing him?"

Deli rolled his gaze up to Carlos and hoped the sniper could at least hit his gun hand. That meant Deli would have to take out the thugs holding him. *Challenge accepted.* They'd gotten the jump on him when he hurried back to the house, but that had been their freebie. He was done playing.

"Señora, I'm going to count to three and then I'm going to shoot your little man. One…" Carlos kept his gaze on the house.

Yup. Mistake number one.

A quick glance up at the thugs showed them focused on the house, too. That would make them easily surprised. Yeah, they had weight on him, but he had unpredictability, training, and determination.

"Copy that. Switching targets to Santo Domingo. Non-lethal." Tanaka's voice held resignation and Deli rather agreed with him.

"Roger. Wait for my signal to take your shots. The go-phrase is 'dog-trainer.' Copy?"

The rest of the team replied with a round of "Copys" and the game was set.

"Two…" Carlos tightened his grip on the Colt pistol.

"Okay, okay. Hold up." Agent Sandoval stepped out the door onto the porch, his hands in the air. He left the door open behind him, but not wide enough to see inside.

"Who the fuck are you?" Carlos didn't move and Deli gritted his teeth to keep from snarling.

"Agent Sandoval. FBI."

"Where is Señora Atherton?"

"She's not available right now. Plus, with all the

shooting, she's scared of talking to you, seeing as how you have a gun." Sandoval kept his hands up as he pointed at Carlos. "Who the hell are you?"

"I'm the one asking the questions here." Carlos scowled and tightened his grip.

"Okay, okay. You ask the questions. Got it." Sandoval nodded and moved one finger to point up at the sky.

"Tell the Señora to come out here or I blow this little man's head to pieces. *Comprende*?"

Sandoval shrugged. "Yeah, I don't know if I can convince her, man." He held up a second finger and Deli recognized the count down. "You already came in here shooting up her place. Why is she supposed to trust that you won't shoot her?"

Carlos smirked. "She can trust that I'll shoot her little man." He took a step closer to Deli.

And there's mistake number two.

"Okay, all right. Calm down. You know she's just a dog-trainer, right?"

Deli dropped his weight, dragging one thug off balance as Trace shot through the open door. A shot rang out and Carlos' hand exploded into a spray of blood. Another shot sounded and the off-balance thug's body rocked back, a bullet through his chest, releasing Deli.

Deli jerked on the arm attached to the second thug and pulled the guy close enough to head-butt him into shock. Then he yanked the AK-47 out of his stunned hands and shot him in the foot. The guy howled and bent to cover his feet, and Deli used the stock to clock him upside the head. The thug dropped to the ground unconscious.

A vicious snarl pulled Deli around to find Trace latched onto Carlo's free arm, tugging and jerking her weight to pull him down. He yelled and scrambled, trying to get free until Deli stomped close to his head. The man stilled and looked up at him with wide eyes as he pointed the muzzle of the AK-47 at his nose.

"Move, and I'll ignore the order to keep you alive. *Comprende?*"

Carlos swallowed hard and nodded.

"Trace. *Poost.* Back."

The dog released Carlos and stood back about a foot, her teeth bared as a low growl rumbled out of her. Carlos whimpered and gathered his injured arms across his chest, one bleeding badly, the other mauled. Deli didn't feel much sympathy.

"Report." Sandoval appeared next Deli, his gun still in his hands.

"All threats immobilized." McAvoy's voice came through the coms. "Tangos on north side of the house down, including the extras who showed up late to the party."

"Copy that." Sandoval nodded. "Tanaka?"

"Yard covered. No other movement currently."

"Roger."

"Y'all aren't gonna forget us now, are you?" Finch's voice carried through the coms and Deli shot a look down the driveway. "We got no less than eight, I say again, eight tangos tryin' to make an appearance on your party. Three are KIA and five are waitin' for transport."

"Roger that." Sandoval looked down on Carlos' bleeding form and grunted with approval. "Thanks for giving me the evidence I needed, Santo Domingo."

The guy blanched as his real name came out, but Deli wanted to know if Caroline and Daphne were all right.

"How's hostage, Senior Chief?"

"Awake and spittin' mad, Chief." Finch chuckled. "Reece had to keep her from goin' Beckham on their asses. I swear she was gonna use their heads for soccer balls."

"Roger that." Deli grinned. "You gonna be okay to make it back or do you need some reinforcements?"

"Sheriff and more FBI agents en route," Murphy reported. "ETA five minutes."

Deli caught movement out of the corner of his eye as Caroline came through the door with her rifle. He didn't blame her. Who knew when another attacker would come out of the woods? He started to offer her a smile when she raised the rifle and fired into the ground beside Carlos' head. He ducked and yanked his hand back from the act of reaching for a dropped AK-47.

"Try it again and I'll put the first bullet squarely in your chest. *Comprende*?" Caroline's lips had pulled back from her teeth and Deli was glad he wasn't on the receiving end of that look.

Carlos responded with a black look. "This isn't—"

"Over? Yes, it is. This is my land and my home, and you're under arrest, you sonuvaprick."

"The cartel will be back to get this land." He sneered the words as Sandoval yanked him up just as the sheriff and an ambulance drove into the yard.

"If you do, there'll be no more warning shots. I'll shoot to kill. And they'll never find the bodies."

"You don't have it in you, Señora."

She cocked the rifle and gave him the blackest smile Deli had ever seen. "Try me." Trace growled and rose to stand beside Caroline, her gaze on Carlos.

"*Mierda*, get that *perro* away from me!" Carlos tried to scramble away, but Sandoval kept a tight grip on him.

"Come on, Santo Domingo. We're gonna have plenty of time to get to know each other better." Sandoval dragged him over to the Sheriff's car and Deli watched Caroline slowly relax.

She turned her head to him. "Are you okay?"

"Yeah. I'm okay. Come here." He opened his arms and she fell into them with a grateful sigh.

The yard filled with cops and FBI as they started the cleanup. Deli moved Caroline and Trace back to the porch, never loosening his hold on her. He'd answer questions if necessary, but dammit, he was on vacation and he wanted to hold his woman out of harm's way. This was Finch's and Sandoval's circus and they were welcome to it.

The rest of the living thugs were rounded up and thrown in the backs of the FBI's vehicles while the bodies were collected by the ME. EMTs checked over Carlos before he was hustled away with an FBI escort. Caroline watched him go with a scowl.

Daphne was given a full examination from the EMTs while Sandoval hovered nearby, his expression anxious. *Oh, man, I think he's smitten.* Not that Deli could talk. He'd already fallen in love with Caroline and he knew what he'd be doing when his tour of duty was up. She was his heart and his soul and the reason he had a future waiting for him.

Caroline took a deep breath and straightened, pushing out of Deli's arms. "I'm going to go make some tea."

Deli nodded. "Everything's better with tea. Right?"

"Yes. Exactly right." She nodded. "Would you like some?"

"Yeah. Make me a cup. I'm gonna go give my statement to the cops and FBI so it's done. But I'll be back soon."

"Okay. I…" She bit her lip. "I'll see you soon."

He noticed her slip but nodded. "Count on it."

She gave him a real smile and it warmed his chest all the way through. "*Here*, Trace. Hup."

Damn, the woman had him by the balls and he wasn't the least bit unhappy about it. He headed over to the sheriff with a grin.

****

The rest of the day wore on a lot longer than Caroline expected what with all the crime scene techs from the FBI and sheriff's office wandering around. Deli had to give multiple statements and verify stories with Finch, Reece, and Sandoval. Daphne had been released to stay at home under supervision and Beryl pressed herself against the younger woman's legs, taking comfort rather than giving it.

Despite the hubbub, relief settled over Caroline as she sat in her favorite chair with Trace beside her. *It's good to have the love of a great dog.* She rubbed Trace's mismatched ears, the black half-mask reminded her of a pirate. *Avast, ye seadogs, shiver me timbers and throw me a bone.* Trace looked up at her and panted in a doggy grin as if she agreed.

At last, the yard emptied of official vehicles and even the Ultimate Recon guys said they'd head to town for the night before hitting the road early the next morning. As much as she'd enjoyed their company, she was rather glad to get her quiet life back.

"Y'all should be good to go now, though the FBI and the sheriff will be keepin' a close eye on your place for a little while." Finch shook her hand with a wince. "Damn, this shoulder is gonna take a bit of gettin' used to."

"Come on, Boss." Reece patted him on the shoulder. "We'll make sure you're taken care of." He rolled his eyes at Tanaka. "You know how these Navy guys need coddling."

"Oorah." Tanaka winked and grinned as Finch scowled.

"Y'all know it's the SEALs who pull your asses outta the fire, so don't hand me that shit." He shook his head. "Damn grunts." But his eyes twinkled. "Anyway, keep me in the loop about your welfare and I'm pretty sure I'll be in touch about gettin' a dog in the near future."

"Just let me know, Cyrus." Caroline nodded as she held out her hand. He shook it gently but firmly. "Thank you very much for all your help."

"You're more than welcome, Caroline." He released her and nodded to Deli standing to the side. "Good to see you, Chief. You let me know what you decide when your tour comes up. I'll be waiting on your call."

"Roger that, Cyrus. But I think I figured out what I'm gonna do."

"Well, if anythin' changes, you let me know."

"Will do."

The Ultimate Recon crew loaded up and said goodbye, McAvoy waving from the backseat. Sandoval had gone as well, but he spent several minutes alone with Daphne, and her niece had smiled more than she had in the last two years. *Could there be more to their connection than just gratitude?* Caroline chose not to pry when Daphne said she was going to her room for some time alone.

Caroline took care of the other dogs and Trace, soothing their concerns and feeding them. When the energy of the kennels had settled down, she retreated to her damaged house, glad all the glass had been swept up and plastic covered the broken windows to keep out the breeze. Tomorrow she'd deal with the insurance adjuster, but for now she just wanted a quiet moment with Deli.

Before he has to leave.

She settled with her fifth cup of tea on the front porch, listening to the frogs in the gully and watching the bats swoop for bugs, their silhouettes flitting against the last light in the sky. She rested on the padded bench, trying to find calm even when the sadness started to set in.

Tomorrow was Friday and Deli would have to return to Coronado. *And to his duty as a Navy SEAL.* A whimper worked its way out of her throat before she could stop it and she smothered the sound with tea. She didn't want him to leave. She'd grown used to having him at the house, even after only a few days.

She held her mug in front of her face as he came out to join her on the bench with his own cup of tea. They didn't say anything for several minutes, though he gave her a smile. Tonight he wore a black dry wicking high performance shirt that molded to his chest, and a pair of black cargo shorts. He left his feet bare as he sat back with them crossed at the ankles.

"You go home tomorrow." She hadn't meant to say it aloud, but now it hung between them like a dark cloud.

"No, I go back to Coronado tomorrow."

She grimaced and waved her hand. "Same thing."

"No, it's not the same thing. Coronado is my duty station. Home is here with you and Trace." He tilted his head and gave her a half-smile. "You know, my dog."

"She is *not* your dog." Caroline rolled her eyes, but there was no heat to her argument. She would've liked Trace to be *their* dog. She sighed and sipped her tea. "What time will you have to leave tomorrow?"

"0800." When she raised her eyebrows, he nodded. "It's a long drive and I want to get back in time to do laundry, shower, and rest." He shrugged. "I'm not as young as I used to be. I need more sleep these days." He winked.

"Shut up." She laughed and bumped his hard shoulder. He lifted his arm to wrap it around her shoulders. "You're not old."

"I am in SEAL years. The younger guys are starting to make me look slow." He grinned and she shook her head.

"Sounds like it might be a good time to retire, then."

He nodded. "Speaking of that, know any good places that have fresh mountain air, a good forest for hikin', and dogs? I'm looking to retire somewhere with all those features."

She didn't say anything for a few moments, letting her thoughts churn like the bats wheeling through the dark chasing bugs.

"Do you really want to come back here, Deli?"

He sat forward and set his mug down on the porch before turning to her. She raised her eyebrows as she met his steady gaze.

"I want to come back here to be with you, Caroline. For the first time in years, I have someone I want to come home to." He took her hands and turned her toward him. "I've been struggling to find a reason to keep doing what I'm doing. Most of my friends have someone waiting for them to come home, now. I was startin' to feel left out." He grinned. "But if you're waiting for me to come off the boat, so to speak, that'll make the time away from you worth it."

She nodded slowly. "How long do you have left on your tour?"

He checked the diving watch on his wrist. "Seven months, eight days, nineteen hours and thirty-one minutes. Not that I'm counting."

She laughed. "Oh no, I can tell you haven't given it much thought."

"Actually, after this week, I still have enough leave to separate a few months earlier, if it makes any difference."

"It might." But her grin faded. "Strangely, I'm finding I don't want you to go."

He nodded. "I don't want to go, either. But you have my cell number and I'll give you my email address. I'll answer you as often as I can when I'm not in training. Just tell me you'll be waitin'."

She gave him her most sincere smile. "I'll be waiting, Chief." She leaned forward and brushed her lips over his. "I promise."

"And you'll bring my dog?" He winked.

"She's not your dog." But she laid her head on his chest and snuggled against him. If he came back to her, Trace just might be his dog after all.

CHAPTER SEVENTEEN

Four months, eight days, twenty-one hours, and ten minutes later...

Deli threw his head back and let the spray of the shower wash away the sweat, the stress, and the uncertainty. Today he'd cashed in the last of his leave, attended his last required separation counselling session, and officially separated from the Navy and the SEALs. He'd signed his discharge papers and filed them with Lt. Commander Whittleton this afternoon. It had been both the right thing to do and an emotional moment. He didn't want to lose the camaraderie and friendships he'd made with the men in his squad, particularly Farkas, Stanton and Bones.

Deli scrubbed his head with shampoo as if to clean out the unease at not being a SEAL. What would he do tomorrow? Where would he go? He rinsed off his head and reached for the body wash. He wouldn't have to wear a uniform tomorrow. Maybe he'd let his beard grow like he did when he'd been with Caroline.

Thoughts of the woman he hadn't seen in more than four months made his cock harden and his heart squeeze with yearning. Driving away from her had been the hardest thing he'd ever done, and that included all the missions he'd been on as well as Hell Week. She'd smiled for his benefit, but he'd seen the tears in her eyes. Or maybe they'd been in his every time he looked in the rearview mirror.

He stepped back under the spray, letting the heat relax his muscles as it washed away the soap. He'd emailed and texted as much as he was able, but there had been weeks of no communication while the squad had been out on missions. The weather had sucked on more than one occasion, and only Caroline's smile had kept him focused on the end goal of getting himself and his team home.

But he'd been back on base for the last couple of days and her responses to his texts had been remarkably short and vague. Had she lost interest? He wasn't usually prone to giving into his doubts, but spotty communication left him uneasy.

This must be what it's like for SEAL spouses.

Hopefully, like the spouses, no news was good news.

He finished his shower and dried off, heading for his bedroom. He still had a couple of months on his lease, but if it all went according to plan, he wouldn't be renewing. *And we all know how well plans go.* He scowled and dug through his closet for a clean t-shirt and shorts.

He glanced at his watch. Beta Squad was having a send-off party for him at the Surf 'n Turf downtown next to Zamora's Think Ink Tattoos shop. Bam-Bam would be there along with Ghost, Magic, Retro, Rimshot, and Farkas. Even Cyrus Finch and his wife Sadie were making the trip down from Issaquah. But Caroline's responses hadn't revealed her plans and he worried she'd changed her mind.

No use borrowing trouble. Can't know what we're really into until we get there.

Bones's voice echoed in his head and sadness bloomed. The older SEAL was still recovering from the injury on their last op together. An old friend had flown in to help him, but it had been a long process after his Traumatic Brain Injury. Deli had checked in on him as often as he could, but he was glad Bones's friend had been there for him.

Deli checked his watch. Almost 1900 hours. He shoved his feet into his shoes and grabbed his keys and phone as he headed out the door. He was as ready as he'd ever be for his send-off. He just hoped he had somewhere to go.

He parked his Jeep in the parking lot behind the Surf 'n Turf and took a moment to scan the area. He recognized Retro's truck and a couple of the other vehicles from the Squad, but overall the lot remained quiet. *I wonder how long it will take me to stop looking for threats.* Probably never. Once a SEAL, always vigilant.

His phone pinged with a text message as he climbed out of the Jeep.

Where are you? It's past 1900!

He laughed at Farkas's words and typed back a quick response as he headed around the front to the entrance. The evening remained warm despite trending toward October and tourists milled through the downtown area in a celebration of the weekend. Deli dodged around a pair of guys excitedly talking about the "hot Navy men" in town and grinned as he headed into the bar.

He took a moment to let his eyes adjust to the dimmer lighting and a chorus of cheers met his ears. Familiar faces had taken position near the windows, sliding three tables together to provide seats for everyone.

"There he is!" Eric Farkas waved at Deli as he rose to his full height. "Someone get the man a beer before he bolts for the hills."

Deli sent him a dry look that morphed into a grin as Todd "Magic" Hunter and Jim "Retro" Waters slapped him on the back in greeting. Chris "Ghost" Hunter shoved her men out of the way to give Deli a hug.

"Congrats on your separation. You deserve to relax." She pushed him back to beam at him.

He snorted. "I don't know if I know how to relax. Do you ever stop sleeping lightly?"

She tilted her head and grimaced. "I'll let you know when I do."

"It's true." Todd winked. "I still can't sneak around quiet enough for her. She hears me comin' a mile away."

"Hell, *I* can hear you coming a mile away." Jim slapped Todd on the back as the other man scowled.

"That's what you get for having roommates, you know." Eric brought Deli a beer.

"You're just jealous 'cause you don't have one, Padfoot." Kevin "Rimshot" Stanton poked their friend, his other arm wrapped around his wife Jaime. "Don't knock it till you try it."

"Congrats on your separation, Chief." Jaime stepped close to give him a hug. "Do you have an idea of what you're gonna do now?"

"I think that's where I come in. At least I hope so." Cyrus rose from his seat beside a woman with sharp eyes and sandy blonde hair. "You still considerin' takin' my offer to come work for Ultimate Recon, Chief?"

"Good to see you, Cyrus." Deli reached out to shake his hand. "How's the shoulder?"

"Eh." The other man grimaced. "It's healin'. Didn't give me near as much hell as Sadie did, though."

"That's because SEALs are supposed to *avoid* bullets, not take them." The clear-eyed woman beside Cyrus gave him an eye-roll filled with love and affection. "We know better in the Marines." She turned to Deli. "Congratulations on your separation, Chief."

"Thank you, ma'am. It's very good to meet you."

"Well I figure if he's offering you a job, I might as well know what he's asking for." She grinned.

Deli laughed. "Yeah, I'm still thinking about it. I just

got discharged today, though. I figure I can take the weekend, at least, to decide."

"Yeah, it's true, but there's nothin' wrong with hedgin' my bet." Cyrus nodded.

Deli snorted. "True enough."

Greg "Bam-Bam" Killian and his wife Zamora Hart bustled in through the doors and waved as they approached the table.

"Hey, sorry we're late, Deli. Zamora was finishing with a customer." Greg engulfed Deli in a back-slapping hug. "I can't believe you're done. Are you sure that's the way you wanna go? You could always be an instructor."

"Yeah, I think I'm ready for something else." Deli nodded as he stepped back. "I loved SpecOps, but I want some time to learn a new skill."

"You need to learn a *new* skill?" Master Chief Gabe "Keys" Szellem snorted. "What, the Navy get too boring for you?"

"Yeah, you know, I'd like to know what it's like to sleep in on the weekend and get good coffee instead of the swill at HQ." Deli grinned as groans sounded around the room. "Oh yeah. Kickin' back in front of the ball game. It's gonna be sweet."

"Yeah, yeah, rub it in." Kevin shook his head. "But you'll miss it."

Deli reached out and bumped knuckles with him. "Yeah, don't tell." And he would. He'd miss all these men and women around him. But he wouldn't miss getting shot at or dodging IEDs and terrorists.

"All right, y'all. Raise your glasses to Deli Rubenovich." Kevin stood up and held his beer high while the others got to their feet. "The smallest man in the Teams and the only one to never get lost. To Deli."

"To Deli!" The crowd cheered and even some of the folks outside of his circle of friends cheered along with them.

It took Deli a few moments to realize someone new had joined their party. Someone with whiskey-colored eyes and golden brown hair. Someone who'd kept his focus on coming home alive when the training missions and ops went long.

"Caroline." He set down his beer and rose to his feet.

"Hey, Deli." She gave him a hesitant smile. "I'm sorry I'm so late. I'm not used to places with so many one way streets."

He didn't bother to answer as he wrapped his arms around her and pulled her to his chest. *Oh, fuck yeah. This is home.* She'd come down to Coronado from her mountain. He wasn't sure she'd come. *But it's a long drive from Cascade Breaks.* He should know. He'd done it four months, eight days, eleven hours, and seventeen minutes ago. Not that he'd been counting.

"I'm so glad you came tonight." He released her and met her gaze. "Thank you."

"You're welcome. I wouldn't have missed it." She squeezed his waist. "Are you really done with the Navy?"

"They have the option to recall me for a short time, but I'm pretty much a civilian now."

"What are you going to do?"

He tilted his head. "I was hoping you'd tell me that position at the Last Chance Dog Sanctuary is still available."

She nodded slowly. "Are you sure that's what you want? Compared to what you're used to, it's pretty quiet and boring."

"I dunno. The last time I was there, I was still dodging bullets and taking down thugs." He grinned as she grimaced.

"Yeah, well, the FBI and ATF got Carlos to talk and he gave them a lot of the cartel's key players in California. Agent Sandoval's words, not mine. It's been quiet at home."

"How is Agent Sandoval?" Deli raised his eyebrows.

She shrugged, a small smile curling her lips. "I can't say how his cases are going, but I can say he's taken a personal interest in the welfare of the Last Chance Dog Sanctuary. Or more accurately, one of its employees."

Deli laughed. "How is Daphne doing after the events of the summer?"

"Better. I think it helps that she was unconscious for much of it, but mostly it's because of Rick." She smiled at his raised eyebrow. "I think he makes her feel normal. Or as normal as she can after what she's gone through. And he likes her. He treats her with respect and kindness. It's good to see."

"I'm happy to hear that." He drank Caroline in, his heart thumping with excitement and pleasure. "I'm very glad you came. I don't even have the words for how good it is to see you."

"What, you weren't counting down the minutes, hours, days?" She winked.

He lifted his arm to show her his watch. "I had an alarm set."

She grinned and pulled out what looked like an old fashioned pocket watch on a chain. Except it had an extra knob that allowed her to set a timer. "Me, too."

Oh my glory, I love you. He wanted to say the words aloud, but a clearing throat reminded him of where they were at the moment.

"Y'all want to let us in on the little secret you got goin' over there? Or did this suddenly become a private party for two?" Todd's voice intruded and the only time he hammed up his Texas accent was when he needed to get someone's attention.

Like mine. Deli winked at Caroline and drew her close to his side before he turned to face the rest of his friends. Each one of them wore expressions of curiosity except Finch. Sadie smiled with satisfaction as if she'd planned this with her husband.

"I'd like you all to meet Caroline Atherton, owner and head trainer at the Last Chance Dog Sanctuary. She trains service dogs for people with PTSD, and she rehabilitates Military War Dogs so they can find homes with civilians after their military service."

"Damn, Deli's goin' to the dogs." Jim shook his head with a mock scowl. "And we had such high hopes."

"Shut up, Retro." Deli grinned. "You're just jealous that I get to play with cute puppies."

"Puppies?" Chris raised her eyebrows. "I thought you rehabilitate older dogs."

"We do, but Tallulah our rottweiler gave birth four months ago so we have some cute rottie puppies running around. We'll need to find homes for them soon."

"Awww." Chris turned her own puppy-dog eyes on Todd and Jim. "We could get a dog. It could help keep me safe while you guys are off saving the world weeks at a time."

Todd rolled his eyes and snorted. "Like you need a dog to keep you safe, darlin'."

"More like you'd keep the dog safe, sweetheart." Jim shook his head, but his eyes had softened. "But I'm okay with getting a dog."

"Please, Todd?" Chris batted her eyes at her husband while Jim spread his hands in mute agreement.

Caroline leaned close to Deli. "What's up with the dynamic between those three?"

Deli turned his head so the others couldn't read his lips. "Chris, Todd, and Jim were very close while in Bravo Squad, but she was medically discharged from active duty a few years ago."

"She was a SEAL?" Caroline blinked.

"Yup. First woman SEAL in the Teams. There are others now, but Chris set the bar. She married Todd after she left the squad."

"And how does Jim fit in?"

Deli gave a one-shouldered shrug. "Jim lives with them. Like I said, they were always close, and they make the relationship work. It's pretty obvious she loves them both, and they love her. Other than that, I don't pry. If they're happy, I'm happy for them."

"Yeah, all right, you can get a dog."

Chris gave Todd a sultry smile as she wrapped her arms around him. "Thank you." She turned to look at Caroline and Deli. "Just let me know when a good time is to come see your puppies and I'll be there."

"You're welcome to come up anytime. I don't think Daphne's put the ad in the paper yet. We still have all nine puppies." Caroline smiled as Chris's eyes widened. "Yeah, and they're all sweet tempered like their mama."

"How many dogs do you have at the sanctuary right now in training?" Sadie tilted her head as her husband wrapped his arms around her waist from behind.

As Caroline described her business, Deli sat back with satisfaction. He might have left the Navy, but these folks would always be his family. He looked over the couples listening to Caroline and he had the sense he'd joined a hidden group of people who'd found their long-term happiness. Todd, Chris, and Jim might be the most unusual connections, but no less loving than Greg and Zamora, Kevin and Jaime, and Cyrus and Sadie.

The only guys still left at the "singles table" were Eric and Gabe. *And Bones.* But something told him Bones might find his one-and-only soon. Eric looked up as if he'd sensed Deli's attention and he motioned to meet him at the bar. Deli excused himself to join him.

"Looks like you definitely got your head on straight during your leave." Eric nodded back toward Caroline. "She's amazing. Have you told her yet?"

"Told her...?"

"That you love her to distraction." Eric grinned as the

bartender gave them new pints of beer.

Deli narrowed his eyes. "How do you know that, Padfoot?"

Eric winked as he tapped his nose. "I can smell it." When Deli laughed, he shrugged. "It's obvious to anyone looking. And I'm pretty sure she feels the same about you. Which is fuckin' awesome."

"Yeah." Deli nodded. "Wait. Are you sure?"

"That it's awesome? Hell yeah."

"No, that she feels the same."

Eric rolled his eyes. "Uh, yeah. I don't think she would've driven all the way down here for this party if she didn't. But here's the thing. You need to tell her how you're feeling so she doesn't have to guess."

"Yeah, I know. I'm kinda waiting for the right time when it's not so—"

"Scary?"

"I was gonna say 'public.'"

Eric snorted. "What's scarier? Telling her you love her or watching her walk away because you were too busy being a stoic SEAL?"

He didn't even have to think about it. "Watching her walk away."

"Bingo."

"I'm gonna tell her. Tonight, but not with all the rest of youse guys around. That's private." Deli headed back toward the table. "Even if you're a fuckin' romantic and want to see it happen."

Eric laughed as they rejoined the group.

"Besides," Chris was saying as she shot a look at Jim. "Having a protective dog around will be good for when the baby arrives."

A stunned silence hit the group before the women squealed in delight and the men cheered, thumping Jim and Todd on their backs. Todd grinned, his shoulders straightening with pride and pleasure. Jim blushed, and

Deli laughed, amazed that the tough, badass SEAL could look like someone had given him his favorite guilty pleasure. *He's excited to be a dad.*

"Congratulations!" Zamora swept Chris up in a hug. "When are you due?"

"June of next year." Chris grinned. "So I have time to train a dog to love me, too."

"Why didn't you tell me? I'm your best friend, for goodness sake!" Jaime gave her a mock scowl and crossed her arms over her chest.

"I just found out today. I figured it would be a good time to announce it."

Deli sat back, satisfaction rolling through him. His family was growing, even as he retired from one profession to start a new one. Caroline stepped back while the members of the Squad took in the news.

"Are you sure you're ready to leave this? We're kinda way out there in Cascade Breaks." She wrapped her arm around his as they watched the others celebrate Chris, Todd, and Jim's news.

"I'm sure. Is the position for a dog trainer still available?" He met her gaze.

She tilted her head. "It is. If you still want it."

"I still want the position. And I want you." He turned her to face him. "I love you, Caroline. You're my calm in the storm, and the one person who can give me a place to clear my head. I want to be with you and work with you. Please say you'll give this a chance."

She nodded at the squad's jubilation. "I don't want to take you away from people who care about you."

"They'll always care about me. It's the way brothers-in-arms work." He met her gaze, his heart pounding in his chest. *What if she doesn't actually feel the same?* "But I need to know you want this, too. Do you want me to come back to Cascade Breaks and help you with the dogs? Do you want me to share your space? Do you want me?"

"Oh, Deli." She placed both hands on either side of his face. "I want you so much it hurts. I've missed you. The house seemed too quiet without you there. Even Trace was looking for you."

He chuckled. "Well, she is my dog."

"She's not your dog...yet." Caroline leaned forward and brushed her lips across his. "But she could be if you come home with me." She pulled back to meet his gaze. "I love you, Eugene, and I want you to help me run the Last Chance Dog Sanctuary. I've missed you and I want you to come home. Please."

That was all he needed. He crushed his mouth to hers and let her taste fill his senses. Caroline was his woman and he'd never have to leave her. He needed her like he needed air to breathe and she'd just given him permission to come home.

When he pulled back, he enjoyed the dazed pleasure in her face.

"Hooyah, ma'am. I can be packed by tomorrow."

She laughed. "That's what I've heard about SEALs. They can go wheels-up at a moment's notice."

"Damn right we can." He shifted to the side. "Hey, Retro. Can I borrow your truck?"

"Why?" Jim raised an eyebrow.

"I'm gonna need it to move my shit out to Cascade Breaks." Deli grinned as Jim groaned. "Think of it this way. You were gonna have to drive out there to get a dog, anyway. This'll be like killin' two birds with one stone."

"Road trip!" Chris shot her hands into the air as Todd laughed. "I'm gonna get a dog."

"Think you could find a place for me by Sunday night?" Deli squeezed Caroline's hand as they rejoined the group.

"If I can't, you can always sleep in the barn." She winked.

"Hey, speaking from personal experience, those digs

ain't too bad, Deli." Finch grinned. "There's electricity and the roof don't leak."

"Hey, as long as I get to be with you and my dog, I'll sleep in the barn."

"She's not your dog." Caroline raised her chin, but she couldn't hide the smile curling her lips. "She lives with me, remember?"

"And I'm hoping to do the same." He winked.

"You have a dog, Deli?" Chris asked. "When did that happen?"

"Before I joined the SEALs. I trained with her as a K9 handler and got to work with her again four months ago." He shrugged. "That's what I want to do again. And now that I'm retired, I have the chance to be with the woman I love and work with a damn good dog."

The Beta Squad crew shared their congratulations and jubilation over all the good news. Chris, Todd, and Jim made plans to help Deli move up to Cascade Breaks while Zamora and Jaime plotted about a baby shower. Finch and Sadie discussed the possibility of getting a dog for Ultimate Recon with Caroline, and Farkas sent Deli a wide, satisfied smile and a nod.

Deli looked around and his heart settled. These people were his to protect and he'd always have their backs. They used to be the Bad Boys of Beta Squad, but now they'd branched out to be more than that. They'd become a family, and now it would include Caroline, Daphne, Finch, Sadie, and possibly Agent Sandoval if what Caroline had told him was true.

Things were shifting, but instead of a bittersweet ending, he sensed it was a new beginning. For all of them.

THE END

AUTHOR'S NOTE

I hope you enjoyed Deli and Caroline's tale. Deli is the last original member of the Bad Boys of Beta Squad, so named by Ensign Chris Brickman in THE NAVY'S GHOST. While DELI'S TAKE OUT is book 4 (of 5) in the Bad Boys of Beta Squad and connects to the other stories in the series, it has direct connections to RIMSHOT'S HARD TARGET (book 2) and DARWIN'S EVOLUTION, book 1 in the Ultimate Recon series. You'll get to see more of the Ultimate Recon crew coming in 2019, with the possibility of some of the Bad Boys of Beta Squad showing up in cameos. Thanks again for reading my Navy SEALs. Happy reading!

Siobhan

Order of the Bad Boys of Beta Squad books:
- BRONCO'S ROUGH RIDE, Book 0.5 (prequel)
- THE NAVY'S GHOST, Book 1
- RIMSHOT'S HARD TARGET, Book 2
- BAM-BAM'S INKED HART, Book 3
- DELI'S TAKE OUT, Book 4

BRONCO'S ROUGH RIDE
BAD BOYS OF BETA SQUAD, BOOK 0.5
SNEEK PEEK

What happens in Vegas, stays in the heart...

Chief Petty Officer John "Bronco" Andrews only meant to stay one night in Vegas for a little R&R before resuming his duties as a US Navy SEAL in Coronado. But someone slips him a mickey in the bar and he finds himself in Madame LeBeau's sex trade. As the product. Doped up on ketamine to keep him docile, Bronco has no choice but to let it ride.

Detective Lindsey Jarvis has been undercover in LeBeau's sex slave racket for two years and she almost has enough evidence to take it down. Between abduction, prostitution, and murder, she has LeBeau by the short hairs. All she needs is a "product". John is the perfect witness if she can get him out before the drugs shut down his heart. Then she'll be free to start a normal life.

Lindsey doesn't count on her overwhelming attraction for Bronco or her need to see him through detox. But she's a cop in Vegas and he's a Navy SEAL, two lifestyles with too much unpredictability to maintain a relationship. Neither have time for more than one wild rough ride, and what happens in Vegas, stays. Forever.

THE NAVY'S GHOST
BAD BOYS OF BETA SQUAD, BOOK 1
SNEEK PEEK

A SEAL is strongest with her Team...

Ensign Christiana "Ghost" Brickman is the only female SEAL to survive BUD/S training, a real Navy Jane. But when an ambush ends her career as an active SEAL, she's free to pursue other interests. Like her two best friends Lt. Jim "Retro" Waters and Chief Warrant Officer Todd "Magic" Hunter. She's wanted them for over a year, but never dared to approach them while in the squad.

Retro has fought his dark desires since high school, certain the need to share a woman unnatural. Magic had never considered sharing before Ghost mentions it, but it solves his dilemma of choosing between his best friend and his woman. But Retro balks at Ghost's offer to share and retreats from both when she marries Magic.

Everyone feels Retro's loss, but he ignores the ache of their broken connection in favor of living 'normal.' When Ghost and the other wives of Beta Squad are kidnapped, Retro must reevaluate how much both Ghost and Magic mean to him. And he must decide how far he's willing to go to save the woman he loves, before she becomes the Navy's ghost.

OTHER BOOKS BY SIOBHAN MUIR

Her Devoted Vampire
Queen Bitch of the Callowwood Pack
Second Chance Succubus
Darwin's Evolution
Wildfire's Heart

Cloudburst Colorado Series
A Hell Hound's Fire
The Beltane Witch
Christmas I.C.E. Magic
Cloudburst Ice Magic
Cloudburst Coffee & Spa

Rifts Series
Take the Reins
A Centaur's Solstice Wish
In Death's Shadow

Bad Boys of Beta Squad Series
Bronco's Rough Ride
The Navy's Ghost
Rimshot's Hard Target
Bam-Bam's Inked Hart
Deli's Take Out

The Ivory Road
A Walk in the Sand
Outback Dreams

Triple Star Ranch Series
Rope a Falling Star
Star Light, Star Bright

Warbler Peninsula Series
Order of the Dragon
The Valkyrie's Sword
Burning Yuletide

Coming Soon
Courting the Dragon Widow (Cloudburst Colorado #6)
My Forever Cocky Biker Rebellion Encounter (Concrete Angels MC #1)
Dude With a Cool Car (Concrete Angels MC #2)

ABOUT THE AUTHOR

Siobhan Muir lives in Cheyenne, Wyoming, with her husband, two daughters, and a vegetarian cat she swears is a shape-shifter, though he's never shifted when she can see him. When not writing, she can be found looking down a microscope at fossil fox teeth, pursuing her other love, paleontology. An avid reader of science fiction/fantasy, her husband gave her a paranormal romance for Christmas one year, and she was hooked for good.

In previous lives, Siobhan has been an actor at the Colorado Renaissance Festival, a field geologist in the Aleutian Islands, and restored inter-planetary imagery at the USGS. She's hiked to the top of Mount St. Helens and to the bottom of Meteor Crater.

Siobhan writes kick-ass adventure with hot sex for men and women to enjoy. She believes in happily ever after, redemption, and communication, all of which you will find in her paranormal romance stories.

Connect with Siobhan online at:
http://siobhanmuir.com
http://www.facebook.com/siobhan.muir.35
http://twitter.com/SiobhanMuir
http://siobhanmuir.com/siobhans-blog
http://pinterest.com/siobhanmuir.35

www.ingramcontent.com/pod-product-compliance
Lightning Source LLC
Chambersburg PA
CBHW031953240626
47153CB00003B/973